HOTEL KOALA

HOTEL KOALA

A novel set in Scarborough, North Yorkshire

MARK HARLAND

Published by MVH Publishing 2025

A CIP catalogue record for this book is available from the British Library.

ISBN 978-1-7397547-5-4 (Paperback)
ISBN 978-1-7397547-6-1 (ePub)

Book layout by Clare Brayshaw

Prepared and printed by:

York Publishing Services Ltd
64 Hallfield Road
Layerthorpe
York
YO31 7ZQ

Tel: 01904 431213

Website: www.yps-publishing.co.uk

FOREWORD

The Covid epidemic, that had brought sadness and misery to millions, did have one unpredicted benefit. It rejuvenated the seaside holiday industry. It gave it the biggest shot in the arm since the invention and development of the railways. For the first time in decades Joe Public started to appreciate the joys and benefits of the British coastline which, at most, was two hours drive from anywhere in the country. Yes, you might have a Bank Holiday snarl-up on the A64 or another road that the Highways Department deemed unworthy of up-grade. However, you were guaranteed to be free of passport controls, delayed flights and the whims of foreign air traffic controllers. All you had to do was get there.

Scarborough, dubbed "Scarbados" by its loyal fans, was reborn. For the Fishburn family, who had moved from Hull to Scarborough towards the end of the lock-downs and the pandemic, a whole new world had opened up. When redundancy and an inheritance gave them the money to buy a small hotel, they had grasped the opportunity with alacrity. After less than one season's trading, a combination of good business and good luck allowed them to sell the 'Hotel Scarbados' and up-size to a fifty room hotel that had a been a landmark for decades – the Clifftop Hotel.

There had sadly been a human price to pay. The matriarch of the family, Mandy Fishburn, did not settle in Scarborough and decided to return home to Hull. The subsequent divorce was as amicable as possible and she still retained a twenty-five percent stake in the new business.

How would the new, smaller, family cope with a much bigger business? Would the eldest daughter, Millie, continue to shine both at College and as the effective CEO of the new limited company? Would her brother, Jamie, achieve his ambition of qualifying as a cordon-bleu chef? And if he did, would he stay in the family business or be attracted to a big city like a moth to a lamp? Her younger sister, Lucy, had already decided that her future was in animal care but her real worry was her father, Peter Fishburn. Freed from the legal shackles of marriage, he had struck up a liaison with a somewhat younger editor of a London-based magazine. Was it just a flash in the pan or the start of a meaningful relationship? Only time would tell.

For all the Fishburns, including the family's labradoodle, Sebbie, a new exciting life beckoned. The saga continues with the first Extraordinary General Meeting of the new limited company.

1.

The Meeting was taking place in the smaller of the two dining rooms in the Clifftop Hotel. At the request of all the family, Clive White assumed the role of Company Secretary and Chairman of the new company. It was the Second of December and the sale of the Hotel Scarbados and the purchase of the Clifftop Hotel had conveniently taken place on the same day. The legal formalities in accordance with Company Law had to be dealt with first. Present were Peter Fishburn, Millie Fishburn and James Fishburn. Mandy Fishburn, although a subscribing shareholder, didn't wish to attend. She had given her "proxy votes" to Clive White. Her share of the sales proceeds had already landed in her bank account in Hull and her only interest in the new company was its future profitability and dividends. In any case it was 'bingo jackpot' night tonight and she didn't want the possibility of a delayed or cancelled train to wreck her chances. In many respects it was almost as if she had never left 'Ull, her birthplace and spiritual home. The Land of Green Ginger was etched on her subconscious for ever.

At precisely twelve noon Clive White banged his Parker ballpoint on the side of the glass of water alongside his note pad. It sent little ripples racing across the meniscus, like a stone thrown into a millpond. Everybody had a pen and a glass of water, like on those films of Board Meetings. Except this wasn't Hilton Hotels plc or Trust House Forte. It was a 'one hotel' private limited company with four family shareholders,

'Item number One on the Agenda is to receive any apologies. I have here a written apology from Mandy, er Mrs Mandy Fishburn. There won't be any others.'

Plainly her solicitor had written the letter for her and it was clearly an indication of her intention to keep an eye on the company as a whole, *and in particular* it's future operations and profitability.

'Item number Two is to appoint the Directors.

Item number Three is to change the name of the company to ...'

'Hotel Koala Ltd. ... ' Jamie had spoken out quite forcibly.

'Do I have a seconder please? Yes, thank you, Peter. Hands up. Thank you. Carried unanimously.'

And so the Hotel Koala was born as a legal entity and, for the first time in over eighty years, the name of 'Koala' was once again to be found amongst the list of hostelries that hosted the many thousands who flocked to the Queen of the Yorkshire Coast. The spirit of Hilda Maude Jewitt, the founder and proprietress of the original Hotel Koala, looked down upon them from the starry firmament and smiled. It was a truly great day for koalas everywhere.

The Meeting over and the necessary signatures obtained on the Companies House pro-formas, the four of them drove into town for a celebratory luncheon. It was a Saturday and the run-up to Christmas was in full swing. Rather than experience the discomfort of a cold and empty hotel that had not been used for its intended purpose for many months, they had chosen to treat themselves to a long weekend in another small, family owned hotel overlooking the Crescent Gardens. It was warm, homely and friendly.

They would start the formidable task of working on the newly named Hotel Koala on Monday. In the meantime, relaxation was the order of the day, starting with lunch.

'I'll commence with the Trio of Yorkshire Puddings please, as a starter of course' exclaimed Jamie.

They all laughed except the waitress who didn't have a clue what had caused such mirth.

They enjoyed separate rooms that night and slept soundly. Sebbie was staying with their old neighbours, the Ritsons. It would only be for a few days at the most, until the new hotel was a little warmer and cosier.

Peter, Millie, Jamie and Lucy all met together for breakfast in the hotel's restaurant dubbed the "Mirrors" due to almost every wall featuring a mirror of every size and description. In the evening it was also open to the public and Jamie had already clocked a poster in the lobby:

Wednesday is Steak Night
Any two steaks cooked to order
A bottle of house wine
Any two desserts
Tea or Coffee
£50 inc. VAT
Gratuities at your discretion

Wow, mused Jamie. That's not bad, not bad at all. He made a mental note. Once they had made a proper survey of the Clifftop Hotel and formulated some sort of schedule to open on a proper footing they could move forward. Right now it was a blank canvas. 'Jamies at the Koala' was his own personal restaurant project which he hadn't even run past the rest of the family yet. He would consult with his course tutor, Samantha Lyon, at Scarborough TEC before anyone else. Pursuing his chosen carer path thus far had been directly down to her advice and guidance.

After the toast and marmalade Peter tried to encourage a mutual discussion about the way forward. Young Lucy was desperate to have her doggie, Sebbie, back with her and her whole world revolved around animals and her future as a veterinary nurse. She wasn't due to start full-time at Mr Wilson's practice until after the New Year – a month away that would seem like an eternity to her.

'Dad, can we go and collect Sebbie please from Mr and Mrs Ritson? I want to take him to near the Clifftop so he can get his bearings, so to speak, for his new home.'

'Well of course we can, love. Just give the Ritsons a call first. In fact why don't we all go for a mooch and leave the car in our own new car park? The car might as well start to find its way to its new home.'

Jamie could have told them that Sebbie had already had a good sniff around the front door of the Clifftop months ago when they had taken the Barbadian High Commissioner for a long walk, firstly to the Scarborough Cricket Club and then onto the road and pathways past the then named Clifftop. Not in a month of Sundays could either Jamie or Sebbie have foreseen that one day in the not too distant future, it would be an asset of the Fishburn family.

'The Ritsons are at home and we can collect Sebbie within the next half-hour. Shirley says the kettle's already on.'

How lucky were they to have had such friendly dog-loving neighbours. They were already missing them but no doubt they would meet up socially and frequently. They couldn't believe that it was almost a year since they had arrived in Scarborough just a few days before Christmas on a bitterly cold day with a second 'Beast from the East' threatening. The estate agent handling the transfer of keys, Charlie Hopper, had fallen ill with Covid on the day of completion and but for the quick-wittedness of the Ritsons, their new home would have felt like an iceberg. The lights and heating had been switched on long before their arrival, just as it had got dark on the eve of the Winter Solstice.

The family estate pulled up outside the Ritsons and already they could see Sebbie in the bay window who started barking as soon as he recognised his own family. He practically jumped onto Lucy when the front door was opened.

'Oh, where's Candy Mr Ritson, and the others?

Well you'd better sit down in the lounge all of you while Shirley brings in the coffees and ginger biscuits. It looks like they've become Seb's favourite too, by the way. Candy was quite unwell yesterday, not herself at all. So I phoned Mr Wilson at the vets. He told me to bring her in straight away.' Lucy looked down-crested.

'Don't tell me it's anything serious, please.'

'Well in fact it is, actually. It's very serious indeed and totally unexpected. She's pregnant! It appears that several pups are due early in the New Year. And you know what that means don't you?'

'Well, that's amazing news. I am so happy for you. Oh heck, you don't think that ...?'

'Yes, exactly! Cast your mind back to the afternoon of the Bar B Q not so long ago. Remember Sebbie making a great fuss of Candy down by the Eucalyptus tree when we were all busy eating and drinking on your sixteenth birthday?'

''Oh naughty Sebbie. I just don't know what to say, Mr Ritson. I'm so sorry.'

'What? There's no need to be sorry at all! We are absolutely delighted! In fact over the moon.'

At that moment Shirley appeared, not with coffees but with an opened bottle of Prosecco and six glasses.

'Cheers Sebbie and Candy! You will of course have the pick of the litter. Sebbie will need to have at least one of his offspring with him when you move into the Clifftop – er what did you say the new name was again?'

'The Hotel Koala. We hope to formally open just before Easter with a big launch party of course' piped up Jamie who was already mentally concocting the culinary fare he would be laying on. They had only sixteen weeks to turn the Clifftop into the Koala. None of the others knew it but 'Big Sis' Millie was already way ahead of the curve. She would wait until after the Sunday Lunch to hit them with her multi-point plan of action.

With the "fizz" consumed and toasts made to their canine families, the Fishburns drove the short journey to the still-named Clifftop Hotel. The sole grey castle-like turret at the southernmost corner of the roof stood out in the wintry, milky sunshine. Was it used as a letting room? Surely it was too small. Perhaps it had been an architect's afterthought, a sort of folly. It was worthy of investigation for commercial potential.

They pulled into the good-sized hotel car park. For many months until recently it had been chained off with padlocks to prevent unauthorised parking while the hotel was in use as a temporary hostel for Afghan refugees. Happily, they had all now been rehoused into proper dwellings inland. Proximity to the usually cool North Sea had not been to the liking of the majority. Landlocked Kabul and Kandahar had been a thousand miles from the ocean. Within a few short months the Clifftop, with a new name, new owners and new ideas would once again play a major role in re-booting the fortunes of the Queen of the Yorkshire Coast. At that point in time nobody knew just how big a role.

2.

Next day's Sunday lunch was an eye-opener for Jamie. Now they knew why Marina, the supervisor of the dining room staff, had asked them if they would be staying in for lunch or going out. It was heaving with both 'Mirrors' and the larger dining room, usually reserved for Residents, absolutely rammed. Peter caught Marina's eye just as she was taking another table's orders to the kitchen.

'Marina, is it always this busy on a Sunday? I'm amazed!'

'Well, Sunday trade is always fairly brisk but the town is busy today with Scarborough's Christmas Lights being formally switched on by a TV personality. It's one of the actresses, from *Emmerdale* I believe, who's going to throw the switch just as it starts to get dark. About six of the regular cast are through in the other dining room. They're not staying over – just here for a long lunch I think. Excuse me but I'll have to press on ...'

Jamie took mental notes as did 'Big Sis' Millie who started fiddling with her iPad as soon as she had made her choice of starter and main course – prawn cocktail and roast beef. Another bullet-point was added to her priority list that she would present to the family, now a Board of Directors, after the coffees.

It was getting on for two-thirty before lunches were finished. Marina asked them if they would like to have their coffees in the small and cosy 'residents' only' lounge, off-set from the larger dining room.

'Yes please', said Millie who was anxious for their confidential discussion to be exactly that. Suitably and comfortably seated, and away from prying eyes and ears, Millie opened up her iPad. It was like going back in time almost two years to when they had made the decision, in principle at least, to make the huge move from Hull to Scarborough and buy the run-down Wendover Hotel. What a lot of water had gone under the bridge since then – almost as much as under the Humber Bridge. Millie opened the batting. Didn't she always?

'Right, we've a fairly long list of things to discuss so let's get a wiggle on. With luck we'll finish in time to go and watch the Lights being switched on too.'

Point number one. The opening day. Easter is early this year. In fact, Easter Sunday is the last day of March. We must be well-open by then but how many letting rooms will we have open? It is unrealistic to expect to have all four floors functioning. Clive thinks we should aim to have floors one and two not just open but fully occupied. Financially we must learn to walk before we run and not under any circumstances must cash flow get out of hand. Although Clive has negotiated a small 'in case of use' overdraft facility at the Blackbird Bank we should aim from the outset not to use it until absolutely necessary, if at all. I make that roughly a hundred and twenty days to formal opening. What does everybody think?'

They all nodded in agreement but Lucy's mind was more on other things – such as how many dogs could the Hotel reasonably house if their intended 'Dog Friendly' strap-line was to become a reality.

'Point number two. At the moment only the owners' accommodation on the top floor is up to spec. Are the letting floors going to be carbon copies of each other or we going to give some of them 'themes' with a bit of character?'

'Like what?' chirped Jamie. Millie sighed. Her brother Jamie was gaining knowledge and experience on the food & beverage front but hopeless, just hopeless, when it comes to design and décor. The one person she would dearly like to consult was Pamela Hesketh, the editor of that posh magazine in London who had taken a shine to her Dad. Perhaps she could suggest to her father that he invited her up to Scarborough for a pre-Christmas weekend when her ideas for the Hotel Koala could be encouraged and discussed. Yes, she would do that but only later when she could have a discreet word in his ear away from the rest of the family. They had always been close and as the first-born enjoyed a relationship that her siblings were at times quite jealous of. She knew most of his little quoibles and secrets – or at least she thought she did.

'Point number three. Staffing. The Hotel has not been operating as a going concern for a few years. Thus there are no employees 'on the books' yet as it were. Time is on our side to select, recruit and train the right people. We have to get it right from the outset. Does everyone agree?'

Before anyone could say anything, in agreement or otherwise, the door opened and the ever attentive Marina poked her head through the gap.

'Sorry to interrupt. More coffee anyone? I'm off duty in ten minutes and I just thought I'd check before I left.'

Nobody did but it caused Peter to look at his watch.

'Millie, this is all vital discussion love, but can I suggest we continue after supper? I really would like to see the …'

'Yes sure, Dad. Let's get our coats on and although its only a stone's throw to the town centre it's very nippy outside as you can see from the procession of folks outside. They're all well wrapped-up aren't they?'

They all disappeared up to their rooms for warmer clothing, hats and scarves. Marina popped into the hotel's little office to 'sign off' and say cheerio to the duty manageress, Nadine.

'Cheers then. See you on Wednesday, as I've got two days off now. I'm off to York tomorrow to do some Christmas shopping while the kids are at school.'

'Have a great time, Marina. Not going on the train are you? I heard the drivers are on strike again or banning overtime or something. It's almost the norm now isn't it?'

'Well if that's the case I'll take that Coastliner Bus. It's still a £2 maximum fare isn't it? By the way, that family from Hull who are staying here a few days. What do you know about them?'

'Not a lot. Why?'

'Well I overheard a bit of their conversations – not deliberately you understand but I was taking in their coffees and they were discussing staffing a new hotel.'

'Are you sure about that?'

'Oh yes definitely.'

'Oh my God, yes. The penny's just starting to drop. The family name is Fishburn isn't it? I'll check the register. Hang on a second. Yes, it's them! There was a couple of column inches in the Scarborough News last Thursday. They're the new owners of the old Clifftop Hotel – you know, the one that was requisitioned by the Home Office for refugees or something. We'd best be careful. They might try to pinch our best staff. Good employees in this sector are like gold dust. If only we had a few more like you Marina. Yes, see you on Wednesday.'

Ten minutes later and the Fishburns were walking uphill past Scarborough Library towards the broad pedestrian precinct. Ornamental lights, hundreds of them, were strewn at a safe height across its width. It had taken Council workers many days to erect them in time for the big day. There must have been well over a thousand folks gathered in front of a temporary stage that had been erected only that morning in front of the entrance to the Brunswick Centre, Scarborough's only shopping mall. Its commercial significance had declined substantially since a major national retail chain had closed its doors – a victim of Covid as much as changing shopping habits. A public address system was in view with an extendible microphone perched atop a tall, skinny tripod. Just before four o'clock a short, somewhat portly, gentleman was assisted onto the stage by two of the Centre's management staff supporting him under both arms. It wasn't easy. The stage was as high as his kneecaps and you didn't have to be a sports presenter to see that this chap would never be a high-jump champion. BBC Radio York had their mobile station in attendance and their affable afternoon presenter, Joanita, was at the radio with her own microphone at the ready. She didn't normally work weekends but she had volunteered, thinking it would be a great afternoon out for her twin boys 'Good afternoon, listeners. It looks like proceedings are about to get under way. Yes, the PA is crackling into life. It's the Town Crier!' He looks like a cross between a beefeater and a Morris dancer but with the girth of a Michelin man.' She has a way with words does Joanita.

'Hear yeah, hear yeah, hear yeah!' He rang a large brass hand-bell that would not look out of place in a row of weights in a gymnasium.

'Good afternoon ladies and gentlemen, boys and girls. Welcome one and all to the big switch-on. Would you please welcome TV star Amy Bennett, a star of our own Yorkshire soap, Emmerdale. who will throw the switch in front of me after a count of ten. Join in with me … ten...nine...'

Everybody joined in … two...one...zero!

Fortunately there were no hitches and at two second intervals the bridges of lights snapped on for over a hundred yards up and down the precinct. The opening bars of the *Emmerdale* theme music were drowned out by the cacophony of screams by a thousand children. But it wasn't over yet and the Town Crier assumed a new role of disc jockey.

'We're now going to play you two tunes, both very different but truly apt for our town.'

His voice was drowned out again by the melodic tones of *Scarborough Fair* which wafted out of the powerful speakers that had been erected. None of the young folk present were old enough to remember the movie *The Graduate* and the lovely tune that had been especially written for it and sung by Simon & Garfunkel. Alone in the crowd only Joanita knew what was coming next.

'And now, by special arrangement with BBC Radio York we are going to play you *Every Kinda People* by the BBC Philharmonic Orchestra. The tune was made famous by one of Scarborough's famous sons – Robert Palmer. The arrangement was specially composed to represent Yorkshire. Take it away ...'

Only a handful of listeners remembered the late Robert Palmer whose other famous tracks included *Addicted to Love*. Everybody over fifty knew that one. The crowd started to disperse towards car parks and the few cafés and coffee shops that were still open and defying Sunday trading hours. Peter came up with a suggestion that was adopted unanimously.

'Come on quickly – let's dive into the Brunswick and get four hot chocolates from Esquires on the ground floor.'

'Dad, you're beginning to think and act like a Scarborian already.'

'I think you mean a Scarbadian!'

3.

By Wednesday that week the Fishburns decided that the Clifftop Hotel was just about habitable enough for them to move into. Collectively, they had still not really got it into their heads that they now owned a fifty bed hotel in Scarborough. Two years ago, redundancy and Covid had combined to effect an uncertain future. And here they were now, albeit minus the matriarch of the family. What would her reaction be today? If she grumbled about the Hotel Scarbados then her moans would probably be multiplied tenfold were she taking part in the planning for the new venture today.

Peter had mastered the heating system sufficiently to isolate the first, second and third floors with only the Ground Floor and the owners' accommodation on the top floor maintained at a comfortable twenty degrees Celsius. Mandy would no doubt have insisted it was seventy degrees Fahrenheit and no amount of argument would have persuaded her that they were approximately one and the same. Not surprisingly, in the same vein she had also failed to adopt decimal currency despite being only a young girl when 'decimalisation' kicked in. She still referred to a 'pennorth' of chips and getting cinema tickets in the 'one and nines' to save a few 'bob' when they all went to see the latest film release in town. As the youngster of the family, Lucy still missed her Mum a great deal and this was probably the main reason she had developed an even deeper bond with Sebbie, soon to be a proud father. Lucy couldn't wait and was eagerly awaiting the arrival of Candy's pups and was determined, if possible, to be there for the birth. Garry Ritson had said he would do his best in that respect.

It was a Saturday morning with just over two weeks to go before Christmas. Lucy was out with Sebbie exploring the plethora of paths overlooking the sea. Sebbie was in his element – so many new smells to explore. Lucy was happy too, in her own way. The future and fortunes of the soon to be re-named Clifftop Hotel didn't really interest her. Early January and her new job at the Vet's Surgery would arrive soon enough.

Jamie made a large cafétiere of Java coffee and brought it into the smaller of the two dining rooms where 'Big Sis' Millie and his father were making notes about the way forward. The permutations and possibles were endless and limited only by their own imaginations – or lack of them. Unlike when they had taken over the old Wendover Hotel, there was no existing client bank or repeat business. Under the terms of purchase, the Home Office had redecorated the Hotel almost in its entirety, but that meant beige and neutral colours almost everywhere – carpets, walls, ceilings the lot. What they did, and in what order, was absolutely crucial. As always, Millie took the lead.

'So you see, Gentlemen, what we decide to do next has to be meticulously planned. This is a completely different ball-game.' It was the first time she had jointly referred to her father and brother as Gentlemen. In Clive White's absence she had, without realising it, assumed the role of ad-hoc chairman.

'Jamie, just how serious are you about having your own restaurant, within the Hotel, as it were?'

Millie had caught her brother off-guard with her no-nonsense direct question. He had expected that to come up for discussion some time after Easter and not two weeks before Christmas.

'Well, I er, thought I'd give it some thought in a few months after we'd started trading and …'

'No, Jamie. You need to think about it now. The shareholders, which include you of course, deserve to have an answer very early in the New Year. I appreciate that you probably want to take advice from your course tutor, Samantha Lyon, but just for once you might like to make a decision off your own bat, as it were.' Peter looked at his eldest daughter and raised an eyebrow. She wasn't normally as demonstrative as this. Perhaps she had inherited more of her mother's DNA than he had hitherto thought.

'You see, Jamie, if you decide, in principle, that you do want your own restaurant then the obvious place for it is the smaller of our two dining rooms. I estimate it will accommodate twenty four covers. This will mean planning the décor for it now, before we spend another penny. We can then concentrate our efforts, not to mention our money, on the residents' main dining room. If we're going to go for a phased and gradual development of the Hotel, perhaps one Floor at a time, then do we start as we mean to go on and spend time and money on the visually important parts of the Hotel and play catch-up with the rest as revenues and income allow? Now, have a look at these spreadsheets and flow-charts that Clive and I have put together ….'

Father looked at son and son looked at father. This time four eyebrows were raised. Where would they be without Millie and her financial guru, Clive White? The meeting broke up around mid-day as Millie and Lucy wanted to pop into the town centre to do a bit of Christmas shopping.

They weren't just sisters, they were good mates too. It was a chilly twenty minute walk into the town centre and the dark, overcast sky, prevalent in the month of December, accentuated the myriad of lights in shop windows and Christmas trees in the bay windows of small, family owned hotels and Guest House that lined both sides of North Marine Road. Most of them were closed for the winter and would not re-open until Easter. Walking past the fire Station on their left they clocked a large Chinese Restaurant occupying a large corner site. No doubt at Chinese New Year it would be lit up like a neon pagoda and be visible for hundreds of yards from any direction. Its Chinese owners, former Hong Kong residents, were meeting the festive requirements of their mainly local patrons and did their very best to emulate Western practices. 'Open on Christmas Day and Boxing Day – special menu available – Sweet and Sour Turkey with deep-fried Brussels Sprouts.' The proprietors were obviously having a laugh. Or were they?

'Hey, Sis, are you thinking what I'm thinking? If Jamie doesn't fancy doing a full Christmas Lunch then how about we …'

'Done! Great minds think alike. Dad can still do his Boxing Day ritual with cold meats, his take on Bubble & Squeak and …'

'Yes and we can invite the Ritsons, can't we?'

'You bet we can. Slowly but surely they were slipping into a Christmas mind-set. It did them both good. Sure, there was a mountain of work ahead over the next three months but a bit of mental relaxation, not to mention retail therapy, would be a sure fire morale booster.

Back at the ranch, Peter and son Jamie were busy in the smaller of the two dining rooms. They had one of those laser tape measures so beloved by estate agents and quantity surveyors.

'So what do you think Pamela Hesketh will make of it, Dad?'

I'm going to give her an outline of the room, dimensions, photographs and views from the windows. The corner aspect gives her a bit of scope. The views are amazing aren't they? But don't forget, this is strictly between us two, OK? The girls don't know I'm in regular contact with her but now your mother and I are divorced there's not really anything to hide is there? '

'No, I guess not, Dad, but when are you going to tell them that you've invited her up from London for Christmas?'

'What?! How the heck did you know? I haven't told a soul.'

'You were in the bath the other day and your mobile was on 'speaker mode.' I could hear her voice with that posh London lilt as I walked past your room.'

'Well keep that bit to yourself will you? It's one step at a time with this lady.'

'Sure, Dad, no problem.'

It was dark and after five o'clock when Millie and Lucy returned from their trip into town. They came in through the front door of the Hotel which had not seen any genuine paying guests, as it were, for several years. It would be three months, around a hundred days, before real customers spending real brass would be welcomed. The girls dumped their shopping bags into the hall and went into the kitchen to make tea where they found Peter and Jamie already enjoying a brew. Sebbie also enjoyed a cuppa from time to time, as many dogs do, and had already slurped his way through a half a bowlful of Yorkshire tea.

'Any left in the pot, Dad?'

'Sorry Lucy. You know where the kettle is, love. Make a fresh large pot will you. Your brother and I have been busy and it's thirsty work.' Millie winked at her sister and kept a straight face.

'Really? So what have you two been doing. All I can see is one of those fancy electronic tape measures and a small notebook!' Jamie rose to the bait like a trout after a Mayfly.

'Well if you must know, we've been looking closely at the smaller of the two dining rooms for my own 'in-house' restaurant. I've decided to go ahead with the project. My course tutor, Samantha Lyon, thinks it's a cracking idea. She says she's never heard of a student having his or her own restaurant before even gaining a Chef's Diploma. She said she'll help all she can when the time comes to open it. I think she foresees some of the students gaining part-time employment from it. They're not all on grants by any means and most of then still live at home and rely on the Bank of Mum & Dad to get by.'

Millie kept schtum. There was no need for Jamie to know that she and Samantha had struck up quite an accord and met for coffee in town for a coffee and a catch-up every couple of weeks. She was only too aware that Jamie had struggled with the idea for many weeks but the final decision had to be his and his alone.

'Right, listen up you two. Unless I'm very much mistaken no planning has gone into what we might eat tonight so I'm suggesting we dine at the Lucky Dragon Chinese. Lucy and I had a peek at it earlier. If we like it we can then book for Christmas Day Lunch. What do you all think? Three unanimous 'ayes' and the deal was done.

'I'll call them now to book a table for four people at, shall we say seven o'clock? I made a note of their number and put it into my mobile. I'll call them now – they'll be open.'

Lucy looked a little unsettled.

'Chinese is OK but they're not exactly top of the class for vegetarian cuisine are they …' Jamie intervened.

'Wrong! They do a veggie version of most of their dishes – even a rat dish!'

'Yuck, don't be stupid.'

'Sure they do. Ever heard of ratatouille?'

Jamie's sense of humour was getting worse but he would need to both cultivate it and curtail it in equal measure in the months and years ahead. Nobody could possibly predict who his future customers would be, or pretend to be.

4.

Dinner at the Lucky Dragon was a great success. They had arrived a little earlier than the booked time and were offered seats in a nicely appointed waiting area until their table became vacant. It was currently occupied by a Chinese family – Mum and Dad and four kids in their teens by the look of it, two boys and two girls. Course after course was being brought to the table which was circular and had one of those 'Lazy Susan' tables within its structure. The youngest offspring seemed to take great delight in spinning it too fast when his Mum requested that the dish holding more fried rice was rotated a hundred and eighty degrees so that she could reach for yet another portion. He received a swift telling off from his father in colloquial Cantonese for his misdemeanour. They seemed to be only half-way through what appeared to be a veritable banquet. The 'front of house' a Chinese gentleman in his seventies and resplendent in a blue blazer sporting at least ten shiny brass buttons, walked towards Peter to speak personally.

'My apologies, Sir. As you can see, we are very busy tonight. Saturdays are always crowded and what with the run-up to Christmas we also have a few works' parties booked in tonight. It won't be long now. May I offer you some complimentary drinks? On the House, as you say.'

'Well Mr er ..'

'Mr Yip. Raymond Yip. Some Chinese beers maybe?' Lucy scowled.

'Or perhaps for you young lady, a Chinese mocktail? It's mostly Kiwi-fruit and Lai-Chi juice served on a bed of crushed ice and ...'

'Oh yes please! That sounds wonderful. And by the way, I'm a vegetarian. Is there plenty to choose from?'

'That's not a problem Miss ...'

'Lucy. Lucy Fishburn and this is my Dad, Peter, my sister Millie and my brother Peter.' Mr Yip nodded politely. He wondered who they were as he hadn't seen them before. Visitors perhaps? Ten minutes later with beers and mocktails almost consumed, Mr Yip returned with some good news. Another table by the large curved window is now available. Please, allow me to show you to your table. Apologies once again. The family at the large round table are the new future owners. They arrived from Hong Kong a few weeks ago and formally take over at Chinese New Year – a lucky and very fortuitous time to take over the business, any business. Their family name is Chan. If you like I can introduce you before they leave. Are you here on a short holiday, can I ask?' Peter replied.

'No, Mr Yip, actually we're the new owners of the Clifftop Hotel.'

'Oh really! Well good luck. I'm pleased to hear it's back in operation as a hotel again. When it was used for refugees it didn't provide any customers for us. None. The taste-buds of Middle Eastern people are very different to our own. One or two of them ventured in but it seems like all they wanted was lamb, lamb and more lamb. Some mutton is eaten by Northern Chinese but to us southerners it is usually shunned. We much prefer pork and seafood. In the olden days we got quite a lot of custom from the Hotel, you know, people who were staying just for Bed & Breakfast.' Millie's ears pricked up. There might be a marketing opportunity there in the not too distant future.

'Now, Miss Lucy, I have asked our head cook to make sure that lots of vegetarian dishes are brought out in the Set Meal for four people. Here it comes now. Enjoy!'

Lucy was amazed. A huge vegetarian platter was placed directly in front of her place setting offering spring rolls, deep-fried seaweed bundles, asparagus tips steamed in banana leaves and toffu chunks on sticks in a honey glaze. And that was just her starter. She took her mobile phone from her shoulder bag and took a quick photo. Later she would send it by WhatsApp to her Mum in Hull just to keep in touch. It reminded her to ask Millie to arrange a lunch with their Mother before Christmas actually arrived. Perhaps at the Beverley Arms Hotel. A train ride would be a little treat for them both.

The meal over and all four bellies full, Peter got up to pay the bill at the little counter near the Bar. The Chan family were leaving at the same time and Mr Yip just managed to catch him. He spoke in rapid Cantonese and then in English to both of them.

'Mr Fishburn, this is Mr Kenneth Chan, whom I told you about.' He smiled and shook hands with Peter.

'Nice to meet you Mr Chan. I hear you're taking over in the New Year, er sorry, I meant Chinese New Year.'

'Yes, that's correct. We'll be having a special grand opening. I will make sure you're invited. Mr Yip here tells me you have taken over the big Hotel facing the sea – the Hilltop is it?'

'The Clifftop, yes. But we're renaming it well before our own Grand Opening at Easter. You will be our guests on that occasion.'

It was smiles all round as both families ventured out into the December chill for their respective walks home. The Chans were in temporary accommodation for the time being and until they knew the town a little better before choosing a home to buy. Like thousands of former Hong Kong people they were still finding their feet in their new, adopted country. Millie suddenly remembered to book the Christmas Day lunch and Mr Yip duly made a note in the Reservations book.

'Table for four – one o'clock – same table as tonight – is that OK?'

Millie rushed outside to join the others.

'I only just remembered to book us in for Christmas Day! Let's walk back home on the cliff-top road shall we? There's a bit of moonlight on the water and although it's cold the wind isn't too bad.'

Two hundred yards later and something suddenly dawned on Peter.

'Oh heck. I've left my reading glasses on the table. I can't read an English menu without them let alone a Chinese one. You lot walk on slowly and I'll catch you up.'

He fibbed. Two minutes later and he was back at the Lucky Dragon and collared Mr Yip at the desk.

'Ah, sorry, Millie forgot that we'll be having a guest over Christmas. Make that a booking for five people will you please?'

'No problem Mr Fishburn. Looking forward to seeing you on the day then. I'll ask Chef to do some vegetarian turkey for Lucy.'

Peter did indeed catch up with the other three just after they reached Queen's Parade overlooking the North Sea. It gave them a view of their new Hotel that they had not hitherto seen. The sole turret atop the roof looked quite surreal. Jamie had already been giving substantial thought as to what they might do with it.

'Did you find your glasses OK, Dad?'

Something didn't quite add up to Millie. Funny but she hadn't remembered her Dad wearing his glasses in the restaurant.

It was nice and warm in their small but cosy staff lounge. Somehow they had managed to leave their huge high-tech TV back at the Hotel Scarbados. Consequently they were squinting at a tiny screen with an indoor aerial perched on a windowsill. Perhaps the purchase of a new set might be an appropriate Christmas gift to them all. And of course, it could go through the books as a legitimate business expense. Couldn't it? Peter was learning fast but he would never catch up with his wily, business-savvy eldest daughter. Lucy brought a large cafètiere of fresh coffee into the lounge with four mugs and a small jug of cream.

'Here we are. Dive in. Dad, we are getting a new telly aren't we? I'm going to buy a telescope soon if we don't, that's all.' Jamie suddenly had a flash.

'Say that again sis. What did you say about a telescope?'

'I said I'll be needing a flipping telescope to watch the TV and …'

'That's it. A telescope!'

'What on earth are you on about? You do talk a load of cobblers sometimes, Bro.'

Jamie kept his thoughts to himself. After Christmas was over he would do some research online. They all turned in early for the night. Tomorrow Peter would phone Garry Ritson for some advice on where to buy a new TV for the family and at the same time extend an invitation for Boxing Day lunch. He slept well and dreamt a lot – mostly about Pamela B. Hesketh. He would have to tell the girls soon, as a matter of courtesy if nothing else.

5.

Shortly after breakfast Peter called Garry on his mobile. He guessed correctly that he would be out with the two other dogs, Candy being confined to barracks in the last few weeks of her pregnancy.

'Morning Peter, how are you all? Settling in OK I hope?'

'Hi Garry. Slowly but surely. We've a long way to go yet, but we'll get there. Millie's rigged up one of those giant post-it notes tear-off things in the kitchen numbering the 'Days to Go' until the opening on Maundy Thursday. There are ninety-two days to go I noticed while I was munching my toast this morning. She drives me mad with her obsessive attention to detail sometimes. She really does.'

'Pete, count your blessings mate. Most family businesses would pay a small fortune to have a daughter like yours to help run it.'

'Yes, you're right of course. I'm a lucky guy. Anyway, Garry, the reason for the call – two things actually.'

'Fire away. I'm sat on the wall near the Sea Life Centre but I've got a good signal just for once. It can be a bit dodgy down here. Go ahead.'

'OK firstly, where can we we buy a top quality 'smart' telly for our family lounge? What about that huge discount warehouse place on the road into Scarborough? Is it any ..?'

'Garry, it's fine but listen, surely you'll be wanting fifty TV sets, won't you? You know, one for each guest room?'

The notion hit Garry like a sledge hammer.

'Oh my God, of course, how stupid of me. So where do you recommend? You've been here forty years longer than me?'

'Well actually, if you had asked me that question forty years ago I would have undoubtedly pointed you in the direction of a family owned business called Williams TV but they're no longer in business. The family retired and sold the building to a Chinese family. It's now a restaurant called the Lucky Dragon. You've probably seen it up past the Fire Station and ...'

'You won't believe this. We ate there last night. You say it was a TV shop?'

'Oh yes, one of the best too. Those two huge curved glass bay windows were crammed with all the latest sets from manufacturers you only see in retro shops today – you know, Bush, GEC, Grundig, Telefunken, Decca – you name it. They would look like museum pieces today but back in the day it was ...'

'So where do we go today for fifty plus modern sets?'

'There's only one place to go if you want personal service. It's called 'Euro something' and it's right opposite the casino, just a few hundred yards from the Lucky Dragon. Mention my name, if you like. I know them through the local Kennel Club. They've got miniature Schnausers – five of them at the last count. I'd wait until after the New Year if I were you, special promotions and all that. Plus you'll have real buying power with an order like that too. You said you had two things to run past me.'

'Oh yes, I've been chatting off-piste haven't I? 'We'd like to invite you and Shirley for our traditional Boxing Day lunch again.'

'Thank you, we'd love to but on one condition.'

'What's that?'

'That you serve up that amazing Bubble and Squeak again like last year. Shirley fairly rabbited on about it for days. She almost drove me nuts. Do you think Peter will give us the recipe? Go on ask him! You know what a nagging wife can be like, I'm sure?'

Garry suddenly realised that he had put his foot in it, momentarily forgetting that Peter's wife Mandy, now his ex-wife, had left Scarborough to return to her native 'Ull.

'Sorry I didn't mean to be crass. I'm always putting my foot in it. I don't think I would have made a good diplomat. Do you?'

'No, me neither mate. Listen, keep this to yourself but there'll be seven of us for lunch not six.'

'You mean seven including Sebbie?'

'No, seven people. Remember Pamela Hesketh that magazine editor from Mayfair who stayed with us in the summer and gave us that brilliant review?'

'Sure I do. A bit of a cracker if I recall. Shirley said she looked a bit brassy but she was probably jealous of her obvious good looks and comparative youthfulness. So how the heck did she wangle an invitation to come for Christmas?'

'Simple, I invited her!'

'You old snake. Or should I say a dark horse. And she accepted straight away?'

'Within five minutes, on WhatsApp.'

'What did the kids say? Do they know?'

'Well by accident, Jamie does, but please keep it to yourself. I don't want the girls knowing just yet. I don't want them yapping to their mother. The three of them are meeting for lunch in Beverley in a few days time. I'll think of an appropriate time to tell them when they come back.'

'Well good luck with that one. Listen I'll just check with Shirley about Boxing Day and then call you back to confirm.

She'll be picking me and the dogs up in fifteen minutes or so. I had intended to walk but the weather's gone pear-shaped in the last half-hour. She wasn't terribly chuffed about it apparently as she was listening to the Sunday morning omnibus edition of the Archers on Radio Four. I told her it was on a pre-tuned spot on the car radio and all she had to do was press button number four.'

'Yes, typical. Mandy was exactly the same. If a radio didn't have a huge manual tuning nob on it she couldn't work it. Anyway call me soon. Cheers, Garry.'

'Will do, bye for now.'

'Who was that you were just talking to, Dad?' Millie didn't miss a trick. He hoped she had only heard the bit about the Boxing Day lunch and not the bit about the seventh guest.

'By the way Dad, Lucy and I are going to meet with Mum in Beverley on Wednesday. We've little presents already wrapped up to take with us. Did you have something from you that you'd like us to take? You know what the Royal Mail is like at this time of year.'

Millie had a job keeping a straight face. Pete gulped and looked a tad embarrassed. He hadn't given it a second's thought. Didn't she already have enough with the former matrimonial home in Hull, "loadsa money" and a twenty five percent stake in the new business – one she didn't even have to lift a finger in the running of? Peter had thought for some time that Clive White's advice to give her all of that to ensure a quick deal on the purchase of the Clifftop Hotel had been somewhat generous. On the other hand, Clive had steered them into a very low price for the new Hotel so perhaps, all in all, it wasn't too bad after all. The adage 'we are where we are' was never more apposite than right now.

'Er, no, to be honest I er, …'

Millie dug her Dad out of a hole.

'Dad, tell you what, why don't you pay for our lunches at the Beverley Arms as a Christmas present to Mum. I'm sure she'd appreciate that as much as anything and that way you don't have to actually buy anything and gift-wrap it. Seventy-five quid should do it.'

'What? Seventy-five quid!'

'In fact make it a straight ton. Then we can have a few glasses of something nice to go with it. It is Christmas after all.'

'But Lucy doesn't even drink and …'

'Maybe not but Aunty Gwen does and you know how she can knock the gins back.'

'You didn't tell me Mandy was bringing her sister, not that it matters. Oh all right then here's a hundred pounds and don't forget to bring me the change.' The last remark was more in hope than expectation.

'And Dad, either you or Jamie will drive us to the railway station on Wednesday morning please won't you? The train leaves at 11:01 so can we leave here just after ten-thirty please? We don't want any cock-ups.'

'Yes, of course. Listen, can we run through those forecasts and spreadsheets of yours. It scares me the amount we're going to have to spend to get this place ship-shape. For a start there's the huge cost of fifty-plus televisions which both you and Clive completely omitted to put into the costings. Garry just happened to mention it in an off-hand remark. Millie just sighed a daughterly sigh.

'Dad, you obviously didn't look properly. We've allocated over fifty grand to be spent on IT and Communications. Surely you didn't think we were going to spend that sort of money on a new office computer did you?'

Peter wasn't sure what to say. It was just as well that his eldest daughter and her Business and Accountancy tutor assumed responsibility for that side of things. Maybe it was time that he started to concentrate more on his own field of expertise – namely food and beverages – after all that was his speciality for two decades at sea as a senior steward. It was high time that he and Jamie had a long sit-down with one of those new-fangled iPads and made a note of what stock they would need to acquire, at a minimum, After an hour and three cups of tea later they began to realise the magnitude of the task and the planning that would have to go into it.

'Dad, we're looking to feed one hundred people max at a time, assuming full occupancy. You've got down here six fifty-litre barrels of lager and the same quantity of no less than four other beers. This is a fifty-bed hotel, not a five hundred cabin ferry. Let's start again.'

By five o'clock it was well and truly dark and the girls returned from Sebbie's afternoon "walkies" cold and hungry.

'What's for tea, Bro?"

'Bangers and Mash with lots of caramelised onion gravy, broccoli and asparagus. Vegetarian sausages for you, Lucy, so don't pull a face at me please. By the way I forgot to tell you the Oxford English Dictionary is changing its meaning of the word 'vegetarian' next year. Did you hear?'

'Er, no. What's the new definition?'

'It's apparently an old Red Indian word meaning 'Bad Hunter.'

Millie and Peter laughed their socks off. Lucy, by contrast, was not impressed and the look she gave him disappeared into infinity.

6.

The next few days flew by as it always seems to do in the run-up to Christmas. More plans were made and boxes ticked. According to Millie's "count-down" calendar there were now less than ninety days to go before the Clifftop Hotel would re-open under its new name – the Koala. Wednesday morning brought a fine day with a clear sky – perfect for a nice train ride to Beverley, the County Town of East Yorkshire. Mercifully, traffic in town was light and Peter dropped off his daughters at the railway station with a generous fifteen minutes to spare.

'Lucy, let's grab a couple of 'flat whites' from the kiosk shall we and take them with us on the train? Which platform is it anyway?' Lucy glanced up at the electronic time-table which displayed train departures, the soonest at the top.

"SHEFFIELD via Bridlington and Hull 11:01 Platform 4"

'It's over there look. We've got oodles of time!'

'Two flat whites please, Sue. Oh yes and a couple of those blueberry muffins. They look yummy.'

'Coming up! Not seen you getting this train before, love. I recognise most of the regulars on this next train. Lots of folks going to Hull shopping today. You know, last minute stuff for Christmas. That's a problem with seaside towns these days – lots of big retailers have either closed or moved to those awful retail parks. The last train that left for York was packed with shoppers. My Gran used to tell me about all the lovely shops there used to be in Scarborough. I think she would be very upset if she could see it now with all these betting shops, charity shops and the like. Do you remember …'

'No, we're fairly new to Scarborough. We moved here from Hull and bought a small hotel in Peasholm but we've taken over the Clifftop and we're going to rename it and reopen just before Easter.'

'Oh wow! So it's you?! I heard something on BBC Radio York weeks and weeks ago. Well good luck to you. You'd better watch the clock. That's ten pounds and fifty pence please.'

Millie swished her contactless debit card from the Blackbird Bank plc across the card reader. Ping!

'Safe journey, see you again maybe.'

'Thanks, Sue.'

Thank goodness for name badges. It made things so much more personal and friendlier. That reminded her to order new name badges for the Hotel Koala to replace those from the Hotel Scarbados. So many things to attend to in the New Year. She would add it to her 'to do' list. Right now it was family stuff, not business.

The train left exactly on time and within minutes it had passed the town's retail park mostly consisting of branches of national chains ranging from cars to DIY to household goods. The first stop was Seamer although it could perhaps be more accurately called Crossgates as it was over a mile from Seamer village as the crow flies. There was a historic reason for this. More than half a century ago it had been the site of Seamer Market where every Monday scores of farmers from over a wide area brought their livestock to sell to butchers. At this time of the year the sight of poultry being unloaded from special livestock carriages would have been a sight to behold. In Victorian times, thousands of geese and turkeys would actually have been walked into town. Imagine what the animal rights brigade would make of that scenario today. Just as well Lucy didn't know. Next stop was the little seaside town of Filey but train passengers couldn't really see any of this quiet but delightful resort, not even a view of the sea. That would have to wait until they could get a view of Bridlington Bay about ten minutes later.

They were not disappointed as a weak, but yellow winter sun shone over the bay, highlighting the white water atop the moderate waves that were coming in from the East. The Tannoy was quickly in action as soon as the train halted.

'This is Bridlington. This train will leave in approximately ten minutes for Driffield, Beverley, Cottingham and Hull Paragon where it will form the twelve-twenty to Sheffield.' Lucy's ears pricked up.

'Hey I didn't know until today this train goes to Sheffield, did you?'

'No, I can't say that I did. Why?'

'Well, just thinking, maybe one day in the New Year you and I could have a day out at Meadowhall – for the New Year sales maybe. Just a thought.'

Millie sighed. She loved her little sister dearly but thinking about her forthcoming new job at the vet's, and probably little else, she had little if any understanding of the enormity of the business tasks in front of them. Perhaps it was just as well. Ever the diplomat though, Millie gave a positive response.

'Yeah that sounds brill. Let's get Christmas and New Year over with first though shall we?'

It wasn't long before the magnificent edifice of Beverley Minster loomed in the distance. Resplendent in the low winter sunshine you could see it for miles. It was loved by residents and visitors alike and was every bit as impressive as York Minster.

'Do you think that Mum and Aunty Gwen will be there already, Millie? I take it they'll have got on a train like the one we'll be going back on later?'

'Oh yes, there's only one line from Hull to Scarborough – or should I say 'Ull, like Mam?' They both giggled.

'We're just about there, look.'

The train slowed down as it moved into the covered station. They climbed off and mounted the steps to cross to the other northbound platform and the main exit.'

'Perhaps Mam and Aunty Gwen have got here before us and are in the tea room?'

Before they had even crossed the bridge Millie's iPhone started to ring in her jeans back pocket. It was her mother.

'Hello love. We've got a problem, Millie. Our train's been delayed and now it's been cancelled altogether. We're on the way in a taxi so we'll meet you at the Beverley Arms, love.'

'What happened?'

'Well, I'm guessing it's another one of those overtime bans by the train drivers' Union. As if they don't get paid enough already. Make me mad they do!'

'So where are you now?'

'We've just gone past that garden centre where you and your father knicked those palm trees from and ...'

'I told you before we didn't pinch them. With the arrival of Covid and imminent lock-down, they were giving them away and ...' She didn't finish. Her mother was obviously in 'one of those Viking moods' again and she was asking the driver how long it would take. 'Ten to fifteen minutes' was his reply.

'OK Mam, we'll see you there. Meet us in the main dining area. The table's booked in my name. See you soon.'

Mandy hung up without another word. She definitely was in Viking mode. The girls walked up past Wednesday Market and Ye Olde Pork Shop next door to one of those cream coloured telephone boxes, a unique feature of the area that encompassed Hull and the immediate surrounding area. Kingston upon Hull had always had its own telephone system quite separate from BT and even before that with the old Post Office.

'Oh look, Lucy, there's the Olde Pork Shop that Dad used to rave about. He drove up here once a month just to fill up on his special sausages then put most of them in the freezer at home to last until the next visit. Let's get some on the way back shall we? Jamie can do that gorgeous 'Bangers and Mash' again for us.' Lucy just scowled.

The lunch with their mother and her sister, Aunty Gwen, went well as far as it went. Mandy didn't seem excessively pleased to see her two daughters. Millie paid the bill at the end with a generous 'Christmas tip' for the attentive waitress who had served them. She reminded them of the obliging Marina at the Crescent Gardens before they moved into the hotel. Where on earth were they going to recruit staff like that? Mandy started to get vociferous after her third gin and tonic. She was more than keeping up with her sister.

'How much was that bill – ow much? I hope your father's paying. He wouldn't be where he is today if it wasn't for my inheritance .... and perhaps he'd like to pay for our taxi from 'Ull an' all, while he's at it. And speaking of brass, do you know when the first company dividend will be paid out? I'm still a quarter shareholder in the new company. Gwen and I want to use some of that to go on a Mediterranean cruise in the Spring, don't we Gwen? I said don't we, Gwen?'

Gwen was busy fiddling with the volume control on her right hearing aid which, unfortunately for her, was facing towards the in-house speaker, blaring out Bing Crosby, Slade and Chris Ria – the usual Christmas stuff.

'So when is the first dividend due? Easter or what?'

It suddenly occurred to Millie that her Mother had clearly not read the Minutes of the first Board Meeting that Clive White had so meticulously compiled and distributed to all four shareholders. She kept her thoughts to herself – for the time being.

'No Mum, the first divi will be paid after the end of the first quarter's trading. So that will be at the end of June.'

'What? Well we'll start to look at brochures in the New Year, won't we Gwen? I said won't we, Gwen? I think we'll order a taxi back to Kingswood. If there's any change left from the bill you might like to put it towards our taxi fare.'

Millie gave another one of her signature sighs. How her Mum had changed from the jovial housewife of yesteryear. It was quite upsetting. She hadn't once enquired about her son, ex-husband or even the business in which, as she quite rightly said, owned a quarter of the company Koala Hotel Ltd. The taxi arrived and the two sisters got in after the briefest of air kisses all round. Mandy's last words before the driver shut the rear door were:

'And I hope that tart from that London magazine doesn't ever venture anywhere near the new business. Quite why your father ever took a shine to her I just don't know. All fur coat and no knickers if you ask me. Typical 'cockney cow' anyway ta-ra. We're off.' And with that they were gone.

The girls called into Ye Olde Pork Shop on the way back to the station. They guessed there was something wrong when they asked for four pounds of pork sausages.

'Crikey! When were you last in here, before Covid easily I'd say?'

'Er, well yes. Dad used to call especially for Mr Hillman's special recipe sausages.. Did I say something wrong?'

'No, not at all love. Sadly John Hillman passed away just before Covid. Nothing was ever weighed in kilos, only pounds and ounces. In fact nothing was ever weighed properly at all. Whatever it was being bought was put on these old-fashioned scales for less than a second and the charge was always the same – four pounds.'

'Oh yes, I can remember Dad telling me now. What a shame Dad will be quite upset when I tell him.'

'You can also tell him that John's funeral was massive. He's actually buried in the Minster. Hundreds of folks still come here and ask for John's special sausages. The recipe itself was part of the goodwill when the current owners bought it. John's photo is up there on the wall. Look!'

He looked resplendent in his butcher's coat, striped apron and straw hat and Millie took a couple of photos on her iPhone.

'Is there anything else I can get for you, ladies?' Lucy dared to ask.

'I don't suppose you do vegetarian sausages do you?'

'Well actually we do, Miss. We cater for all palates these days. You can have a choice of tomato, chive, spring onion or fennel flavourings. Which would you like?'

'Wow! I'll have a pound of each please.'

'You mean half a kilo, Miss?'

The cost was eight pounds. Seems like little had changed.

'Thanks, goodbye, and a Merry Christmas to you, ladies.'

'And the same to you. We'll be back again I'm sure.'

Twenty minutes later and they were both on the train home to Scarborough. Lucy was almost in tears.

'You know what really upset me? Mum didn't once ask after Sebbie. That really hurts.'

7.

Jamie cooked a nice supper of 'toad in the hole' with roast potatoes and broccoli. The girls didn't want much to eat, being still full of the excellent haddock, hake and halibut served up at the Beverley Arms. Lucy announced that she was taking Sebbie out for a short "walkies" along the cliff top towards the castle. It was easy to see where the name of the hotel had come from.

'I'm going up to the Albert Hotel for a game of darts now. I won't be late. See ya later.'

Peter was glad that his son was starting to find a few new friends in the town. It had been very unsettling for him in the early days but over a year after the big move from Hull he was more than finding his way.

'Have a good evening, Jamie. Score a few 'one hundred and eighties' won't you!'

Millie went to make a fresh pot of coffee and soon returned to the lounge to find her Dad semi-reclined on a sofa fiddling with a TV remote control that seemed to have more buttons on it than a Space Shuttle instrument console.

'Oh my God. The new telly's arrived! Wow! When did that come?'

'This afternoon while you and Lucy were away in Beverley with your Mother and Aunty Gwen. This TV is just amazing. We haven't even had to pay for it yet, it's on approval over the Christmas period to see if we like it. The young guy that delivered and fitted it was a really pleasant chap – only in his early twenties. He said he'd pop back after Christmas with a matching "sound bar" – whatever one of those is. Any idea?'

'Dad you are a total dinosaur with technology aren't you? Pass it over here. Which channel were you looking for anyway?' As usual Pete surrendered with no hesitation.

'Here. Anyway how was your day? By the look of Lucy's long face I'm guessing not according to plan or expectations. Am I right?'

'You could say that, Dad. Our train was bang on time but Mum and Aunty Gwen's was delayed and finally cancelled. They eventually arrived in a taxi from Paragon Station and this will make you laugh.'

'What will?'

'She's invited you to pay for the fare!'

'Cheek! By the way, was there much change from the money I gave you for the lunches? Not that I'm bothered, just curious that's all.'

'Then this will make you laugh even louder. She demanded the surplus from the lunch money for the taxi fare all the way home too!'

'Good grief. She came out of the divorce settlement a lot better than I did!'

'You and I both know that, as does she. But Dad, she's changed. It's now just like that ABBA song "Money, money, money." Then she asked when she'd be getting her first dividend from the new company. She and Aunty Gwen want to go on a Mediterranean cruise with it, so she said.'

'I can't believe how someone I thought I knew so well could …'

'Dad, people change and money can be a catalyst for changes for the worse. She's my Mother but right now I feel as if she's just a name on a birth certificate, not the lady who gave me my birth and infant nurture. Honestly, it's so sad.'

'How was she with Lucy? They always had a special bond, you know, Mother and the youngest of the litter so to speak.'

'I might as well tell you. Apart from a peck on the cheek on arrival and an air kiss on departure she practically ignored her.'

'Oh dear, poor Lucy. Still at least right now she's out with her favourite man – Sebbie!'

'Well that's another thing that really upset her. Mum didn't ask after you or Sebbie at all. Not once. That really got to her and she had a little weepy on the train home.'

'Oh, poor lass. Did anything good come out of today's reunion?'

'No, to be honest. We stopped by Ye Olde Pork Shop in Beverley before we got on the train home.'

'Oh no, don't tell me it closed and never reopened after Covid?'

'No Dad, but the even sadder news is that the former proprietor, John Hillman, has passed away.'

'Oh no! I'd been going there for years. I can't believe it. It might have seemed bonkers driving from Kingswood to Beverly just for sausages and ham but .... oh dear me. I'm a bit shocked.'

'What made you go there in the first place?'

'Long story, but as you might expect I met hundreds of regular passengers on the Pride of Bruges over the years, hundreds. One of them was an ex-Royal Marine called Terry McMahon – a dapper little chap with a handlebar moustache and he always wore a black cap. He drunk like a fish. He must have had hollow legs. He was retired and lived in Scarborough. Anyway, one evening before the ship docked in Hull the next morning, during a lull at the Bar, we were chatting about meat of which he was obviously something of a connoisseur. He just happened to mention that he and his travelling companion always stopped at Beverley on the way home for a coffee and to buy some sausages at Ye Olde Pork Shop. You should try them, Pete. Mention my name if you do. Just say that Terry the Marine from Scarborough recommended you. So I did, simple as that.'

'Goodness me. How long ago was that? Can you remember?'

'Crikey, probably since about 2004, shortly after I joined the Pride of Bruges. I can't believe he's gone. He was an absolute institution and a gentleman to boot. The tragedy is that his secret recipe probably died with him too.'

'No, apparently not. It actually formed part of the goodwill of the business when it was sold. Sadly his son didn't want to carry on the family business. We brought a couple of kilos back for you. I've put them in the freezer. And Lucy got the same weight in vegetarian sausages in four separate flavours.'

'Well that's a sign of the times. Old John would have had no truck with this veggie lark – ha ha!'

'I can't wait to tell Jamie. He might be able to make something of it on a Specials Board one night. You know how much Pamela Hesketh encouraged him to be descriptive. Oh yes, and before I forget, Mum's parting words were not about any of us. They were about Pamela.'

'What? You're kidding me. Why, what did she say?'

'I can't repeat exactly what she said but she was most unpleasant. Just jealous if you ask me. Have you kept in touch with her by the way? I liked her. When we're a bit more settled it might be nice if you invited her up here again. Why didn't you invite her up to join us for Christmas? I don't think she has any ties to London any more. Dad, why are you looking at me like that. Your face looks as if it's going to burst.'

'I already have done, love. She's arriving on Christmas Eve just after lunch – that is if these bloomin' trains are on time.'

Millie crossed the room and gave her Dad a huge bear hug.

'Go for it, Dad, just go for it.'

8.

Over breakfast the next morning Peter formally told them all of his invitation to Pamela to join them for Christmas. Jamie had to pretend to look surprised. A sly wink to his father was the only signal.

'Dad, that's great news! I want her advice on my new restaurant – when it eventually opens – you know, what name to give it, the décor – in fact just about everything. When did you say she's arriving?'

'Tomorrow, Christmas Eve. Sometime in the afternoon. She'll text me tomorrow when the train is leaving York so about fifty minutes after that I guess. Lucy, say something love. Anything.'

She was uncharacteristically silent for a few seconds and then blurted out.

'I'm pleased too. I'm glad you didn't hear what Mum had to say about her in Beverley. Horrid things. I'm glad you weren't there. She was nice to me when she came up for my sixteenth birthday party wasn't she? And Sebbie liked her too so she must be an OK lady. I remember that she even brought some "doggy treats" in her shoulder bag.'

'Millie, are you happy love?'

They pretended not to have had a conversation the previous evening.

'Dad, it can only be good news. How long is she staying with us anyway?'

Peter looked blank.

'Do you know what, I think I forgot to ask. Does it matter?' They all smiled but Millie had the last word on the subject. She had a job keeping a straight face.

'Dad, shall I make up one of the spare rooms for her? Maybe the one under the turret at the end of the corridor? You know how noise carries at night!'

'That's quite enough young lady. Now what are our plans today? It's almost Christmas after all.'

Jamie was the first to react.

'Well, I'm going to roast the small fresh turkey that the butchers in the market dropped off yesterday. Five kilos will be just about right for the eight of us to have cold on Boxing Day, now that we know that Pamela's coming and of course the Ritsons. And a lovely piece of York ham to boil too. I'm going to do it in the slow cooker and use Coca-Cola not water. Dad, don't forget to prepare your special Bubble and Squeak too. And the betting slips for the big race. Don't forget the palaver we had last year. Mind you we didn't know our way around then did we? That bookies is right opposite the train station so if you go early you can kill two birds with one stone .... well you know what I mean. What about you, Lucy?'

'Well Millie and I are going to decorate the small dining room. We've got some of that artificial snow spray to make the windows look festive and some real holly that I found on one of our "walkies" a few days ago. Sebbie stopped for a wee against a small tree down by the miniature railway line and 'hey presto' guess what sort of tree it was? I had to go back later with those secateurs from the tool box but I got several bunches.'

Where would they all be without that dog's predilection for trees? Suddenly, Peter had a flash.

'Jamie, you just mentioned about asking for Pam's advice on the possible name for your restaurant. Well would you mind if I made a suggestion? The final choice would be yours of course but what about this?'

'Go for it, Dad.'

'How about the Four Seasons Restaurant?'

''Any particular reason? What made you come up with that one?'

'Well it was the name of the main restaurant on the Pride of Bruges – until they renamed it something silly like the Kitchen Café or something equally unappetising. Just think, you could then change the menu, indeed the whole ambience, four times a year. It would give you enormous scope would it not?'

'Dad, do you know what, I think you might have something there. Let's talk it over with Pamela shall we?'

Jamie's head was already buzzing. Four new menus a year – wow!

Father and son spent the next few hours in the kitchen together. Jamie prepared the small but juicy fresh turkey for the oven with almost a pound of fresh streaky bacon coated to the outside with olive oil to make it look like it was one of those bizarre items of clothing once worn by lady Ga-Ga. Lucy, of course, would not be partaking in the "meat-fest" but without telling her, he was also preparing a magnificent vegetarian nut roast. When completed it would resemble a "Swiss Roll" in appearance. He had cannibalised two of the veggie sausages she had brought back from Ye Olde Pork Shop in Beverley. In fact it would be triple favoured with fennel at one end, chives at the other and chestnut stuffing in the middle. He would have to come up with a name for it if indeed it met with Lucy's approval on Boxing Day. He could already envisage it being served in slices like a cold Beef Wellington, perhaps with a warm cranberry jus trickled over it. He would make the final decision on the day.

Peter diligently peeled five kilos of Maris Piper potatoes – a job he never relished but he knew it had to be done. That alone took almost an hour and he wondered how sailors of yesteryear in the Royal Navy had fared when punished with several days potato peeling after some minor misdemeanour. What a good job he had never been in the "Andrew" like his grandfather. The discipline would probably have finished him off. Two numb thumbs and fifty minutes later he filled the biggest double-handled pan in the kitchen with tap water and placed it on the biggest gas ring. Adding a healthy tablespoonful of sea salt, he turned up the flame to its maximum and patiently waited for it to come to the boil. In those intervening minutes he cleaned and trimmed the entire crop of small Brussels sprouts on one of those stalks that Jamie had acquired from the Market Hall and similarly put them in a large pan of water to bring to the boil.

'Jamie, let's make a brew shall we? This is thirsty work. I'll put the kettle on. How are you doing with that turkey?'

'Ready to go into the oven in a few minutes then it's a slow cook for three hours followed by a hot blast for the last twenty minutes and I'll add the honey glaze just before I do that.'

The water for the potatoes came to boil just before Peter was about to pour his second cup of tea. He gently lowered the spuds into the boiling cauldron whereupon of course the water died down as the temperature temporarily lowered. Within thirty seconds it once again resembled a hot geyser in Yellowstone Park and Peter turned down the wick to obtain a nice steady simmer. Time for more tea, but mindful of the need not to overcook the "Pipers" he looked at his watch and reached for a sharp twin-tyned carving fork. They need to be just firm in the middle. He wasn't making fish-cakes!

Fifteen minutes later and both potatoes and sprouts were done, drained and cooling down. The turkey had taken up temporary residence in the oven at one hundred and forty Celsius and Jamie stared at his father's two pans with just a whisper of steam emanating from both pans which were now lidless.

'So what do you do now, Dad?'

'You go and help your sisters in the dining room whilst I perform my alchemy, Go on, off you go.'

Peter cubed the now cooled potatoes and halved the sprouts. Adding both back into the largest pan he then added a small tin of Jolly Green Giant sweetcorn and a cupful of halved fresh cranberries. Stirring them altogether, liberally drizzled with extra-virgin olive oil. He was then ready for his final secret ingredient – a few pinches of Cayenne pepper. He popped the lid back on and joined the others in the dining room. What a sight to behold. Every window looked as if it was from a Charles Dicken's novel with lookalike real candles operated with miniature batteries to give flickering flames. Two smallish tables had been pushed together and covered with a large cream coloured linen table cloth. There were three place settings down each side with one at one end. The best canteen of Arthur Price Sheffield silver cutlery had been opened and the contents polished like the Crown Jewels. But who would sit at the head of the table? Nobody would know until Boxing Day. Jamie had already made the decision but kept it to himself.

'Girls, this looks absolutely fabulous. Well done. I just can't wait until Boxing Day when we'll act as hosts. Tell you what, let's have a little pre-celebration drinkipoos shall we? Millie dashed into the kitchen and took out a bottle of Avery's finest Prosecco. It was almost Christmas after all. Wasn't it?

But Christmas Eve was going to prove a little more trying than envisaged.

9.

As always, the DAB Radio in the kitchen was pre-tuned to BBC Radio York. It was just after the eight o'clock News and Georgey's mystery voice competition was still unsolved for the twenty-fifth day, leaving listeners bemused and irked in equal measure. As usual, the voice was familiar but oh so elusive to guess correctly. It had taken over forty days for the soothing tones of Jools Holland's voice to be recognised and it caused hundreds of family arguments and spilt tea over the whole county of North Yorkshire for weeks.

Georgey's dulcet tones wafted over the airwaves with the latest offering:

'So, who is the new mystery voice then cooking bacon and eggs in the frying pan? Uh-oh, it's going to have to wait. I've just been told down my headphones that there's an urgent travel newsflash just come in so the mystery voice will have to wait. Over to you, Bek.'

The news had caught Bek Homer unawares too. She wasn't ready for this – in fact nobody was.

'Travel news just in and it's not good. Trans-Pennine Express have just announced, with regret, that they might have to curtail some services today due to a shortage of train drivers. Can you believe that on Christmas Eve with thousands of people on the move for the festive holidays?'

Peter looked horrified. All the blood drained from his face.

'Oh my God. What if Pam gets stuck at York? Will they lay on a replacement bus service?'

'On Christmas Eve? You must be joking, Dad.' Millie took charge, as always.

'Look, let's assume the worst. How about this for a plan? Dad, you drive to Malton which is about half-way and meet Pam there. If her train to Scarborough is indeed cancelled then you are already half-way to York. In any event it will then give you both some chatting time together. It's a few months since you saw each other after all, isn't it? Will she have left London Kings Cross yet?'

'I've no idea, Millie. Why?'

'Dad, just text her now and tell her what the plan is. It might put her mind at rest too. Just do it!'

Millie sighed once again. Sometimes he just needed a little prodding from daughter Number One.

Peter went to get his mobile phone which was "on charge" in his bedroom on the top floor. Thank goodness the hotel had two electric lifts each able to accommodate eight persons or one thousand kilos, as the brass plate advised on the inside of each one. That equated to one hundred and twenty five kilos per person. Surely not. Maybe the lifts were of Japanese manufacture and designed for Sumo wrestlers. No matter. Five minutes later and Peter emerged into the lobby with a smile on his face.

'I just spoke with Pam. Her LNER train is due into York at thirteen-fifteen that's, er, quarter past one to you lot.' His old maritime habit of using a twenty-four hour clock would never leave him.

'She has a twenty minute wait in York for the connection to Scarborough and it's due in Malton at fourteen hundred hours and …' It was Jamie's turn. He didn't want any cock-ups either, so keen was he to see Pamela and discuss the new restaurant.

'Right then, Dad. That A64 road can be very unreliable and frequently gets jammed up with holiday traffic. Did you listen to the Prime Minister being interviewed by Georgey earlier this year? *Mark from Scarbados* had phoned into the program to ask why the busiest resort in England had the worst road access.'

'So what was his reply?'

'Well of course it was the usual bumf, typical of politicians. You know – 'We're looking closely at the situation, the situation is being monitored, it will be dealt with under the levelling-up plan etc.'

'You mean he said bugger all. You kids weren't born but I remember it took decades to finally sanction the building of the Humber Bridge. They only actually do something when there's votes involved.'

'Anyway, Dad, if I were you I'd set off for Malton just after one o'clock to be on the safe side. The weather report's coming up next. Shush everyone. Georgey's back.'

'Well the travel news wasn't terribly encouraging was it? Let's hope the weather is a bit better. Over to you, Katerina.'

'Morning, Georgey, and morning everyone. Sadly it's not terribly good news from me either. Cold air from Iceland has moved south-east much quicker than expected and is hitting much milder air that has moved up from the Azores. As many of you amateur meteorologists will know, this can often mean snow. It's very hard to predict but there could be moderate falls from lunchtime onwards starting in the west of the county, so Skipton and Harrogate will be the first to be affected followed by York in mid-afternoon. It might just peter out by the time it reaches the coast at Scarborough and Bridlington. Sorry I can't be more specific than that.' Peter reacted first.

'That's all we bloody need. I'll leave here just after twelve noon to be on the safe side. I can always get a cuppa and a sandwich in the tea-room at Malton and read a newspaper. Right I'll get changed into something a bit smarter. I don't want to look like a schmuk in front of Pammie. Now do I?'

Millie and Lucy exchanged a grin and a smile. He wouldn't be 'dressing up' if he was going to meet their mother, that's for sure. They had both also noticed that these days he never called her Pamela. It was either Pam or Pammie. Cupid was certainly active – thus far anyway.

Ten minutes later and Peter re-emerged from his temporary makeover in the bedroom. He wore a Harris tweed jacket, complete with matching tie, and even the top button of his shirt was done up – possibly for the first time since he had discarded his smart Steward's uniform for the last time. His black,toe-capped, Clarks shoes shone like two mirrors.

'Well girls, how do I look? Do I pass muster?'

By the looks on their faces neither Millie nor Lucy knew what muster meant. Lucy broke the silence.

'Dad, you look fine but you'll need a top-coat. It looks freezing out there. Take your sheepskin, the one with the woolly collar. It will go nicely with your jacket.'

'Yes, you're right. I'll need it once I get out of the warm car. Right, I'm off. I think I'll stop at the Shell Garage at Staxton on the A64 and fill up the tank. There've been lots of accounts of cars stuck in snow with no heating recently because they've run out of petrol. And as for those crazy folks with electric cars whose batteries have run flat .... anyway that's their problem. I'll call you when we're on the way back and maybe you could rustle up some nice hot supper, Jamie?'

'Leave it to me, Dad. Off you go. And mind the road – lots of drink drivers around at this time of year.'

And he was gone. Something nagged Peter all the eight miles to Staxton. Twenty minutes later he pulled up at pump number One and suddenly remembered what it was. With a change of plan to pick up Pamela at either Malton or York, the original plan to place the bets of the big race on Boxing Day, the King George the Sixth Chase, was now in the bin. Before even getting out of the car to fill up he grabbed his mobile phone and speed-dialled Jamie.

'Jamie, it's Dad. Listen, can you get on your bike and go and place those bets for us?'

'Just like we did last year? A £1 bet to win on every runner, right?'

'Yes that's right. Oh, one other thing you can do for me please which I completely forgot about. Can you also pop into that perfume shop in the Brunswick Centre and get a small bottle of Chanel Coco Mademoiselle perfume. The real McCoy not the eau de toilette.'

'Dad, what are you on about? Odour what?'

'Just ask the girl in the shop, she'll know OK. And ask her to gift-wrap it please. You know, Pukka.'

Jamie didn't have a clue what his Dad meant half the time. Twenty years on a P & O Ferry had changed his old Hull vocabulary almost beyond recognition. He had once tried to explain to him what the acronym POSH (port out starboard home, to avoid the heat of the sun) really meant but Jamie was totally bamboozled. 'What the heck has travelling to India got to do with it? You only went as far as Zeebrugge.'

'And don't tell the girls, it's between me and you. I'll settle with you when I get back OK.'

'Yeah, OK Dad. You owe me one.'

Peter filled the tank, paid inside then zoomed off on the A64. It was looking bleak in the west, to put it mildly.

Katerina the weather girl had been spot on. It seemed like he was the only car heading west. All the oncoming traffic seemed to have their headlights on with intermittent wipers engaged.

He turned the car's radio onto Radio York's pre-tuned channel and by good fortune the traffic and travel news was next.

'Hello, Good afternoon, this is Abbie Dewhurst with your travel and weather update. To be frank, it's not good. Let's deal with the weather first. That predicted snowfall has arrived sooner than expected and two inches has already fallen in Harrogate and it's started snowing here in York too. It's looking like a white Christmas for the first time in over twenty years. Snow will reach all areas of the east coast by midnight with moderate to heavy falls forecast – quite a change from earlier predictions. As you might expect travel news isn't much better. LNER have said that all trains from London should arrive on time but services further north to Newcastle and beyond might be subject to severe delays and even cancellations. Even worse, Trans Pennine Express have just announced that all trains from York to Scarborough will terminate at Malton. Replacement bus services will be provided – subject to availability.'

Peter put his foot down. There were still twelve miles to go to Malton. It started to snow and he noticed more and more cars coming towards him had white rooves. Twenty minutes later and he pulled into the station car park and headed for the single platform. Malton Station was only single track. He glanced up at the electronic display.

'The next train will terminate here. Passengers heading for Scarborough to wait in the Waiting Room. A coach will be provided.'

Yeah right, well there weren't any buses or coaches in the car park. Who was kidding who? Suddenly the PA system crackled into life.

'Trans Pennine Express regret to announce the delayed arrival of the thirteen thirty-five from York. This is believed to be due to an incident on the track at Haxby Station. No further details are available but we will make another announcement as soon as more information is to hand. Crikey, thought Peter. What a good job Millie had come up with the idea of him driving to Malton. At least she was on the way. He hoped that back in Scarborough son Jamie was having a better time.

Jamie had parked his motorbike and placed the bets without any problem. There were nine runners and nine betting slips were tucked safely into his leather jacket. He strolled the two hundred yards down to the Brunswick Centre and soon found the Perfume Shop. He had forgotten to bring the scribbled note he had quickly made following the conversation with his Dad. The shop was busy and the two assistants behind the counter were serving non-stop.

'Yes love, can I help?'

'Thanks. I'm doing my Dad a favour. He wants something called Odour Toilet by Channel sounded like Cocoa something ...'

Both girls exploded with mirth.

'It's OK love, we know what you mean and I bet you're really buying it for your girlfriend aren't you?'

'No, honestly, it's for my Dad. He's trying to impress a lady from London who's staying at our hotel for Christmas.'

'Which hotel is that?

'The Clifftop not far from the cricket ground. We're not officially open yet, in fact not until Easter.'

'Oh yeah, I read summat in the Scarborough News about it. Will there be a big opening party, like?'

'We'll certainly be doing something. Now how much do I owe you?'

'That's just seventy-one pounds please, love. Ta. Donna'll wrap it for you. I've just had my nails done and I don't want to risk it tying the gold string. I'm Chloe by the way.'

'Hiya Chloe. And I'm Jamie, Jamie Fishburn.'

'Can we be very cheeky, Jamie? Will you invite us both to the opening Party?'

Jamie was caught totally off-guard. Were all Scarborough girls as forward as this? Perhaps he'd been spending too much time on his Chef's course and not studied enough of the local wildlife.

'Well, I don't see why not. Here, write down my mobile number and send me a text after Christmas. Donna and Chloe did you say? Anyway, thanks for your help and Merry Christmas.'

Twenty miles to the south-west things were not nearly as cheerful. In fact quite the opposite. The public address system had just squawked into life again.

10.

'Trans Pennine Express are pleased to announce that the problem on the line at Haxby is currently being attended to by North Yorkshire Police and the service has now restarted. The train is expected to arrive here at Malton in approximately twenty minutes time.'

Peter glanced at his watch and was horrified to see that it had stopped altogether more than half an hour ago. It had been a birthday present over a decade ago from his then wife Mandy. To be honest he had never particularly liked it – far too garish. He had often wondered if she had won it as a bingo prize. Peter stepped into the Tea Room and looked up at the wall mounted clock that looked as if it had been there forever. It said two-thirty PM. Time for quick cup of tea and perhaps a scone.

'Sorry love, I can do you a tea but food's finished now. Milk and sugar?' Oh well, not long to wait. He unfolded his *Daily Express* and read the headline:

'It's a white Christmas for the North. Mild and sunny in the South.' So much for levelling up.

Peter had barely finished his tea when the lady behind the counter blurted out – 'That train's just coming in now love. I take it you're waiting for your wife are you?'

'Thanks, er no, just a friend. Cheers and Merry Christmas.'

'The same to you. Have a good one.'

Within twenty seconds the mug was in the dishwasher and the lights turned out. Everyone was keen to get home and beat the oncoming poor weather – that is if Abbie on Radio York had been correct. Peter strode out onto the platform just as the shiny blue steel locomotive purred to a halt almost opposite where he was standing on the platform. There seemed to be five or six carriages behind it. There was a 'ping and a whoosh' as two electrically operated doors opened on the lead carriage. He saw several elderly people with small suitcases being helped onto the platform by fellow travellers and a member of staff. There was no sign of Pamela. Don't tell me she missed the connection at York? No, surely not. His disquiet didn't last long. The member of staff reappeared and headed for the third carriage whose doors had failed to open automatically.

'Leave those cases, Miss. I'll get them down for you.'

It was Pamela. First one then two long brown boots appeared through the door and descended gingerly onto the platform. Peter quickened his pace and soon threw both arms around her slender waist. He pecked her on both cheeks in turn and froze. He completely forgot the lines he had practised. For the first time in over thirty years he felt like a love-struck teenager. He needn't have worried. Miss Pamela Hesketh took command.

'Oh, Peter, I am sooo pleased to see you again. It's been too long, babes.'

'Babes? Babes? When had anyone ever called him Babes? Certainly not Mandy, not in a million years.

'Crikey, Pam, how much luggage have you got? Are both these cases yours? And you have a chunky shoulder bag too. Here let me take both of those cases. It's a good job they've got wheels on them. Did you know that we put a man on the moon before we put wheels on suitcases? Unbelievable when you think about it.'

That's one of the things she like about Pete. You never knew what he was going to say next but it was usually something interesting. She hadn't even been born when Neil Armstrong had taken that 'one small step for man but one giant leap for mankind.' he was always coming up with things like that. Pete opened the tailgate of the family estate car and picked up the first of Pam's two cases.

'What's in here, gold bars? It's a good job you're not on one of those airlines and paying an excess baggage charge.'

The second case was, if anything, slightly heavier and the rear suspension visibly dipped. Why women always carried so much clobber he never knew. It would be a while before he found out. It was almost dark, although it was only three o'clock. It was best not to dilly-dally.

'Plot a course for Scarborough, Captain Fishburn.'

'Yes M'am, but I think you mean Scarbados. We'll be on a heading of zero four five and increase revolutions to make fifty knots.'

They both laughed the easy laughs of two people who were totally at home in each other's company.

'Oh Pete, before we start off can you just bung this empty sandwich carton and Costa coffee cup in that green bin over there please. I don't like carrying trash around.'

'Sure, pass them to me.'

Now why hadn't she done this before they got in the car? Women!

Peter never knew, even years later what made him do it. It went against all his natural instincts. He lifted the hinged lid on the bin and paused momentarily for just a couple of seconds. Rolling up the cuff on his left arm he slid off his wristwatch and stuffed it into the Costa coffee polystyrene cup and replaced the snap-on lid. He hurled it into the dark recess of the bin as though running out a world-class Test batsman. He almost forgot to ditch the triangular sandwich wrapper at the same time. The cathartic effect on him was instantaneous. He was a new man. He got back into the car to be met by a wave of Chanel No. Five which hit him like a tornado. Now he knew why she wanted him to leave the car. They headed out towards the A64 and kept fingers crossed there would be no more hold-ups from the weather or anything else for that matter. Some hope.

They had gone less than six miles when the blue flashing lights of a Police vehicle hinted at trouble. They slowed to a halt and a uniformed Officer approached the driver's window.

'What's up, Officer? Don't tell me the road's blocked. That forecast snow has petered out, seems to me.'

'You're right, Sir. No snow. A sink-hole has suddenly appeared in Rillington village a mile ahead. The road is impassable. Where are you headed?'

'Scarbados, er I mean Scarborough.'

'Well Sir, you have two choices. Either you can double back to the by-pass and then take the road to Thornton le Dale via the High Marishes or you can take the next right and go via the Wolds and come into Scarborough via RAF Staxton Wold. I strongly recommend the first option. The Wolds being on higher ground will almost certainly have had some snow so why take the risk? Scarbados did I hear you say? I like it! Her indoors is always badgering me to take her to Barbados one day. I'll try to see if I can get away with Scarbados. It'll be a bit cheaper! Safe journey, Sir.'

'Thank you. Merry Christmas, Officer, and if you do make Scarbados look us up at the Hotel Koala not far from the Cricket Club.'

'Do you recommend it?'

'Gosh I hope so. We own it!'

'The Koala? Then I'll bear it mind, Sir.'

They all laughed at the traffic cop's pun, not normally a profession noted for its humour. Peter carefully negotiated a U-turn and headed back towards the by-pass and the road to Pickering and Thornton le Dale. The words – 'we own it' stuck in Pamela's mind like the ear worm of a popular tune. We own it. We own it. We own it.

It was fully dark now as they approached the little town of Thornton le Dale. On the right hand side was a broad but shallow stream illuminated by a thousand miniature white lights where artificial swans faced upstream, themselves lit up by discreetly hidden neon lights. It was mesmerising and magical. To Pamela, born and raised in the big city, it was like being on a different planet. She broke the silence and surprised Peter:

'Pete, can we stop here a few minutes please? Look, there are spaces on the left here'.

Without saying anything, Pete slowed the car to a stop and then neatly reversed into an empty slot so that they faced the river, the lights and the swans. A hundred yards away the village church clock chimed four times. The place was almost deserted. Slowly she turned towards him and with a tear-drop running down a cheek said:

'Peter, darling, kiss me then take me home please. Just take me home, Babes.'

Three 'babes' and a 'darling' in one day and it wasn't even over yet.

11.

They were almost inside the Borough of Scarborough's boundary and were approaching St. James's Church at the top of Valley Road where it joined the A64.

'Pete, if we go right here where does it take us?'

'Down the Valley to the South Bay. Why?'

'Can we go that way, please? I want to see both Bays. Do you mind? It's just that I haven't seen the sea since I was here at the end of last Summer. That's the problem with London. It's a train ride to Brighton or Southend to see the sea.

'You mean the oggin!' They both laughed. Pam was getting used to "Jack Speak." Another few weeks and she'd be fluent.

Indicating 'right', Pete changed lanes at the last minute and turned down the hill past the church famous for its three bell tower – but no bells. The green copper lightning conductor that ran down from the spire and the weather vane glowed in the street lights like a green mamba. Passing beneath the railway bridge of a million bricks they headed down towards the Bay. The ancient iron footbridge twixt town and the Spa had stood guardian for almost two centuries and the soft green lighting under its arches glowed like peppermint Aero. Pamela was in dreamland. If she wasn't gazing at the sea illuminated with soft moonlight, then she was looking at Pete with nervous sideways glances.

'Is it always like this, Pete?'

'Er, well no but it's not far off a full moon. It's due in a couple of days I think. Let's keep fingers crossed for a clear night and we can go out and moon-gaze.'

'Moon-gaze. Wow! I've never done that.'

'Will you still be here, Pam? How long do you plan to stay – not that there's any rush?'

Pamela didn't answer and continued to look all around her. The ancient castle walls rose to her left beyond the houses of the Old Town. Then suddenly they were gone as the road swept sharply facing the North Sea or the German Ocean as Sexton's map of Yorkshire called it. That latter moniker had swiftly fallen into disuse, even dislike, a century ago following the German Navy's bombardment of Scarborough in the Great War. Innocent civilians had died and there were still repercussions to the present day.

They were soon into the North Bay and within a couple of minutes Peter once again resumed his role of tour guide.

'There it is Pammie, that large building up there atop the cliffs with the turret on the corner. Voila! The soon to be christened Hotel Koala. It's hard to believe we own it.'

There's that phrase again, mused Pamela. We own it. We own it. That was the problem, so did his ex-wife. Well, twenty-five percent of it. For now anyway. When was she going to put all her cards on the table? She wasn't even sure herself.

'It's a sharp left here, Pam, up Prince Albert Drive followed by a right hair-pin up to the top.'

Pamela tried to take it all in. The smart white building on her left glowed 'Boston Hotel' and she wondered how on earth somewhere on the Eastern Seaboard of the USA had lent its name to small but picturesque hostelry on the East Coast of 'Ingerland.' Mind you, she had yet to learn why an appropriately named Clifftop Hotel was soon to be re-named 'Koala.' It was a mystery to her.

'Nearly there, Pam.'

They drove past a string of small hotels one of which was sadly boarded up having fallen into disuse. It was an eyesore and Peter was yet to learn that the whole issue was being taken up by a self-appointed committee of local residents.

'Here we are, Pam. Home sweet home. Welcome to the soon to be Hotel Koala.'

Before he had barely turned off the ignition she had unclipped her seat belt and gyrated to the right. A 'starboard ninety' as Pete might have called it.

'Thank you, honey. I can't tell how pleased I am – just to be here. I can't wait to see the kids again – and of course Sebbie.'

She didn't have long to wait. Jamie had been in the rear facing kitchen at the moment his Dad had swerved into the hotel car park, the headlights projecting twin beams across the ceiling. It had to be them. Nobody else was expected. He opened the rear door just slightly and before he could even shout a welcome 'Hello' Sebbie shot out between his legs and dashed towards the family car. It was fifty-fifty. Would he head for Peter, the head of the family, or the lady from London whom he had met on only two previous occasions? Peter didn't stand a chance. Sebbie knew which side his bread was buttered and made a bee-line for Pam and her shoulder bag which had the sniff of a hundred doggy treats – not totally masked by the Chanel No. Five.

'Oh, Sebbie. Good boy. Look, what I've brought for you. Yes, Fortnum and Mason doggie treats. You weren't supposed to get them until Christmas Day.'

The girls rushed out, oblivious to the chill easterly, both giving Pamela a homely hug then each grabbing a case that their father had lifted from the tailgate. Millie pulled the larger of the two cases, not that there was a lot in it, and smiled inwardly. If this lady was planning to stay for a weekend then there were fairies at the bottom of her garden – not that the Hotel had a garden.

'I've made you up one of the guest rooms, Pamela. It's up there right under the turret – look. It's very secluded and romantic isn't it?'

Was that a statement or a question? They exchanged the briefest of smiles. Pamela could only dream that, one day, Millie might make the loveliest of step-daughters. One day.

Stepping inside, Jamie blew Pamela two exaggerated air kisses. He was in his 'Chef's uniform' with his black and white chequered trews and little white hat. It was more of a gesture than a necessity but he wanted to give the right impression to Pamela.

'Hello, Jamie! Getting some practice for Master Chef I can see! Tell me, what's for supper?'

'You'll just have to wait and see Ma'am. I don't think you'll be disappointed. Aperitifs will be served in the lounge at six o'clock followed by supper at six-thirty. Now, if you don't mind, our staff will escort you and your luggage to your room.'

Millie groaned the groan of a mistreated sister. 'Staff' indeed. She would get her own back on little brother. Just you wait!

Pamela tried to take as much in as she could as they walked through the spacious public spaces and into the lobby and the two elevators. The highly polished wooden reception desk looked to be made of Douglas Fir unless she was very much mistaken. A blast from the past and probably taken from salvaged timbers in long disused cotton mills in West Yorkshire or Lancashire. Millie and Pamela chatted animatedly in the lift for the fifteen second ride to the top floor. They looked fairly new and had almost certainly replaced the pre-War examples that required inner and outer metal doors that looked like something from an old black and white movie starring Carey Grant or Audrey Hepburn. Journeys end was met with an electronic 'ping' not unlike a microwave.

'Here we are, Pam. We've put you in the end room underneath the turret. The views are amazing – look. Two windows with very different vistas.'

'Wow this one faces due east, right out to sea. I can actually see a ship despite the fact it's dark now. I wonder where it's headed for? And is it going north or south?' Millie just grinned.

'Well if you ask my Dad he'll probably be able to tell you even without a pair of binoculars.'

'Really? How?'

'Well if you can spot a red light on the side of it, that means its the port side so it's heading north – a green light is the starboard side and means it's heading south. Can you make out which?'

'Oh yes, I can now – now I know what I'm looking for! It's a green light.'

'Then it's definitely heading south. Tell Dad over supper and he'll probably tell you its name, heading and where its bound for.'

'You're kidding.'

'No, Dad really misses his life at sea in so many ways. He spends many an hour up here doing a bit of ship-spotting. Anyway look, I'll leave you to unpack and see you downstairs soon. No rush. We'll both need to change too. I think Jamie has rustled up something nice and festive for us. He wouldn't tell me what it was.'

''Lovely, Millie. See you downstairs soon.'

Half an hour later and all of them except Jamie were in

the lounge enjoying a mulled wine with some extra herbs that Jamie had blended earlier and allowed time to merge into the wine. It smelt slightly orangey but nobody was quite sure. Would he reveal his little secret later? They would have to wait. Peter assumed command and raised a glass.

'Cheers everybody, a very merry Christmas to you all. And Pamela, can I say how pleased we all are that you are able to join our family this year. To think we didn't even know you this time last year.'

'Thanks, Peter. I can't tell you how pleased I am to be with you all. I have a little gift for you all but I'm not handing it over until tomorrow. After you told me about your family tradition of watching the big race on Boxing Day I just couldn't resist it. It's a secret!'

It wasn't the only secret she was keeping to herself but she sincerely hoped that one would never come out. Jamie had just arrived from the kitchen, minus his chef's garb and now in black trousers, a frilly dress shirt, a festive bow tie and a 'holly and ivy' waistcoat. He looked every inch a Master Chef presenter. Gregg Wallace, eat your heart out.

'Ladies and Gentleman, would you please proceed to the dining room where supper will be served. For your delectation on this Christmas Eve I have prepared my own version of Toad in the Hole from the rarest breeds of Yorkshire pork sausages. Wolds bred, hand fed and organically reared they represent the finest agricultural traditions of the East Riding of Yorkshire. Served with a jus of caramelised onions and red wine they ...'

They all started to laugh, Pamela the loudest.

'Oh Jamie, what a star you're going to be on TV one day.'

The Toad in the Hole, made from the remainder of the purchase from Ye Old Pork Shop in Beverley, was accompanied by mashed suede and carrots and Dauphinoise potatoes – all grown on the chalky soil of the Yorkshire Wolds.

'Nothing has travelled more than thirty miles including the dessert to follow – baked Bramley apples stuffed with mincemeat and drizzled with brandy and Madagascar vanilla custard.' It was time for Millie's revenge.

'OK smart arse. And how many thousand miles is Madagascar from here? That'll teach you not to refer to me as your staff ever again, Bro. Got it?!'

'OK Sis, you win. But this local produce tag has a lot of merit these days, doesn't it Pam?'

'It certainly does, Jamie, and it works nicely with your Dad's idea of calling your restaurant the Four Seasons. I love it.'

It had been a long day for everyone and they all retired to bed long before the clock in the hall struck midnight. Peter decided to be a gentleman and stuck to his own room despite the obvious temptations of the flesh at the end of the corridor. His sleep was short lived as shortly after one o'clock he was awoken by the opening of his bedroom door by Pamela wearing only the flimsiest of diaphanous nightgowns. She was trembling as she slipped under his duvet.

'Peter, didn't the crying awaken you too? How could you not hear it? It was absolutely haunting. A young girl maybe?

12.

It was dawn on Christmas morning. A brief but beautiful sunrise splashed orange beams through the chink in the curtains of Peter's bedroom. Awakening only slowly, he stirred and moved an arm across to where he had expected to find a warm woman. In fact Pamela had risen an hour earlier, still haunted by the human cries that had disturbed her. She had gone back to her own room long before dawn. Although filled with trepidation she didn't want to give Pete's kids the wrong impression. She was cultivating the persona of a possible future step-mother, not a promiscuous trollop from London out for a good time on the coast with her fancy man.

An hour later and the whole family, plus Sebbie, were in the large kitchen where Jamie was about to start preparing their traditional Christmas Day breakfast – scrambled eggs with smoked salmon. Only thirty minutes earlier he had received a text from his mother in 'Ull complete with festive emojis and exploding stars.

'Happy Christmas Jamie love. Don't forget the traditional family breakfast. Mam. xx'

He wouldn't dare. The table was laid for five people and they all settled down to mugs of steaming hot Yorkshire Tea. Lucy poured a half a bowlful for Sebbie and was mindful to add some cold water lest he burnt his tongue. Whist she was doing that Sebbie looked up pleadingly at Pamela. Surely she wasn't going to keep him in suspense much longer.

'Oh all right, Sebbie, here you are then.'

She handed a small gift-wrapped box for Lucy to open. As soon as she had cut the string and removed the outer wrapping Sebbie went into bonkers mode. He ran around in circles and barked loudly twice. He must have recognised the box from when Pamela had arrived in the car park less than twenty-four hours earlier. Lucy was over the moon, let alone Sebbie.

'Oh Pamela, you are SOOO kind. You'll have to be careful or he'll be expecting them every time you come up to visit.' Pamela said nothing. She just couldn't at this stage.

'Right everybody. Choose what kind of toast you want – there's rye, farmhouse white, wholemeal, granary or French and a choice of real Yorkshire butter or ....'

'Pack it in Jamie! You're not on TV yet. You'll be giving us a choice of either Scottish, Swedish or Norwegian salmon next.' Everyone laughed but Millie had the last word.

'And don't try telling us that the salmon is local either!'

'Funny you should say that – have you ever heard of Filey Bay salmon?'

'Pull the other one, it's got bells on it. More tea and toast anyone?'

With lunch at the Lucky Dragon set for one o'clock they mutually decided that a nice walk would do them all good and would work up an appetite. It was the first time that anyone, including Pamela, had ever eaten Chinese food on Christmas Day.

'I'm so looking forward to it, Pete. I just love Chinese cuisine, particularly Northern Chinese with lots of pork, duck and seafood. Darling, you must come down to London in the Spring and I'll take you to Chinatown in Soho. The food is exquisite.

Millie looked a tad puzzled. The Yips at the Lucky Dragon had said that type of food was favoured in the south, not the north. Perhaps it was a slip of the tongue and she was just trying to appear more knowledgeable than she actually was. Lucy's main concern was Seb's morning "walkies" and once he had finished his tea and three more up-market posh doggie treats she fetched his lead.

'Right, well I'm going to walk with Seb down to the Watermark Café, along the sea front towards the castle and then up to the top and back. So I'll be an hour or maybe a bit less. Shall we exchange presents then, Dad?'

'Oh heck yes, er why not? Then after a café cognac we can set off to the lucky Dragon end …'

'I can offer you Martell, Remy Martin, Courvoisier or …'

'Shut up Jamie. You're beginning to sound like an old food and beverage nerd like your Dad.'

'Oi, less of the old. I'm not even sixty yet!'

The day was going swimmingly and only Sebbie had received a single present yet. Pete, Jamie, Millie and Pamela chose a different route for their morning stroll. They turned down the hill known as Victoria Park and crossed over the road towards the main entrance to Peasholm Park. It was quiet, very quiet, with just the odd lone doggie walker probably trying to work up an appetite too. Pamela was still trying to find her bearings and familiarise herself with the area.

'Hey, can we walk all the way round the lake and end up where we first started?'

'Sure we can. We'll turn left at the boathouse and follow our noses past the Tea Rooms. It's not open in the winter though or we could have had a toasted teacake and a cuppa. Tell you what, we'll do that straight after Easter if you like. Yes?'

Pamela didn't answer. Twenty minutes later and one clockwise circumnavigation of the lake they were indeed back at the main gate.

'Pete, what's that building over near the pagoda, over there?'

'That's where they keep the battleships for the Naval Warfare. It only operates in the summer though. It's one of England's oldest tourist attractions, I understand.'

'What? Even longer than the Mousetrap in the West End? Are you sure, honey?'

'Yep, beyond a shadow of a doubt. Anyway come on. Just past this little café on the right and then we have to walk up a million steps to get us up to the cliff top and home.'

'Oh look what a lovely name for a café – it's called Peaches and Cream. Your ex-wife even mentioned it on Lucy and Jamie's birthday party last year, didn't she?'

'She did? Are you sure?'

'Oh yes, she said something like 'I can't believe my little girl is sixteen – sweet sixteen, peaches and cream.'

'I can't say I remember, Pam. She hadn't taken much notice of me for months and to be honest I probably wasn't listening to her anyway. I'm surprised it stuck in your memory.'

He didn't dare tell her what Mandy had said about her. Ten minutes later they were all at the top of a hundred plus steps and it prompted Pamela to make a remark.

'Phew! You'd have thought that the Victorians would have built a funicular or something wouldn't you? It would make a nice tourist attraction, even today.'

'I've got news for you. Some local resident told me a while ago that there used to be one but that the Council tore it up and sold it to another Council in Cornwall. Nobody really knew why. It was just one of those mysteries.'

Pamela took it all in and more. She gazed back at the mini-mountain they had just climbed.

'What on earth is all that rough land over there on the other side of the road. It's all fenced off. Why?'

'Well apparently it was originally a huge outside lido called Atlantis with water chutes, slides and other aquatic attractions. The Council owned it and then closed it to make way for a massive business development including a cinema, hotels, shops, apartments and you name it.'

'So what happened? Why didn't it come off?'

'As I understand it, the only bits that got built were those two smart new apartment blocks that you can see clearly from here. Very popular they are too. They fetch high prices and are rarely on the market I'm told – high rentals too from those that are let out.'

'So what happened to the cinema? I noticed a small one just around the corner from our … er, the Hotel. Does it do well?'

'Yes, I think so and all the major new releases eventually reach there – you know Bond films and the like. It's old fashioned and family run with popcorn, ice creams in the interlude, but it fills a niche in the market. As for that gaping waste of a site over there I just don't know what's going to happen to it – seems like nobody does. It's just crying out for development, if you ask me. Come on, lets get weaving. I want that coffee and brandy!'

Once back at the Hotel Pamela, went to her room and immediately updated her Notes on her iPad. It was for her eyes only. For the time being anyway.

Java coffee and Remy Martin were served in generous measures in the lounge and gifts were exchanged. Pamela was so surprised with the perfume, and the anecdote of the "Odour Toilet" caused mirth all round. Pamela waited until last for her turn and produced a flat-shaped parcel about eighteen inches square wrapped in a copious thickness of bubble-wrap. Had she taken a leaf out of Mandy's book the previous year with another photograph of Sebbie? Surely not.

Lucy was given the task of removing all the packaging. It was a fine photograph of two horses in a field, one brown and the other brilliant white. They were surrounded by fox-hounds, probably a couple of dozen of them. Both riders wore the brilliant red traditional jackets and the rider of the brown horse was about to blow on his post-horn. Tally Ho! There was a little caption screwed to the bottom of the frame and Lucy read it out loud.

'The famous racehorse, Desert Orchid, is pictured here in his retirement with the Sinnington Hunt in North Yorkshire.'

There was an awkward silence which Pamela felt she had to break.

'When Pete told me that we'd all be watching the King George the Sixth Stakes on the TV tomorrow I decided to do a little research. Apparently Desert Orchid was the most popular winner ever in the history of the race and a stunningly beautiful animal to boot. I contacted a racing correspondent at the Daily Telegraph and he managed to obtain this photo for me via a contact here in North Yorkshire. "Dessie" was a Yorkshire colt I believe. Anyway I hope you all like it?'

Lucy was the first to respond.

'Thank you, Pamela. It is a beautiful photo of a beautiful animal but I must tell you that I totally disapprove of hunting. In this day and age it's just barbaric. Sorry, but thank you anyway.'

Peter had to think quickly.

'Tell you what, let's compromise. We'll hang the picture up every single Boxing Day while we watch the race on TV. Everyone agree?'

They all nodded and smiled except Lucy. Pamela had just gone down a couple of notches in her opinion. Still, at least she'd be going home to London in a few days time. Wouldn't she?

13.

The Christmas 'Lunch for Five' at the Lucky Dragon was just splendid. They all agreed on that. The place was packed, absolutely rammed, and the waiters and waitresses, all Chinese, were working non-stop. Mr Yip had managed to save them the circular table with the "lazy Susan" which was more or less in the centre of the four thousand square feet restaurant. Lunch was more of a meze or a "dim sum" with trolleys not unlike those used by airlines being pushed around from table to table. It was Europeanised Chinese cuisine at its best. The deep-fried sweet and sour turkey was probably the most popular food on offer and the Yips had made sure there was an adequate supply. The "Gweilos" would never forgive them if they ran out of turkey at Christmas. It would be tantamount to running out of duck at Chinese New Year.

There was another tradition that the Yips also dare not forget – Christmas pudding. Every luncher was served with a small individual pudding by a waitress and within seconds a hovering male waiter poured a generous stream of brandy over it and clicked a disposable lighter to produce the expected blue flame. The lights were dimmed and everybody gasped at the effect of dozens of flickering puddings in the mid-afternoon dimness.

Peter was about to drain the last drop of Remy Martin from his extra tot when he spotted the Chan family over in the window – the Hong Kong Chinese family they had briefly met a week earlier.

'Oh look, there's Mr Kenneth Chan over in the window at the table we had last time. I'll just pop over and say Hello. Won't be a mo everyone.'

Fortunately for Pamela she was facing the other way and hadn't seen the Chans. But just the merest mention of the name caused her heart to skip a beat.

'Kenneth, hi and happy Christmas.'

Kenneth rose from his sitting position to shake hands.

'I didn't think we'd meet again so soon. Have you had a nice lunch?'

'Yes, you too I trust. The best of English and Chinese foods together maybe?'

Peter wasn't sure if it was a question or an answer.

'Would you like to come over to our table and meet my friend Pamela from London? She's staying with us for a few days, perhaps even until the New Year.'

'Ah yes but which one, Peter, the Western or the Chinese New Year? Actually, we're a little pushed for time and so if you don't mind we'll leave the introduction for a later date if you don't mind.'

Kenneth Chan was as keen as Pamela not to reveal that they already knew each other. After lunch the walk in the fresh air back to the Clifftop Hotel was enjoyable. It was cool and the sun had already set in the west towards the town and it would be a week or more before there was any visible difference to the timing of the sunset. One or two hardy folks could be seen walking dogs down on the Marine Drive but with almost no natural light left they would all soon be turning for home, a warm fire and perhaps a re-run of the King's Speech on TV. The practice of millions of people watching the old Queen's broadcast at precisely three o'clock seemed to have fallen by the wayside. Everyone knew it was pre-recorded at Windsor Castle several days earlier but it was one of those rituals that had pertained since nearly every house in the land had a TV. Sebbie was waiting for them as soon as they got back home and within seconds Lucy had grabbed his lead and taken him straight outside. She had saved some chilli beef, Char Siu pork and sweet and sour turkey for him but he would have to wait a while for his Christmas Dinner. She didn't want to be out long as it was almost dark now. Peasholm Park and back would be long enough. They all dressed down and went into snooze mode.

Pamela retired to her room pleading a bad night's sleep. That was only partially true. She had some more Notes to make on her iPad. The accidental meeting with Kenneth Chan could have been disastrous. She had believed him to be in Whitby or Bridlington, not Scarborough. She would need to get an urgent message down to "The Chairman" in London at the earliest opportunity. It might be tricky as although he was also Asian, in all probability he too would be taking a long break over the Christmas and New Year holiday. Just to be on the safe side she would avoid the Lucky Dragon for the rest of her stay. The major hurdle to clear now was Pete's ex-wife, Mardy Mandy. By hook or by crook she had to acquire her shares in the Koala Hotel Ltd. But how? How do you force the shareholder of any private limited company, particularly a family company, to sell their stake? She would sleep on it.

Later in the evening they overdosed on a repeat of Morecambe & Wise Christmas Special (1980), an Only Fools & Horses Christmas Special (1999), The Great Escape and a repeat of the King's Christmas Message to the nation. Everyone was bored stiff, except Pamela whose brain was in overdrive. Shortly after ten o'clock, one by one, they started to drift off to bed. Soon only Pete and Pamela were left and she canoodled closely to him on one of the several sofas.

'Dahling, I've been thinking. There is no possibly of a reconciliation between you and Mandy is there? Well is there?'

'None, absolutely none, Pam. I promise you. The divorce was final and relatively clean. Apart from our three amazing kids, the only thing we have in common is our twenty-five percent shareholdings each in the Hotel, the limited company. Why?'

'Well, I've been thinking Dahling, wouldn't it be great if I could buy her out? Then she would be out of the frame and out of the picture for good. Wouldn't she?'

'Babes, in an ideal world that would be wonderful, but she hates you. She would never agree to selling her shares to you. Never.'

'She might you know, she just might. If she was frightened or greedy enough. I heard the girls saying that all she wants is the dividends every quarter so that her and her sister, Gwen is it, can go on more winter and spring cruises?'

'Yes, so I heard. They want to fly to South Africa and then cruise their way back on the Queen Mary via the Seychelles, Mauritius, Oman, Egypt and the Mediterranean. Top-deck cabins of course all the way – the thick end of ten grand each so Millie reckoned – plus spending money of course. It'll be twenty five grand in total I'll bet you.'

'Right, let's fix it then. Tell her that it is costing a lot more money to fit out the Hotel than expected and that the company will therefore be looking to the existing shareholders to each inject, say, ten thousand each to make up the deficit.'

'But the kids haven't got ten grand each and for that matter neither have I and …'

'You won't have to if she swallows the bait. You tell her an interested third party has come along wanting to invest and is prepared to pay her two hundred and fifty thousand for her shares – twenty five thousand now and the balance before the end of the financial year. I can pay the twenty five within a few days and we can draw up an agreement with solicitors to transfer the shares and pay the rest by April 5th. If required her solicitors can take a lien on the shares, dahling.'

'A what?'

'A lien. It's like holding it in safe keeping pending the deal going through. It's all kosher.'

'Can you raise the balance in that time?' It was time for a few fibs, white lies and not a little subterfuge.

'My flat in Pimlico is worth well over twice that and my private bankers will advance me what I need.' She didn't tell him it wasn't a real bank. He didn't need to know.

'Wow! So when shall we put the proposition to her? I'll bet you she and Gwen are poring through those glossy brochures now. She must have already blown her share of the surplus from the sale of the Hotel Scarbados.'

'Let's start the ball rolling straight after Christmas but before New Year, shall we? There's no point in contacting her solicitor in Hull. They'll be on holiday until the first week in January. You know what bloomin' lawyers are like. No, let's strike while the iron's hot. We'll draft the letter straight after Boxing Day. Come on let's go to bed and you can remind me why you excite me so much.'

Their passion was so noisy that they both failed to hear the wailing of a child from the turret above them. They were too absorbed in each other to note even if they had heard it, on the stroke of midnight, the cries ceased. Tomorrow was another day and it was going to be unforgettable for more than one reason. Just as he got into bed Jamie's iPhone pinged twice. It was a text from Chloe the young assistant in the Perfume Shop.

'Merry Christmas Jamie. Meet soon for a coffee? Chloe.'

14.

It was barely light on Boxing Day morning when it was Peter's phone's turn to ping twice. Pamela had insisted that he returned to his own room before dawn. She didn't want the kids, especially Lucy, getting the wrong idea, or even the right idea.

The incoming text was short and to the point. It was from Garry Ritson.

'Good morning and congratulations to Sebbie on becoming a Dad. Photo follows. Garry.'

Thirty seconds later and a picture arrived of Candy and three tiny little puppies. Peter switched on his bedside lamp and fiddled with his phone. He just had to send this to Lucy immediately. She, more than anyone else, would be over the moon. Send – whoosh! A few seconds later Lucy was awakened by her own phone's pings. She was almost in tears with happiness and within a minute was on the landing in PJs and dressing gown.

'Wake up everyone! Wake up! Sebbie is a Daddy. Look – aren't they just gorgeous. Oh wow.'

'Dad, can we go and see them straight after breakfast, please'

'Hey, steady on young lady. Let's just think carefully about this. Candy will be needing rest, not excitement. How about this for an idea. The Ritsons are coming here for lunch around one o'clock anyway. So how about I drive you down to their place say just after mid-day, and then I bring the four of us back? They can either walk back after the big race on TV or they can get a taxi. We'll all be having a few sherberts no doubt with the news no matter who wins the big race. Deal?'

'Done, Dad, done.'

She gave him a "high five" and they went back into their respective rooms to get dressed. Peter almost went into the wrong room!

There was a joyous and festive atmosphere over breakfast and coffee. Everyone wanted to congratulate Sebbie who took not the blindest bit of notice of any of them. His only interest was in his half-bowl of Yorkshire Tea and some Toad in the Hole left over from Christmas Eve. By mid-morning Lucy had taken Sebbie out for his constitutional, this time down the steep paths to the Oasis Café, along the Drive then back via the big hair-pin bend and home. There was a stiff easterly blowing and the horizon looked dark and very murky. The tide looked ominously high too. It didn't bode at all well for the traditional Fishermen versus Firemen football match on the South Bay beach scheduled for two o'clock. The match was one of Scarborough's institutions and the organisers would be loathe to cancel it. Lucy and Sebbie had just got back to the top of the hill when the first flecks of the white stuff started to appear in the sky. Herring gulls screamed their annoyance as they rode the winds back and forth along the clifftops.

'Come on, Sebbie me boy, not far to go now. Then I'm going to see your little family. I wonder if you've got sons or daughters? Mr Ritson didn't say.'

Shortly after eleven o'clock, Lucy was chomping at the bit with her excitement at going to see her new "grandchildren" at the Ritson's house. It would feel a little strange visiting the property next door to the Hotel Scarbados that they had only so recently vacated.

'Come on, Dad – hurry up can't you?'

'Lucy, just be patient please. I'll call Garry Ritson now and tell him we'll be on the way in a few minutes. Jamie, Pam will be here if you need a hand in the kitchen, I'm sure. Right then we'll probably be about an hour. Let's be off.'

In fact Lucy was already in the car and had she been old enough to drive would probably have set off without him. It was only a five minute drive to the Ritsons for which they were both grateful as more snow had started to fall. It immediately invoked memories of that awful day just over a year ago when they had moved from Hull and had only just "beaten the weather" as they say. It wasn't anything like as bad as that today – not yet anyway.

The Ritsons were at the door as soon as they heard the car in the drive.

'Come on in you two before you get nithered. It's turned nasty hasn't it? We've moved Candy and the puppies into the front room where we've got a nice little log fire going with a metal fire-guard in front. In you come, Lucy.'

Lucy almost cried with happiness. She immediately reached for her iPhone and started taking pictures – snap, snap, snap.

'Oh Mr Ritson, I almost forgot to ask – are they girls or …'

'Two bitches and one boy puppy. I checked on Candy about four this morning – nothing to report – and then again just after six and hey presto suddenly we have six dogs in the house can you believe that? So they were all born sometime before six – Boxing Day babies so that's easy to remember isn't it?' So, Lucy, we now have a surprise for you.' Garry winked at Peter although he genuinely had no idea what was coming next.

'As Sebbie is undoubtedly the father, Shirley and I have decided that you can have the pick of the litter. You don't have to choose now, there's plenty of time. Give it some thought in the days ahead.'

At that point Lucy actually did burst into tears and threw her arms around first Garry and then Shirley.

'Oh my God, thank you, thank you, thank you. This is the bestest Christmas present ever, and I do mean ever.'

Outside the sky was even darker and Peter looked a tad apprehensive.

'Garry, I think we should be setting off back now. Our car isn't terribly good in snow. The back end starts to slide at the slightest excuse. What about yours?'

'Ah well, I didn't tell you that a week ago there was a promotion on with those small four by four jeepy looking things at that garage on the way into town. They put us a steel dog-guard in the back as a freebie. There's more than enough room for three Yorkies and two er.... well what are they? What's Labradoodle Yorkie cross called? '

'Do you think they'll grow as big as Sebbie or stay more like Candy?'

'Well I would say that the dog will take after Sebbie more in stature. Look, you two , you'd best set off. We'll follow you soon. I hope we're going to have your special Bubble & Squeak just like last year?'

'You bet we are! See you soon. Come on Lucy!'

It was only five minutes drive back to the Clifftop Hotel and Lucy didn't say a single word until Peter turned the engine off.

'Dad, I'm going to choose the little boy doggie. I've decided. He'll be great company for his Dad too. Now, what are we going to call him?'

First they had sampled a delightful seafood cocktail of

prawns, crab and mussels bathed in Rose Marie sauce. There wasn't the slightest morsel left in any of the seven glass cocktail dishes. Peter rose from his chair and disappeared into the kitchen. Nobody but nobody was even allowed to watch as he put the finishing touches to the two huge cast iron skillets full of his own creation. Turning both gases up to full flame it looked like the full blast of an Elon Musk rocket engine under each one. With a wooden spoon, he made a hole in the centre of each one right through to the metal itself and then poured extra virgin olive oil into each hole until they were full to overflowing.

'The main course will be served in two minutes. Top up all your glasses!'

Waiting sixty seconds, Peter then deftly grabbed a skillet handle with both hands and, sliding the mixture from side to side to make sure it was lubricated, he tossed the entire contents in to the air like a pancake. Bingo! It was perfectly golden brown. He repeated the exercise with skillet number two. The lunch was amazing with cold cuts of turkey, Yorkshire ham, sausage-meat and of course a four flavour nut roast for Lucy. It was all washed down with Prosecco and a New Zealand sauvignon blanc called Oyster Bay. Everyone had "seconds" of Peter's signature dish and even Sebbie, not normally noted for any vegetarian tendencies, enjoyed a half a bowlful. And he didn't even know yet that he'd become a daddy!

Time just flew and it was Pamela who noticed that it was two-forty five and time to settle down in front of the TV for the big race from Kempton – the King George Sixth Stakes. All eight betting slips were passed round in a wine glass and unfurled to reveal the name of the horse on which they had a one pound bet. Unbelievably, none of them was the winner. The eighth betting slip was still in the glass. It was left for Sebbie and it was called AlfieBoy, a winner at twenty to one. Lucy smiled.

'That's it, everyone. It's fate. Sebbie's little boy will be called AlfieBoy.'

Everyone cheered except Pamela who pleaded a migraine and went to her room – alone.

The big race had barely finished and the horses and jockeys were heading for the Winner's enclosure when Garry Ritson took a look out of the dining room window.

'Oh heck even more snow. Look please, don't think badly of us but if you don't mind we'll set off now before it gets even worse.' Shirley was not amused.

'I think we should get a taxi, love. And how many glasses of wine have you had? Three, four, five? You'll be over the limit. I'll phone Z-Cars Cabs even if it is double fares on Boxing Day. Now, where's my phone?'

'Z Cars. A taxi from the Clifftop Hotel did you say? Sorry love it will be over an hour's wait, maybe more. The big footy match on the beach had to be abandoned at half time because of the weather and now scores of folks want a taxi home...'

'Don't worry I'll drive. It'll be a doddle with this new four by four. No problem.'

He didn't tell Shirley he hadn't quite mastered the drive controls of their new motor just yet. There were hugs, kisses and "see ya soons" all round and then they set off gingerly down the hill towards Peasholm Park. About two inches of snow had settled and Garry was confident that the new motor would handle the conditions without a hitch. Wrong! The right hand turn at the bottom looked simple enough and there was absolutely no other traffic in sight. Not yet anyway. Garry indicated right and let in the clutch too quickly, in fact far too quickly and the vehicle leapt forward and spun to the right before it had cleared the centre of the road, not that the dotted white lines were visible given the snowfall. Shirley was not amused.

'Are you sure we're in four wheel drive? It didn't feel like it to me!' Suddenly some bad news appeared in the rear view mirror – blue flashing lights. No siren, just the blue flashing lights of a North Yorkshire Police vehicle.

'Oh my God, Garry. I told you not to drive. How many glasses of Prosecco and wine did you have? Three, four or even more? You'll be breathalysed, charged with drink driving, fined, banned for a year and you know I can't drive at the moment until I've had my cataracts done. How long is that bloomin' waiting list? Anyway that traffic cop has stopped behind us. You're for the high-jump in about sixty seconds time and ..' Garry just smiled and said nowt. He hadn't told her he'd only been drinking zero-alcohol Prosecco.

'Don't worry, love. I can see who it is now. It's the dog handler PC George Anderson. We go back a long way.' He wound his window down.

'Hiya George. Happy Christmas mate. Are you having a good one?'

'Hey-up Garry. Not really mate. Too few of us on duty and appalling weather too. I was about a hundred yards behind you when you cocked-up on that turning. I recognised your plate R1TSO and I thought I'd put the blue lights on and have a laugh. So, you've changed your motor I see. Nice one, mate. What made you change it?'

'The family's growing! Three more pups arrived today actually but we're giving one to the Fishburns, you know, our old neighbours at the Hotel Scarbados. They've taken over the Clifftop, had you heard?'

'No I hadn't, to be honest. Thanks for telling me. I'll pass that news on to Inspector Mort at PHQ in Northallerton tomorrow – that is if the buggers are back on duty after the holidays.'

'Why will he need to know, exactly?'

'Right, you'll have to keep this right under your hat mate. Promise?'

'Of course.'

'PI – Police Intelligence – have just informed us of new information concerning the goings on at the Hotel Scarbados long before the Fishburns bought it. Details are still being confirmed but it seems like there might be a Caribbean connection to the Class A drugs cache that the Fishburn's dog dug up.' Garry gave out a long whistle which in different circumstances would have called all his dogs to heel from a hundred yards away.

'You're kidding. Well we never saw any Caribbean folks staying there in all the time we lived next door, did we Shirley?'

'Anyway, Garry, Mums the word. By the way, you see that little nob next to the gear lever? If you press it down then forward it engages four wheel drive. Read the brochure next time. Cheers!'

15.

The next morning was little better weather-wise. Lucy was keen to go and visit Candy and her puppies again but it would have been a nasty walk and Peter was not keen on getting the car out. Maybe Garry's investment in a small four x four had been a wise one. Winters in Hull had not been as severe that's for sure, the Humber Estuary being quite protective of Hull from the worst that the North Sea could throw at it. They were just finishing a late breakfast when the Hotel's land-line telephone started ringing. It was the first time it had rang since they moved in and it caught them all totally by surprise. Millie reached it first.

'Er, hello, er the Clifftop Hotel. We haven't actually officially opened yet and ...'

'Good morning. It's Inspector Mort here from North Yorkshire Police. Is that young Millie Fishburn?'

'Yes it is, good morning.'

Millie suddenly remembered that Inspector Mort had been the senior investigating officer following the unexpected turn of events at the Hotel Scarbados. She had accidentally on purpose called him Inspector Morse which had triggered his ire at the time. Rinse and repeat was Millie's motto.

'Oh, compliments of the season to you Inspector Morse. This is an unexpected surprise.'

Fortunately she could not see the scowl at the other end of the line, fifty miles away as the crow flies.

'Yes, well we'll put that behind us shall we? Compliments of the season to you too. Now, it's your father I'd like to speak with if I may, if he's available. Actually, it is rather urgent – not life or death you understand, but urgent nonetheless. Is he available please?'

'Er yes, Inspector, he's in the building somewhere. Shall I ask him to call you back on this number in say ten minutes?'

'That would be great thank you. If he had pen and paper to hand that would be good too and please ask him to make the call in privacy please. Thanks again. Goodbye.'

Wow! That was not the sort of call you might expect to receive at any time, let alone the day after Boxing Day. Where was her Dad anyway? He found him outside washing the underside of the car down with warm soapy water to remove any salty slush. They never seemed to have this problem in Hull.

'Dad, there you are. I've just taken a call from that Inspector Mort at North Yorkshire Police in Northallerton. You know, the cop who handled the enquiry about the drugs and money that Sebbie dug up last summer.'

'Crikey, I thought we'd heard the last of that lark. We were so lucky being able to keep the money. It looks as if your mother has already spent her share on cruises in the sun. Did he say what he wanted?'

'No, but can you call him back as soon as possible, in private and with pen and paper to hand. I dialled 1471 and wrote the number down for you. It's on the dining room table. I'll make some coffee and bring it to you. Go!'

'Good morning, Inspector Mort. Belated compliments of the season to you. This is an unexpected pleasure.'

'I'm sorry to bother you before the festive season is really finished and if the weather wasn't so squiffy I would have preferred to drive through to Scarborough to appraise you of developments in the case of the drugs and money found at the Hotel Scarbados. I did promise to update you if more information came to light.'

'You did indeed. Don't tell me the new owners have found more money and we can keep that too ..only joking.'

'No, Mr Fishburn. It's rather more serious than that. Please bear with me and take notes as you please. This will take some time.

It seems that the US Coast Guards, acting in conjunction with Royal Navy units in the Caribbean last week, have intercepted a massive cache of heroin that was destined for your old hotel and ..'

'What? You cannot be serious. I mean to say …'

'Yes, of that we are one hundred percent certain. Stencilled on the side of the waterproof packaging were the letters W E N ****D O V E R . Initially the Americans naturally thought that it's ultimate destination was the City of Dover in Delaware. That was quite understandable. Enquiries drew a blank and it became obvious that it was a red herring. Cross checking with the Serious Crimes Agency here in the UK and deleting the four gaps in the stencil, our own PNC – Police National Computer – came up with a possible match. I refer of course to the Wendover Hotel, the previous name of the Hotel Scarbados before you renamed it following the end of Covid restrictions. We had uploaded a Report on our own enquiry to the PNC in accordance with standard practice today. A few years ago that would not have been possible.

Anyway, to continue. Over the last twenty-four hours the Barbadian High Commissioner in London, Malcom Morgan, has been interviewed under caution.'

'No way! He and his wife Marlene were absolutely charming and are hoping to visit the Hotel again when the cricket season starts. There was a distinct possibility that their nephew was going to play a summer season with Scarborough Cricket Club and ...'

'Well he still might but let me finish please. He has been interviewed at length, grilled even, by the Serious Crimes Agency. We are now convinced of his total innocence. Seems he was duped too. However the two so-called Treasury Officials from Bridgetown are anything but Government employees. They were imposters and represented only themselves and the cartel they represented. The Wendover, er sorry, the Hotel Scarbados, is not owned by the Barbados Government at all, but by the cartel in the form of a shell company in the British Virgin Islands.'

'This is a lot to take in, Inspector. Don't tell me that our sales proceeds are at risk? We've already spent it when we acquired the Clifftop. I would not know how to start breaking that news to the family. Oh my God.'

Suddenly there was a knock at the door. It was Millie with a steaming mug of Java coffee.

''Come in Millie love and sit down.'

'Inspector, my daughter Millie has just entered the room and I'm quite happy for her to remain if you are? I'll put my cellphone into "speaker" mode. Just give me a minute to bring her up to speed with what you've told me.'

'Very well. While you're doing that I'll grab a cup myself although I suspect that as mine will be from a vending machine in a polystyrene cup it will not be a patch on the brew I had when I visited you at the Hotel Scarbados.'

''That's fine, look I'll call you back in five shall I?'

'That's fine. Cheers.'

Peter repeated almost verbatim what Inspector Mort had just told him. Millie immediately started to take notes.

'Look, Dad. This could have serious consequences for us.

He'll be asking us lots of questions but we must ask him some too. Stay cool and play it by ear. OK?' Peter rang back after five minutes as promised.

'So, Mr Fishburn, events have moved very quickly indeed over the last few days, despite Christmas. From our point of view, and acting on advice from the SCA, if that huge drugs cache hadn't been intercepted then if previous patterns were to be repeated, it would arrive at its final destination four to six weeks after it had been dumped into the Caribbean. It was discovered outside Barbados territorial waters and was almost certainly due to be picked up by fast motor boats. Of course it will now never reach it's intended destination but somebody here might still be expecting it to arrive.'

'Like who?'

'Like the two "Treasury Officials" who are anything but. Don't you see? That's why they wanted to buy your Hotel. We now have reason to believe that they were not Barbadians but Jamaicans travelling on false passports. I don't suppose you had any CCTV records?'

'No, we never thought it was necessary.'

'Anyway look, we now need to have access to the Hotel Scarbados for further forensic examination. We will also be setting up covert motion-triggered cameras in the Hotel like those that film animals in wildlife programs. Do you still have any keys?'

'No, but the selling agent called Charlie Hopper might be able to help you there. Hang on. Millie has a question.'

She spoke towards the microphone of her father's cellphone.

'Inspector, right now, who actually owns the Hotel Scarbados and who was responsible for performing due diligence as to the origin of the funds?' Inspector Mort wasn't sure.

'Well er, let's leave that until I come to see you, hopefully tomorrow if the weather clears. I'll need to take formal statements from all of your family who spoke to either or both of the Jamaicans.'

'They didn't actually stay at our Hotel. We were full.'

'Even if you weren't, they wouldn't have stayed with you anyway. We'll have to try and find out where they did actually stay. You might just be able to help us? Is about eleven o'clock tomorrow morning convenient for me to come and take formal statements, weather permitting of course?'

'Yes, that'll be fine Inspector. We'll have coffee ready and it won't be presented in a plastic cup. Goodbye for now.'

Peter looked at Millie and Millie looked at her father. Unusually both were stuck for words. Millie eventually broke the silence.

'I just can't believe how many twists and turns can affect our family. Dad, we're going to have to appraise Jamie about this development. After all he is a Director and a shareholder.'

'Agreed, but we'll keep Lucy out of all of this. She starts her new job at the veterinary surgery in a week's time and I don't want her to be upset and lose focus. Where is she right now anyway?'

'She's out with Pamela taking Sebbie for a long walk. I won't be surprised if they end up at the Ritsons – you know how thrilled she is.'

'You might be right but, Dad, can I suggest that we keep all this between the three of us? Pamela is neither family nor a shareholder, after all is she? Let's be right.'

'So where is Jamie? Has he gone AWOL as well?'

'Not really. Apparently he's gone into town to meet some lass called Chloe who works in a perfume shop.

He's meeting her in her lunch break in that coffee shop. Remember, when we went to see the town's Christmas lights formally switched on?'

'Can you text him please and ask him to pop into WH Smith and get us a copy of the latest English Hotels Monthly. The January edition will be in the shops now and I want to talk with Pamela about doing a feature on this place when we formally open and change its name to Hotel Koala.'

'Er, yes OK leave that with me, Dad. And on the subject of the opening etc. don't you think that we should just tread water on our plans for that until the Hotel Scarbados fiasco is well and truly sorted?'

'You're probably right, Millie, but you scare me when you talk like that. I hope you don't know something that you're hiding from me?'

'Er, no Dad. But let's wait to see if the Inspector Morse has any more information tomorrow.'

Millie hoped that cracking the joke again was just enough of a diversion to hide her hesitation. She texted Jamie as requested but it was a formality as her mentor and tutor, Clive White, had just a couple of days earlier scanned a short article in the Financial Times and emailed it to her personal address.

> *'In a surprising development to players in hospitality industry shares, Best Eastern Hotels Ltd. has announced that it is planning an IPO early in the new year and is going to float its shares on the AIM – the alternative investment market. Far Eastern investors are believed to be behind this idea and millions are expected to be invested in a rapid expansion of its property portfolio on the east coast of England. The board further announced that it had head-hunted the*

Managing Editor of English Hotels Monthly, Pamela Hesketh, who had joined the Board with immediate effect.'

Millie had kept this information to herself, for the time being anyway. No wonder Pamela had brought so much luggage.

16.

Jamie had got a bus into the town centre as services were just about back to normal again after the Christmas and Boxing Day Holidays. He got off as close to the railway station as he could as it was still a bit slippery underfoot with most of the snow having turned to slush. At the last minute he had remembered to bring the winning betting slip from the big race on Boxing Day – *AlfieBoy £1win at 20-1*. He had also remembered to photocopy it before leaving the Hotel and had secreted it in his room. It was a surprise gift for Lucy for the day the newest addition to the family finally came home. That would probably not be for a couple of months. The girl in the betting shop remembered him.

'Hiya, it's you. I knew you'd be in soon 'cos you backed every horse in the race didn't you? The bookies did well as the favourite was pulled up. Right, let's see. Yep, you've won twenty quid plus your one pound stake back. A twenny pound note and a one pound coin. Is that OK?'

'That's fine, thanks. Actually our dog won it, Sebbie. It's my sister's dog really and she'll probably spend it on treats or something. She spoils him rotten.'

The teller gave Jamie one of those looks and wondered how on earth a dog could have placed and won a bet. Oh well. Jamie crossed over the road and headed towards the Brunswick Centre. He had texted Chloe and they had arranged to meet during her lunch break – half an hour starting at one o'clock. He glanced at his watch. It was just a couple of minutes after one and he quickened his pace. Glancing sideways as he passed the perfume shop he recognised the other girl, Donna, the one who had gift-wrapped the perfume for his father. She looked a bit Goth for his liking with two whole sleeves of tattoos of bats and vampires. He was secretly pleased that it was Chloe he was meeting.

He spotted her at a vacant table and waved from twenty yards away. She smiled and waved back at him. Jamie felt slightly nervous. After all, this really was the first time he was going to meet her, apart from the purchase of the perfume. What should he do? Shake hands? Give her a kiss, or what? He needn't have worried. Chloe stood up and pecked him niftily on both cheeks in rapid succession.

'Hi Jamie. So tell me, how did the "Odour Toilet" go down with your father's lady-friend?'

They both laughed. The ice was broken.

'Er, very well I think. He didn't say anything to the contrary and to be honest I forgot to ask. Anyway, while I'm on my feet what can I get you, Chloe? Coffee? A Latte or a Capuccino maybe?'

'Ooh no, I'm not all that keen on too much caffeine. How about a Mocha – they're just fab in here.'

'One Mocha coming up and would you like anything to eat? A toasted tea-cake maybe?'

'Oh no thanks, Jamie. I've got some turkey and pasta salad in a plastic lunch box behind the counter and I grab a bit in between serving customers. Our cold turkey will last until Easter at this rate. Why my Dad bought such a big one, I really don't know. There's only the three of us – me, Mam and Dad.'

'You live at home then I take it?'

'Yes, but I'll tell you more in a minute. Look, there's no queue at the moment so dive into the café while it's quiet. It can wait.'

Three minutes later and he was back with a Mocha and a large frothy Cappucino.

'Here you go. It's really nice to see you again, Chloe.'

'And you too, Jamie. Cheers! So where were we?'

'You live with your Mum and Dad and you'll be eating turkey until Easter and …'

'Well, they will anyway. Not me. I've only got a few days left working at the shop and then straight after New Year I'm heading back to Uni.'

Jamie's heart sank. He was just starting to get really friendly with a smart, intelligent and attractive girl of his own age and already she was telling him that she was leaving shortly. What's the odds she's at St. Andrew's or Bristol or a University on Jupiter?'

'Yeah, this is just a holiday job to top up my depleted bank account. I travelled by train every day to Uni initially to minimise accommodation costs – I'm at York Uni.' Jamie's relief was palpable.

'But to be honest the trains got so unreliable what with strikes, staff shortages and a host of other excuses that it was becoming intolerable and my studies started to suffer. I share a little house with three other girls in Heworth. Do you know York at all?'

'No, not really. What do you study?'

''I'm reading Marine Biology and Environmental Studies.'

'Oh wow! You must be a real brainbox.'

'Not really, I only just scraped the required 'A' level grades to be honest. I did it to please my Dad more than anything.'

'Is he a scientist then?' Chloe laughed out loud and almost spilt her Mocha.

'Good Lord no. He's in the fishing industry. When you told me that your family was taking over the Clifftop Hotel soon he asked me if I would pass you one of his business cards. Hang on a mo and I'll fish it out of my purse – excuse the pun! Here it is – careful though, it probably reeks of crab or something.'

Jamie took the card from her outstretched and perfectly manicured hand. It read:

Fred Cammish & Sons
Finest fresh shellfish
Wholesalers & Distributors
Telephone XXXXX

'Gosh, so no wonder you're studying those subjects. So you didn't fancy following in your father's footsteps then?'

'What and getting smelly fingers five or six days a week? No thank you. Everybody on the East Coast here operating in the industry is very concerned. Every so often there's a pollution related crisis of some kind but the authorities never seem to be able to get to the bottom of it. When I eventually graduate in over two years time I want to join one of those research companies that delves into that sort of thing. It'll be a while yet though as I'm still only in the first year. I'm only eighteen – nineteen just after Easter. You?'

'Hey, we're the same age, almost anyway. Can we meet again soon? Perhaps on your day off?'

'That would be great. Crikey, look at the time. I'm due back in the shop in two minutes then it's Donna's turn for a break. Knowing her she'll be out in the precinct for a sandwich and several fags. I've never smoked have you?'

'No, never. Right off you go then and I'll text you in a couple of days. OK?'

'No. I'll call you. I've got you on speed-dial now.'

She smiled and gave him three kisses this time and

zoomed back to the perfume shop where Donna, fag and lighter at the ready, was waiting for her. Right on cue Jamie's iPhone pinged twice in his jeans pocket. It was a text from Millie.

'Don't forget that magazine. Stop in the Viking Café round the corner on the way home and text me when you get there. Important.'

Something must be up. He had never received a text like that before from his eldest sister. He was more than a bit concerned. Jamie drained the last of the froth from his cup and re-donned his furry anorak and gloves. It was still bitter outside. A waitress stopped to collect the empties.

'Excuse me, love. I'm new around here. Is WH Smith's far from here?'

'Go outside and turn right. Then it's on your left past Superdrug. But if its a paper, magazine or a vape you want the Brunswick News Kiosk just over there is nearer. It's run by a guy from Brid called Mark but it looks like his assistant Vicky is on duty today.'

'Thank you, the Cappucino was great by the way – see you again.'

Twenty seconds later and Jamie was in the queue at the News Kiosk.

'Hi, can I help? I saw you looking at all those magazines. There's so many of them these days.'

'Er, yes, thank you. I'm looking for the January edition of English Hotels Monthly – if you've got one that is, please?'

'Who's a lucky boy then? The wholesalers delivered tons of stuff this morning. I've only just opened and sorted it all. It's days late because of the bad weather. Here you are – that's four pounds ninety-nine please.'

Jamie carefully rolled the magazine and held it tightly inside his anorak. He didn't want Millie complaining it was wet or cold. Now, where's the right bus stop for the route back home? Stepping outside Jamie spotted three separate bus stops, each with their own shelter. They were all full of folks sheltering from the icy wind. He approached a lady who was desperately trying to force her way into the first shelter.

'Excuse me. Which is the right bus to go past the cricket ground please? I'm new here.'

'It's this one love. It goes to Scalby Mills right past the fire station and the cricket ground. Hey-up it's just coming now. You're in luck, I've been waiting fifteen minutes in the bloomin' cold.'

Jamie was last onto the bus and occupied one of those tip-up seats near the front used by wheelchair users. Ten minutes later and he jumped off the bus right opposite the Hollywood Plaza cinema and just a few yards from the Viking Cafė. He texted Millie before he even went inside.

'I'm at the cafė. J.'

'Order two mugs of tea. I'll only be a couple of minutes. M.'

In fact she was there in slightly less than two minutes.

'Right, Bro. We've got two major issues to discuss. What a day. We've had North Yorkshire Police on the phone with Dad this morning. Firstly though, have you got that magazine?'

'Of course I have. Here it is.'

'Right Bro, let's take a look inside shall we. Never mind the front cover, that's just wallpaper. I want to see what changes there have been since the December edition. I've got a copy here. Ah-ha I was right.'

Millie opened both magazines to the first inside page, inverted them and put them under Jamie's nose on the formica table top.

'Now, tell me how they differ. Look closely mind.'

'I haven't got a clue what you're talking about – oh hang on though. December's Managing Editor is Pamela Hesketh and, well, January's is Nazareen Akbar … what the f… '

'Language please. You're not watching the Tigers now.'

'So Pam's gone. But where?'

'Right, now read this that Clive White emailed to me last night.'

'So who else knows apart from us and Mr White? Does Dad?'

'No, and he mustn't yet either. He's deeply worried about something else. Put that issue to one side for the moment and listen to me carefully. This is the gist of the call from that Inspector Mort this morning.'

Millie recalled, as best she could, the whole of the conversation to which she had been privy. Jamie looked glum and barely sipped his tea despite the fact he was trying to warm up from the short but freezing walk.

'So Morse is coming to take statements tomorrow is he? Well I don't know about accurate descriptions – two black guys, early to mid thirties, well dressed and partial to roast beef and Yorkshire puddings isn't exactly going to go down well on "Crimewatch" is it for God's sake?'

'You must try not to be so flippant when you make the formal statements. It's important that these guys are caught. There's a small but distinct possibility that our whole sale of the Hotel Scarbados might be illegitimate. Although we are entirely innocent, if the money we received ended out to be dirty money then it could open a whole new can of worms.'

'OK sis, I promise to treat it seriously.'

'Did you hear any of the conversation relating to where they might be staying? We were full, remember?'

'Actually, I do. Something about a headland or similar.'

'I'll bet that's the Headlands Hotel up the road and round the bend near to where that swimming pool was that the Council demolished. Remember to put that in your statement. In fact as soon as we get home I'm going to call Inspector Mort.

Now, back to the other problem. Obviously we need to tell Dad. However, I think I'll have another chat with Clive White first. Is that OK with you?'

'Agreed, Sis, agreed.'

'I'll call him after supper. I don't suppose that he and Mrs White will be out. This weather seems to be affecting the whole of the East Riding now. I had actually thought about inviting them up for a day or two over New Year. What do you think?'

'That sounds like a plan but we'd have to be very careful indeed what we said in front of Pamela.'

'You can say that again. Come on, let's get home and make some tea.'

'I thought I could rustle up some nice Turkey á la King with some pilau rice. There's still tons left. OK? Chloe reckons that her family will be eating turkey until Easter.'

'Sorry I forgot to ask, how did you get on with "Chanelle?"

'Ha ha! She's a smart young lady and we'll definitely meet again. I like her a lot. Hopefully, we'll meet again soon.'

'That's nice. Right lets be off home. I'm going to call "Inspector Morse" first before he leaves the office and then I'll see if I can raise Clive White.' She was on the phone to Northallerton within five minutes of taking her coat off.

Inspector Mort please, if he's available?'

'Who shall I say's calling?'

'Millie Fishburn from Scarborough.'

'I'll put you through, he's in his office. Hold the line.'

'Thanks, I will do.'

'Good afternoon Millie. This is an unexpected call.'

'Good afternoon to you too. Yes, I just wanted to give you a snippet of information after I had managed to speak with my brother Jamie. His description of the two black guys will be almost useless but he did say they mentioned something about a headland. To me that can only mean the Headlands Hotel just a few hundred yards away from the Hotel Scarbados.'

'Wow, thank you. I'll be onto that straight away. We've got the dates on file. It's just luck now but my best guess is that they have already left the country on false passports. They probably have a collection of them. Anyway, thanks for the heads up and I'll see you tomorrow to take formal statements. Bye for now.'

'Bye, Inspector.'

Switching to her mobile phone which had Clive White on speed-dial, Millie went to her own room on the top floor. Top floor and top secret. He took her call within seconds but it was going to be a much longer and in-depth conversation than she could possibly have envisaged.

17.

'Hi Clive, can you talk?'

'Yes, Betty's making some tea – turkey something I think.'

'Ha, sounds like we're all at it! Right then we've got a hold of a copy of the January edition of *English Hotels Monthly* and guess what?'

'Pamela is no longer the Editor?!'

'Yes, you're right. So what made you think that?'

'Well, since I emailed you that scan of the short article in the FT I've done a bit of digging, a bit of research and asked around a few mates in the City and …'

'Clive, before you go any further, can you tell me what an IPO is please?'

'Sure, it's just City jargon and it stands for Initial Public Offering.'

'So what on Earth does that actually mean?'

'Quite simple really. It means exactly what it says. It's a company's first time of offering its shares to the investing public. It's something we'll shortly be covering in your Diploma but in this case you're actually experiencing it first hand. Young companies do this when they want to raise money after they've established themselves and have a plan for business expansion. It's a ground floor opportunity to invest in a company's future.'

'OK I think I get that. So what else have you come up with?'

'Millie, there is no way that Pamela Hesketh would have left a hundred grand a year job at the magazine without a massive incentive. You know, salary, shares and goodness knows what other perks. I'll bet right now she'll be in the sun somewhere plotting what the company can buy next to expand its portfolio prior to the IPO going live as it were.'

'Well Clive, I can tell you you're definitely wrong there.'

'How do you know?'

'Because right now she's staying with us. She arrived on Christmas Eve. I don't know whether Dad invited her or it was a mixture of both. Anyway she's here and from the amount of luggage she brought with her I don't think it's gonna be a short stay.'

'Millie, I made some notes after I did my research but they're not immediately in front of me. I started a little pop-up file and it's on my desk in my study. Tell you what, lets both put the kettle on, make a brew, and regroup in five. I'll call you OK?'

'Yep. Speak soon.'

Millie did indeed go downstairs to make some tea. Jamie was in the kitchen making his Turkey á la King and the aroma was just amazing.

'Hi Bro, listen, I'm half-way through a long chat with Clive White. I'm taking tea back to my room and then Clive's going to give me a lot of information about Best Eastern Hotels. I'll bring you up to speed later.'

'Where's everyone else?'

'Out with Sebbie I think.'

'Supper won't be until six-thirty, is that OK Sis?'

'Great, that's fine. This might take a bit longer than I thought.'

Five minutes later she was back in her room and her phone's caller ID told her that the incoming caller was Clive.'

'Hi again, Millie. Got your tea and a pen and paper?'

'Hang on, you never mentioned that last bit. Give me half a tic. OK fire away.'

'Right, the name of the Company is actually Best Eastern Hotels (UK) Ltd. It was registered and incorporated at Companies House just over a year ago. It's registered office is in London at one of those firms of Accountants that also act as Registered Offices. There'll be a little brass plate on a wall in the lobby. It's in Hill Street in Mayfair so it's probably kosher.'

'Huh?''

'Legitimate, you know, legal. Anyway to continue, the company hasn't had to file any accounts yet but I can tell you that half the shares are owned by Best Eastern Hotels (Asia) Ltd. registered in Hong Kong and the other fifty percent are in the name of one Kenneth Chan, who is also a Director. There are several other Chinese names and a couple of others that sound Oriental which I think might be Malaysian or Vietnamese. And then, lastly is Pamela Hesketh who was appointed on 1st December just gone.'

'Wow, Clive, this is all hard to take in. I'm scribbling my own notes with one hand and holding my phone with the other.'

'Take your time, stay cool, as you youngsters say today, and don't let your tea get cold.' Clive was an old-school retired bank manager and never did anything of import without a mug of tea by his side.

'So what do we do now, Clive?'

'OK, Millie, this is the tough bit. Not for you but for your Dad. I know he's your father but I think he's a really nice guy too.'

'This sounds ominous. What's coming next?'

'Millie, I think the main reason, possibly the sole reason, she's here is to ingratiate herself into your Dad's mind and body and thence to acquire your Mother's twenty-five percent stake in Koala Hotel Ltd. When she's achieved that she will then recommend to the Board of Best Eastern that they buy the whole of Koala Hotel Ltd. possibly before it's even started trading. She'll make a killing overnight, but there again you all will. I'll just let that sink in.'

'Dad is so happy. Since he and Mum split, Pamela has filled the missing hole in his life. What do we do now?'

'I haven't finished yet. I have further discovered that there is a Board Meeting of Best Eastern on the 3rd of January in London, the first working day after the New Year. There's no way she will want to miss that. It's her chance to put some runs on the board and impress the Board – excuse the analogy!'

'Actually, Clive, we were wondering if you and Betty would like to come and spend New Year with us and stay over a night or two. If the weather doesn't interfere that is. But if Pamela is here we'll have to be very careful not to talk out of turn.'

'I'd love to join you as I'm sure Betty will too. I'll bet you a pound to a pinch of the proverbial that sometime in the next day or two she'll concoct an excuse to travel back to London for a few days. In the meantime, however unfair it might seem at this moment, I think you should keep your Dad in the dark. You can share this with Jamie of course.'

'This is so tough, Clive. By the way there have been developments on the Hotel Scarbados front but we'll talk about that if and when you come up. Speak tomorrow when you've checked with Betty?'

'You bet, Millie, and keep your eyes and ears wide open. Bye.'

A few minutes later and Millie was in one of the elevators taking her empty mug down to the kitchen when something dawned on her like a ton of bricks. Kenneth Chan … Kenneth Chan … Kenneth Chan. Could it be the same Kenneth Chan they had met at the Lucky Dragon restaurant? The guy who said he was buying the restaurant and was living in rented accommodation while his family searched for a house. Surely not, after all Chan was a very common Cantonese family name.

She had just stepped into the kitchen when the back door opened. First through the door was Lucy who unclipped Sebbie's lead, followed by Peter and Pamela who had to un-clinch their arms before walking through the narrow door that was one half of a double door to allow access by industrial sized wheelie bins so common in hotels and catering establishments. Pamela sniffed the air and murmured appreciatively.

'That smells gorgeous, Jamie baby. What a talented son you have, Peter dahling. I'll go and change for supper now I think. See you all later.'

'Supper is served, Ladies and Gentlemen. Bong Bong!

Jamie so wished he had remembered to bring the dinner gong from the Hotel Scarbados. It had obviously been left behind in the rush and confusion of moving just before Christmas.

Pamela appeared last at the table and had changed into a snazzy cocktail dress and reeked of Coco Chanel. She looked more than a little upset or worried and it showed immediately to the concerned Peter who immediately placed a comforting arm around her waist.

'What's the matter, darling. What's up?'

'Oh Peter, I'm so sorry but I've just had a bad bit of news. My sister Margaret has had a stroke it seems. She's in St.

Barts in London. They just called me – I'm down as next of kin as she's a widow. She's ten years older. I think I must have been an accident or an afterthought or something. Anyway look, I'm going to have to go back to London for a few days.'

She sat down at the table, sniffed and reached for a tissue from her small Armani handbag which she seemed to carry everywhere with her.

'I'm sorry to be a party-pooper but I'll have to skip the festivities on New Year's Eve. I'll check trains in the morning. I'll just take the smaller of my two cases and hopefully Margaret will improve and I'll be back here soon. I just can't believe it …'

Millie certainly could. Clive White was bang on the money.

18.

Peter drove Pamela to the railway station straight after breakfast the next morning. They had a brief clinch and a hurried kiss as he lifted her small case from the back of the family car.

'Safe journey, Pam, and let me know about Margaret as soon as you can. We'll all be wishing her well.'

'I will, babes, and thank you.' Sniff sniff.

And with that she disappeared onto platform number three and boarded the end carriage – First Class of course. It would go down as expenses for Best Eastern Hotels (UK) Ltd., not that Peter would know that. He drove back to the Hotel via the "scenic route" copying the journey he and Pamela had taken just a week earlier. The weather had "ummed and ahd" in the interim between awful to acceptable and Peter hoped that Pam's journey to London, via York, would not be disrupted. She had promised to message him as soon as she had visited her sister Margaret in St. Bart's that same evening. If only he knew the truth. He decided to break his relatively short journey at the Watermark Café for a hot chocolate. Parking was free in the winter months and to his astonishment the place was very busy. Lots of dog-walkers had the same idea including his youngest daughter Lucy whom he spotted almost immediately at the far end near the welcoming wood-burning stove. Needless to say that Sebbie was with her on the end of a short lead and he had his eye on a lady who looked to have far too many sausages on her plate. With luck, one would be proffered his way soon if he tried to look hungry. As if! Lucy soon spotted her father.

'Dad, I didn't expect to see you here. I thought you were taking Pam to the train station?'

'I just have done. According to the electronic board her train was on time so I decided not to hang around – no point.'

'Cheer up, Dad. I know you're disappointed that Pam had to leave in a hurry before tonight's New Year celebrations. But families come first in cases like this, don't they? Here, take Sebbie's lead and I'll go to the counter. A hot choc like me?'

'Please love.'

Meanwhile, back at the ranch, it was a very different story. Millie and her brother Jamie were alone for the first time since their illicit meeting in the Viking Café. They needed to talk in confidence and they thought they wouldn't have long before their father returned from the station. They were wrong. Millie's mobile pinged twice in her jeans back pocket. It was an unexpected text from Peter.

> *'Stopped at the Watermark for a hot drink on the way back – bumped into Lucy and Sebbie. We're going to visit the Ritsons for a quick visit. She wants to see the puppies again. What time is Inspector Mort arriving? Is he still coming? Dad.'*

'Oh my God, I'd forgotten about "Morse!" and he hasn't called to say whether he's coming or not. Well, we'd best assume that he is, in the absence of any news to the contrary. Anyway look, apart from that, what are we going to tell Dad about what we now know about Pamela? If anything. What's your gut feeling, Bro?'

'I think we should tell him everything we know. He's smitten and it will hit him hard but it's best in the long run that he is fully in the picture now. Do you agree?'

'I do, yes. And later, perhaps after supper, we can discuss it with Clive present as well. It might help to soften the blow about Pamela's Machiavellian intentions. What time are Clive and Betty arriving anyway?'

'They're leaving Beverley straight after lunch so they get here well before it gets dark. The weather's OK over the Wolds apparently – according to the weather girl Abbie on BBC Radio York.'

This was definitely not the case in north North Yorkshire where another three inches of fresh snow had fallen in the Northallerton area. Inspector Mort looked out of his office window and groaned. There was no way he was going to spend the New Year stuck in a snowdrift even if it was a Police 4 x 4 Range Rover. No way José. He reached for his mobile and hit the speed-dial for Millie Fishburn's number. Millie was extremely relieved to learn that the meeting would have to wait until after the New Year break. Didn't they already have enough on their plate with Pamela, Best Eastern Hotels plc, and how to delicately handle their Father?

'Hey, Bro, I've just had a thought. In Pamela's absence there'll be a spare place at our dinner table tonight.'

'Meaning?'

'Meaning why don't you ask your new friend Chloe if she'd like to join us?'

'Oh, I'm sure she'll already have something arranged – New Year's Eve – out on the razz with her friends, surely!'

'Well, you can only ask. Go for it Bro. You said you really liked her!'

Once again, her little brother need a sisterly push in the right direction. She diplomatically went into the kitchen to leave him alone and kept her fingers crossed. Ten minutes later and he joined her with a smile as wide as the Humber Bridge is long.

'Guess what? She said she'd be delighted to come. She said the 'staff night out' didn't appeal to her at all and it was a perfect excuse to get out of going. Wow!'

Millie gave her little brother a sisterly hug. Actually, she had an ulterior motive. If Jamie was going to get involved with this new girl in his life then she wanted to make sure she was a nice person.

'This will focus your attention tonight, Bro. Don't forget you're the Head Chef. You'll have to impress her! Anyway, to slightly more immediate problems. What and how are we going to update Dad? Let's do it straight after lunch and before the Whites arrive. In fact let's have a little "dummy run" in the lounge before he and Lucy get back.'

'Dad, this is very difficult information to impart to you but ....'

They didn't have long to wait. The sound of the family car arriving in the hotel's car park followed closely by a few barks from Sebbie as he rushed towards the back door quickly brought them back to reality. Peter looked visibly downcast and before anyone could say a word came out with his own monologue.

'Listen everyone, I know we're all so disappointed that Pamela has had to leave us for a few days but her family must come first. We are still all going to enjoy ourselves tonight and ...'

He reached for tissue from his pocket and had a little sniffle. His eyes had dampened in the corners too. Millie broke the awkward silence.

'Jamie, tell Dad who else is coming to dinner.' Jamie took the hint.

'Oh yes. Dad, my new friend Chloe is coming to join us. I hope you don't mind – do you? We just thought that well, you know, with a spare place at the table it would be a shame to ...'

''Great! So this new lady friend, is she a blonde or what?'

'Er no, Dad, she's a shiny brunette and don't get any ideas. She's just a new friend and ...' Suddenly Lucy chirped up.

'Well I hope she likes dogs 'cos Sebbie is missing Pam already – especially those little doggie treats she always seems to carry around with her. Does she have a dog of her own?'

'Lucy, I have no idea. Anyway, look you lot, I've got a lot of work to do in the kitchen.'

It suddenly dawned on him that he had no idea if Chloe was a vegetarian, a pescatarian or what? Two minutes later and the question was partly answered when his mobile phone rang. The caller ID told him it was 'ChloeMob' – Chloe's mobile.

'Hi Chloe. What's up? Please don't tell me you can't come tonight.'

'No, of course I'm coming. Dad's giving me a lift to your place in his fish truck. That's what me and Mum call it anyway. It's got big wheels and it's a 4x4 so the weather won't beat us. No, the reason for the call is this. A few local restaurants aren't opening tonight because of expected bad weather so he has a surplus of shellfish and is asking if he can donate some for our dinner tonight.'

'Wow! You bet. Tell him thanks very much. Any idea what it is exactly?'

'You'll see, it's a surprise. Catch you later, alligator.' And with that she was gone.

Millie suddenly appeared at her brother's side.

'Jamie, we cant tell Dad anything yet can we? He's still disappointed that Pam's not here. Let's you and I have a quiet chat with Clive later, or even tomorrow. Agreed?'

'Agreed, sis. Let's all have a great evening.'

Jamie repaired immediately to the kitchen and glanced at his watch – almost three o'clock – he'd better get a 'wiggle-on' as they say. He'd already decided to do a roast loin of pork as a main course with an apple and mustard jus when it dawned on him that he needed more information from Chloe. He needn't have worried as within two minutes his mobile pinged twice. It was an incoming message from Chloe:

'Sorry I forgot to ask you – how many people will be at the table? Dad wants to know? He's doing a seafood starter for us. What time are we eating? Chloe x'

Jamie breathed a huge sigh of relief. That's one less thing to worry about. He texted back within seconds.

'It's seven and seven. See you soon. Jx'

It was the first time he had ever sent a text to a member of the fairer sex with a kiss at the end of it – apart from his mother and two sisters. He felt on top of the world.

19.

Just as Jamie was turning his attention to the evening's culinary matters, a sleek red and white Azuma train of the LNER company was about to pull into Kings Cross Station in North London. Pamela Hesketh, needless to say, was in the First Class coach at the front of the nine-carriage train. It was almost two hours late as it had been stationary on the track just south of Stevenage due to a 'signalling problem' according to the public announcement. Thousands of people were travelling to celebrate New Year and there was a collective groan from over four hundred passengers when the bad news came over the Tannoy. Oh well, at least Pamela had some reading material that she had purchased at the WH Smith kiosk in York during the twenty-minute wait for the connecting train south to London. Unusually, she had actually had to buy a copy of *English Hotels Monthly* now that she was no longer an employee. She was curious to see how her successor was doing as Editor in Chief and paid more than a little attention to the centre-spread feature – a converted oat house in Kent. She assumed, wrongly, that none of the Fishburns would have bought the magazine, let alone seen the new management structure on the inside cover. The extra time on the train, in a quiet First Class coach, afforded her the chance to collect her own thoughts and update the Notes on her iPad in preparation for the all-important Board Meeting of Best Eastern Hotels plc in just a few short days time. She would be able to make a very realistic and persuasive case to the Board that the company invested heavily in real estate and businesses in the Scarborough and surrounding area. Pamela disembarked the train on Platform 8 and headed straight for the Taxi Rank and the ride to her apartment in Pimlico. The Tube would be heaving and anyway the company would pick up the tab for the taxi fare – as long as she remembered to get a receipt. A half an hour later and she was nicely ensconced in her half-a-million quid apartment and she turned up the central heating thermostat to twenty-five Celsius. Sod net zero – she was paying the gas bill not the new Energy Secretary. She dressed down to a cosy 'onesey' that made her look like a snow leopard, made a pot of coffee and chucked a frozen 'chicken ping' in the micro-wave. It was time to chill after the tiring and delayed journey. She wondered momentarily what she was missing in the culinary department two hundred and fifty miles north but after consuming the only food she had immediately available she dozed off on the sofa. She clean forgot to make 'that call' to Peter. Up in Scarbados it was a different scene altogether.

Clive and Betty White had arrived from Beverley just before it got dark and had managed to avoid any really bad weather as they drove over the Wolds. There had been a few snowflakes but nothing serious enough to make them divert to the coast road via Bridlington. The plan was to spend one night at least in Scarborough with the Fishburns but they packed a few extra clothes just in case the weather deteriorated. Betty was secretly wishing that it would as she rather fancied a mini-break on the coast, and apart from the previous stay at the Hotel Scarbados, the last time she had done that was when she and Clive had attended his Bank's 'Scarborough Weekends' in May every year. Clive and Millie had shared a short conversation on the subject of Pamela as soon as they had taken their cases in from the car. They agreed that Peter should be kept in the dark about their findings – at least for the foreseeable future. After unpacking and freshening up in the double room that Millie and Lucy had prepared for them on the top floor, they came downstairs to the warm lounge for some hot tea and shortbread. It already had the feel and ambience of a Hotel despite the fact it would be three months or more before it started officially trading. Ever the chancer, Sebbie appeared before Betty with one eye on the shortbread and another on her right hand. Waiting until nobody was looking she surreptitiously held the last inch of a shortbread stick down the side of her chair. Sebbie moved in like a terrestrial great white shark and removed it in less than a second without even touching her fingers. If he thought he'd got away with it, he was wrong. Lucy had spotted him.

'Sebbie, stop that! You won't want any tea! And it's your favourite pork tonight.'

Suitably chided by his mistress, Sebbie slid into the kitchen to seek sympathy, and perhaps a tit-bit, from Jamie. He was out of luck. Jamie was just too busy.

Just before seven o'clock there was a flash of headlights from the car park which illuminated the whole kitchen and half of the ground floor. It was Chloe's father's van with the logo Cammish/Shellfish embossed on the side in gold lettering from what Jamie could make out from the sole light in the Hotel's car-park. Suddenly, he felt nervous. What should he say to Chloe's father? Hello, how to you do, or pleased to meet you? He needn't have worried. Mr Cammish jumped out of the driver's side of the van looking like a Lifeboat man on duty wearing a bright yellow sou'wester, rubber boots and a waterproof hat. Dashing round to the rear of the vehicle he opened one of two doors that looked remarkably like a large domestic fridge freezer and slid out a large plastic tray.

'Don't just stand there lass – get that kitchen door open!'

Seconds later they were both inside the kitchen. Chloe looked nervous too.

'Er, Dad, this is Jamie Fishburn. Jamie this my Dad and ...' She didn't finish.

'Hey-up Jamie lad. Ow do. Now where do you want this tray? On't top o'this table or what? Me hands are freezing.'

Mr Cammish put the tray on the work-top and removed a soggy glove from his right hand.

'Now we can shake hands.'

His grip almost tore Jamie's hand right off.

'I'm Fred, please. None of this Mr Cammish lark. I'd best get back. Her indoors will have our tea about ready then we'll head down to the seafront and have a few scoops. You'd best book a taxi home Chloe for just after midnight. Look after her, lad. She's the only one I've got. Enjoy the starter with my compliments. Happy New Year.' And with that he was gone.

Chloe slipped off her coat to reveal a stunning black trouser-suit with Cuban heels. At work she always wore her hair either 'up' or tied back but tonight it cascaded past her shoulders and danced merrily in the modest cleavage that she dared to show. Her Dad hadn't seen that bit. Jamie turned to stone and hadn't a clue what to say or do next.

'Thanks for inviting me, Jamie.'

She almost jumped on him as she planted him a smacker on his lips.

'Now, are you going to introduce me to the rest of your family or what?'

As if on cue, Sebbie trotted into the kitchen. He had smelt a stranger. Would she prove as affable as the previous lady who dared to venture into the family fold? Only time would tell. Lucy soon followed.

'Oh hi, you must be Chloe. Welcome to Fawlty Towers – I'm only joking! This is Sebbie. Here, give him one of these doggie treats.' Gulp! See, now you've got a friend for life. Let me take your coat. Wow, what a fab outfit. I feel almost scruffy. I'll go and get changed but let me take you into the lounge first where the rest of the gang are.'

Jamie was quite relieved that his younger sister was going to do the introductions for him. In any case he still needed a while in the kitchen and what was in the mystery tray anyway? He peeled back several tea towels that had protected the mysterious contents. He was taken aback. Seven small lobsters had been dressed and lay on a bed of crushed ice surrounded by alternate quarters of lemons and limes. Each one was accompanied by two languistines that almost resembled baby lobsters. How generous of Mr Cammish – er Fred. It made him wonder what Chloe's mum had prepared for their own tea.

Ten minutes later and they were all in the lounge having a glass of mulled wine. Peter's tongue was hanging out and had his ex-wife Mandy been present he would have got black looks and a severe tongue-lashing later.

'Jamie, you didn't tell me that Chloe modelled for Vogue magazine when she's not studying.'

Everyone chuckled except Chloe who looked a tad embarrassed. Millie came to her rescue.

'Chloe, you look lovely, absolutely gorgeous.' She winked at her sister.

'I'll tell you later about his previous girlfriends in 'Ull shall I? Tattooed trollops most of them, if you ask me. No wonder Mam never asked any of them to tea.'

This time it was Jamie's turn to blush and he quickly rescued himself.

'Right, I'll just go and check how dinner's coming along. Give me five, folks.'

Chloe followed him and this time he got two full smackers on the lips.

'Jamie, your family are just lovely. Everyone's being so nice to me.'

Dinner was served with as much panache as Jamie could muster – with the assistance of his new girl-friend Chloe, of course. She clung to him like a limpet to a rock, much to the amusement of Peter who was almost envious in the absence of his own beau.

'OK listen up everyone. The seafood starter is courtesy of Chloe's Dad, Fred, so let's raise a glass of thanks to him shall we before we actually start eating. The wine I have selected to accompany the lobsters by the way is a French La Nantaise Muscadet which always goes well with seafood, especially shellfish. Note the long, smooth finish which is accentuated if it's not served too chilled.'

Peter momentarily raised an eyebrow and wondered where on earth his son had picked this information up from. Then he remembered the Tasting Guide from Crombé Wines in Kortrijk that he had brought back from the MV Pride of Bruges. His mind flashed back to the many happy lunches he had spent with one of their Directors, Balder Vandenbroucke. Perhaps he could invite him and his charming wife Jill over to the formal opening of the Hotel Koala in the Spring. The arrival of the main course, roast loin of pork, propelled him out of his daydream. Lucy looked horrified.

'Jamie, you know I'm a veggie so I hope you've made something separate for me and Sebbie?'

'Lucy, of course I have. I've grilled some of Mr Hillman's fennel and leek sausages for you but you'll share the mustard and apple jus, I trust. And as for Sebbie, he is not a vegetarian dog, I'll remind you!'

Everybody laughed except Lucy. At the very mention of his name Sebbie's ears pricked up. He'd already taken up station in one corner of the dining room and was speculating which of the diners might be the first to offer him a chunk of juicy crackling – his particular favourite. Jamie continued with his presentation as if he was already on Master Chef.

'The pork, which incidentally is from the Greene's Farm on the Wolds, is served with mange tout, a mash of Swede and Carrot and Dauphinoise potato. The wine is a German hock which complements the pork perfectly and …' Lucy cracked up.

'Jamie, sit down and stop this please. It's all yummy so let's just eat can we?'

The conversation around the table flowed easily. Millie had arranged the table plan and had deliberately put her father at one end on his own so that he could talk to everyone easily. She knew he would be feeling a bit of a gooseberry without Pamela. He felt a bit like a quiz show compere.

'So, Chloe, have you been in this hotel before?' She looked a bit uneasy.

'Well, er no actually. But did you know that its got a bit of folklore attached to it – you know the ghost? Don't tell me you hadn't heard?'

'No, we're all fairly new to Scarbados, as I'm sure Jamie told you. Tell us more.'

'Well, during the First World War Scarborough was shelled by two German battleships lying a couple of miles offshore. There were lots of casualties. One was a young girl who was badly hurt when her school was hit. She was brought here to this Hotel which was turned into a makeshift hospital. The poor girl eventually succumbed to her injuries and died here ten days later on Boxing Day 1914. Rumour and folklore has it that her spirit returns here on that day every year just for one day. All four Fisburns looked at each other in total silence. Perhaps there had been more than a shred of truth in Pamela's claims to have heard the cries of a young girl. Chloe was astute enough to instantly realise that she had put her foot in it and needed to say or do something quickly.

'Does Sebbie like crackling? I'm not keen myself.'

Like greased lightning Sebbie, launched himself to Choe's right hand which was proffering a four inch sprig of a hog's hide beneath her seat. He immediately decided that this newcomer was a bit of all-right.

The dessert of the last of the Season's Christmas pudding was dished up with a perfect brandy sauce and coffees were brought in. Millie looked out of the window towards the illuminated ruins of Scarborough Castle. It was invisible.

'Oh my God. Have you seen the snow outside? We've been eating, drinking and talking so much we hadn't noticed. There's no way there'll be the customary fireworks display in this. Last year's was cancelled because a bloomin' walrus had dragged itself up onto a slipway in the harbour and the animal rights people didn't want to upset it with the bangs and flashes. Chloe love, how are you getting home? And where exactly do you live anyway?'

'Dad said to order a taxi in advance and I forgot. We live in Quay Street in the Old Town – Harbour Haven House. There's no way I'll get one now. Every man and his dog will want one after the midnight countdown and celebrations won't they? That is if taxis will even operate in this.'

Millie seized the opportunity to get to know her little brother's girlfriend a lot better.

'Look, tell you what, Chloe. Call your Dad now before

you forget. Tell him that with the deteriorating weather you've been invited to stay with us overnight and he can collect you in the morning when the weather will be better. OK? There's a spare single bed in my room that's made up. It's even got an electric blanket. Neither Peter nor Jamie knew what to say. The girls had taken over. It was time for another brandy. By the time they all retired to bed, Peter had completely forgotten that Pamela was supposed to have called him with an update on her sister Margaret's condition. No matter, she was probably fatigued after a long day. He would call her straight after breakfast.

But Pamela was very much awake. After a bit of supper and a short forty winks on the sofa she felt a lot better. She had given a great deal of thought as to what her message to Peter should say. She had to plan ahead, that's for sure. She made a few corrections and amendments before saving it as a draft on her iPhone. She would send it in the morning at roughly the time she estimated they would all be round the breakfast table.

'Pete, dahling.

Good morning and a very Happy New Year to all of you.

It was so late last night after I had seen Margaret at St. Bart's I thought I would leave it until this morning.

The news is that Margaret has survived the stroke but her Consultant has recommended that she goes into Care as soon as possible after the New Year. She needs twenty-four seven attention from now on. The onus of responsibility will of course fall on my shoulders. I could well have to stay back here in London for a week or more.

I'll call you tonight babes.'

Mwah!

Pammie xxx

20.

The next morning brought a break in the weather. Occasional gaps in the clouds revealed a weak, milky sun that was struggling to gain altitude, It was, after all, only ten days since the winter solstice.

All seven in residence were gathered around the same table as the previous evening. Nobody had much of an appetite and tea, coffee and toast was all that anybody wanted. Peter had barely buttered his second slice when his mobile pinged in his shirt pocket. It was an incoming text – from Pamela of course. He read it silently to himself twice.

'It's from Pamela. It's not really confidential so I'll read it to you all.'

Clive White looked at Millie and Millie looked at Clive. Neither said anything but the silence was broken by the back door bell ringing. Sebbie rushed to it first as he was wont to do. It was Chloe's dad, Fred. Jamie was next at the door after Sebbie.

'Morning all. Has my little girl survived a night in the Haunted Castle? I take it she told you about it?'

'Morning, Fred. Come in please. Coffee?'

'Aye, milk no sugar please. Did anyone hear her then on Boxing Day?'

'Hi Dad. And Happy New Year.' Chloe gave her father a peck on the cheek.

'You were right about the taxis stopping working shortly after midnight. At least your Mam and I didn't have far to walk from the Newcastle Packet to home. We were home by twelve-thirty.'

Jamie was staring out of the window at Frank's van.'

'That looks a useful vehicle, Mr er, Fred. I don't think I've ever seen one quite like it.'

'Aye, it's a belter. It's got eight quite separate compartments, all individually temperature controlled from minus five Celsius to plus thirty-five. It means you can transport frozen, chilled or warm foodstuffs over about a fifty mile radius. Most of my seafood is just chilled and I deliver to restaurants locally and as far afield as York and as far south as Beverley and even sometimes to Hull where you lot come from!' Jamie was intrigued.

'Is it petrol or diesel, Fred?'

'Neither, it's actually electric! Nowt to do with being 'green' or net zero or any of that lark. Come outside and I'll show yer.'

The boys went outside and talked engines and batteries for five minutes.

'You'll find nowt like this in UK – at least not yet. No, I imported it from Malta two years ago. Me and Chloe's mother were on holiday when we saw one delivering fish to the hotel we were staying in. I had a chat with the driver who actually was the owner and he put me onto the firm that built it in a village called Burr-Marrad. They had to cope with hot temperatures from May right through until the autumn. It was the bright red lobster logo on the side of the van that caught my eye. Anyway, one thing led to another and I arranged to get one and had it shipped to UK – King George Dock in Hull to be precise. Why, do you want one?!'

They went inside and finished their coffees. All five women were talking shopping and New Year sales. Peter and Clive were just observers.

'Right, Chloe, let's get yer home. By the way, Jamie, her indoors says you've to come to tea at Harbour Haven House next Saturday if you're free. It's easy to find.'

Farewells were said and hugs were given and received all round. Jamie got two kisses and a hug but big sis Millie had the last word just as Chloe climbed into the passenger side of the van.

'I've got your number in my iPhone now, Chloe. We'll fix that shopping day and lunch in York as soon as you've gone back to Uni. OK?'

Jamie wasn't sure whether he was annoyed or pleased.

Lucy, Betty and Peter got their coats on and prepared to take Sebbie for a walk along the cliff-tops. As soon as they had gone Millie summoned Clive and Jamie into the dining room.

'Well, Clive, you're spot on with Pamela. Do we all agree that we have to keep Dad in the dark, at least for the immediate future? Pamela's message was worthy of the Pulitzer Prize for fiction wasn't it?'

Clive paused, as retired bank managers do, before uttering his opinion.

'No. I say we tell him what we know as soon as he returns from the walk.'

'What? Why?'

'Well two things. Morally he should be told that Pamela is only in London for one reason – to attend that Board Meeting of Best Eastern Hotels plc in two days time. Look how cleverly she has already bought herself some more time. She has left it open for her to make as many trips as she likes to London, ostensibly to look for Nursing Homes or whatever. There could soon be more Extraordinary General Meetings if things start to hot up. In fact we could actually add grist to the mill, couldn't we? Let me give it some thought over the next few days. One thing is for certain – Pamela is a consummate actress. Look, this break in the weather might only be temporary so I think that Betty and I will set off sooner rather than later if you don't mind. Get your Dad settled in the nice warm lounge this afternoon and put him completely in the picture. Your Dad's a lovely guy and you owe it to him. Tell him he can give me a call any time he likes.

And secondly, once he's in the picture he won't be caught off-guard. He'll be mentally prepared for anything that Pamela might come up with.'

'Thanks, Clive. Where would we be without you? I just don't know.'

By mid-afternoon it was time to spill the beans.

'So that's it, Dad. Now you know as much as we do. And if it wasn't for Clive we'd all still be in the dark.'

'I feel a total eejit, as Terry Wogan used to say. How could I possibly have been taken in by her? She was charming, intelligent and …'

'Dad, you were only human and vulnerable. After the split with Mum and the subsequent divorce it was only natural that you should seek solace in another lady's company. And you've had a bit of fun – wink wink – and nobody's been hurt. Well only your pride anyway.'

'So what do we do now, if anything?'

''Clive says do almost nothing for the time being. The hotel is ours and Mum is still a twenty-five percent shareholder. Clive's best guess is that she will put in a glowing report to the Board concerning the potential of the hospitality industry in the "Scarbados" area in general and the Koala Hotel in particular. To make her own killing though she will first have to acquire a shareholding of her own. Our Mother's shares are the obvious target. I think you can stand by for a lot of pillow-talk as soon as she gets back.'

'Well even if your mother does agree to sell her shares, which I suspect she will initially reject, what do we do then?'

'Dad, you're a bit slow on the uptake here. If and when Pamela owns Mum's shares, she would then almost certainly recommend that Best Eastern buys a serious stake in the business. It's "ker-ching" time! We all win, including Pamela. Get it?'

'I think so. I need some more tea. Any left in the pot?'

21.

Two days later, at precisely ten o'clock in the morning, the Group Chairman of Best Eastern Hotels called the meeting to order. Stephen Fan had arrived back in the UK on the non-stop overnight flight from Hong Kong, Cathay Pacific Business Class of course.

'Good morning everyone and a warm welcome to the company's first Board Meeting outside Asia. First of all I would like to formally welcome Miss Pamela Hesketh to the Board. Pamela brings with her many years of experience in the hotel & hospitality industry. Her knowledge, experience and we hope, subsequent advice, will be invaluable. I will be asking her to make a short Report later in the proceedings but first of all we have to comply with UK Company Law and pass certain resolutions. It's all a bit boring but please bear with me.

The first item on the agenda is to appoint the Auditors. May I have a proposer please.' A hand went up. 'Thank you. And a seconder please.' A different hand went up. 'Carried thank you.'

Several further Resolutions were proposed and carried. It was all very boring but very necessary.

'And now to the meat of the whole business. May I introduce our newly appointed Finance Director, Mr Kenneth Chan? Mr Chan, the floor is yours.'

Pamela smiled. She hadn't even considered that Mr Chan might be here today. They had of course inadvertently bumped into each other at the Lucky Dragon restaurant in Scarborough so very recently and had made a good job of failing to recognise each other. It been a bit too close for comfort though and they both knew it. This time it was different. They smiled and grinned broadly to each other.

'My main job this morning is to appraise you of the financial situation today and the prospects for the immediate future. The necessary banking arrangements have been established and the necessary protocols completed. We have to be careful. As a new kid on the block we don't want some smart-arse "cookie boy" telling us that we are going to be de-banked because they don't like us. Not that we couldn't pay them off of course!' Ripples of laughter rattled around the long table for several seconds.

'No, liquidity will not be a problem. Funds in excess of twenty-five million Sterling have already been remitted to our London account. The next step is to decide where and how to spend it as we build up our property portfolio up and down the East Coast of England. I have already secured a contract to buy a large and successful Chinese Restaurant in the town of Scarborough. I believe Miss Hesketh has already been taking a close look at this area too but no doubt we'll hear more from her soon. A second tranche of another twenty-five million will become available soon. In six months time we must establish holdings in many successful businesses in the hospitality industry. Only once we have done that will we 'go public' and offer shares to private investors. We will review the situation in three months. Any questions? ' Nobody had and so the Chairman moved his pencil down the Agenda.

'Next, Pamela, would you like to give us your Report on the research you have done thus far please.'

'Mr Chairman, thank you. I have completed the first stage of my research and I am happy to report as follows:

The town of Scarborough, more commonly given the moniker Scarbados these days, offers unlimited upside potential to our company. Historically, Scarborough is the oldest seaside resort in England. Commercially, it reached its heyday in the Sixties. The advent of cheap air travel and the guarantee of foreign sunshine took its toll however, and it declined both in popularity and prosperity a little bit with every year that passed. When Covid arrived five years ago it spelt the death knell for many businesses, mostly family owned and established for many years. Like 'natural selection' only the fittest survived. I have my eye on one particular business – the soon to be re-opened Koala Hotel. It was requisitioned by the Home Office during the immigration crisis but has now been returned to the private sector. A fortune of tax-payers' money was spent on it to the advantage of the new owners, the Fishburn family, formerly of Hull. I think that another review in six months to synchronise with Mr Chan's own review would work well. Would the Board be kind enough to leave that one with me?'

There were positive mutterings all round the table.

'On other matters, my research reveals that there is much potential in the immediate area from non-hotel investment. The old Borough Council has been merged into a new 'Super Council' which has left many development situations unexplored. In fact, looking at old postcards, you could be forgiven for thinking that the Victorian developers had more business savvy over a century ago than the current lot today. Don't just take my word for it. Go and visit Scarbados for yourselves. Wait until the worst of the winter weather has passed then take a look. Go and stay at the Hotel Koala, under cover as it were, then we'll collectively decide to take a look and make a decision. Maybe a short "staycation mini-break" as they call them now? What do you all think?'

To Pamela, the remaining items on the Agenda went by in a blur. The expensive lunch that followed at the Mountbatten Hotel, paid for by the company of course, was exquisite. If she had her way then the future *Jamie's at the Koala* would be just as good but perhaps less expensive. Time would tell. She got a taxi back to her Pimlico apartment, put the kettle on and composed an update text to Peter.

'Hi dahling.

Margaret's condition remains the same, neither better nor worse.

Her Consultant has advised that we start looking for a suitable Home now.

She says she liked one in Isleworth when she visited a friend there last year.

I think I'll take a look myself over the next few days.

Miss you all so much.

Give Sebbie a pat and a treat from me please.

Pammie xxxxx

When Peter's phone pinged twice a second later he read the text. He didn't know whether to laugh or cry. In the event he did both – copiously. When he showed it to the kids they all had a little group hug like footballers who were about to take penalties. Lucy came up with a bright idea.

'Cheer up everyone. Let's go to that little cinema round the corner. The latest Disney film has just come out and tonight's the first screening. Listen, I'll take Sebbie out for a little walk and I'll pop in and get four tickets for the seven o'clock show, OK? I walked past the other day and it looks like they've got a real popcorn machine in there too. Who's up for it? Hands up!'

Half way through the film Jamie's phone pinged as he'd forgotten to switch to silent mode. It was a text from Chloe.

'Don't forget you're coming for tea tomorrow. Meet me in the Flamingo Bay Café on the seafront for a hot chocolate at say half-past three. You can't miss it. We can have a chat and then walk from there it's not far to Quay Street. Yes? Chloe xx'

It took Jamie all of five seconds to text back 'you betcha see you there.' Then he switched his phone off and settled down to watch the film. His social life, in fact his whole life, was starting to take on a brand new perspective.

22.

After breakfast the next morning Millie once again assumed her role of head mistress and clerk of works.

'Right you lot, the festivities are over and we now have to knuckle down. We've got serious planning to do. Easter is quite late this year, April 20th to be precise. Which gives us just over a hundred days if we're going to officially open for Easter. We need to put together a full marketing plan just like we did to open the Hotel Scarbados over a year ago. Any thoughts?' Jamie cut in first.

'I won't have finished my Chef's Diploma by then as it doesn't officially complete until the end of June. That's when I would like to officially launch my 'in house' restaurant as we discussed a while ago. Did we agree that the Hotel would open one floor at a time?'

'Yes, we did, Jamie. As Clive reminded me yesterday, we mustn't run before we can walk. Smooth cash-flow is imperative.' She reached for a large ring-binder file.

'Remember this everyone? This was the master plan for taking over the Hotel Scarbados – well over a year ago now. I've started a new file which I've called Operation Koala. We have more experience than when we first came to Scarborough, in fact a lot more, but many of the tasks and principles are the same. The banking arrangements are already in place so we won't have to go through all that palaver again. We are liquid, that is to say we have money in the bank with no need for any borrowing requirements, thank goodness. I think our main problem is going to be a human one. Don't forget, we had Mam on board before. I can't see Lady Pamela making up beds and cleaning WCs can you?' They all laughed, particularly Peter.

'You're right there! And don't forget that Lucy is starting her work experience at the veterinary clinic next week. That's another pair of hands we'll have to make up for. Where is she anyway?'

Jamie interjected.

'Where do you think? She's taken Sebbie out for a walk. You can bet your bottom dollar that she's walking down to the Ritsons to introduce Sebbie to his son, Alfie-Boy.'

Peter raised an eyebrow.

'Let's hope it's quite a few weeks before they let him join us. We've enough on our plate for the foreseeable future. I'll have a word with Garry without Lucy knowing. Now, where were we, Millie?'

'Staffing. There are agencies that we could use but I understand that they're expensive. Tell you what, I'll pop in for a chat with Nadine at the Crescent Gardens Hotel. If they've had applications for employment but not enough vacancies to fill, then they might care to pass them on to us. It's worth a go anyway. Who knows, we might be able to work out some sort of reciprocal arrangement.

Digressing, my mate Katya in Hull is arranging a new website for us and she's already reserved the domain name. Once that's up and running, and the sooner the better, we can start advertising for bookings, say from the first week in April. The clocks will have gone forward to British Summer Time and folks start to get in a more holiday-like mood.

'Dad, will you get in touch with that Miles Carter at the Cricket Club please and ask him if the season's fixture list has been arranged yet – and if not can he please let us know when it will be out. We still have that arrangement in place where we have a free link on the Club's website to our own website. We should fill the hotel for the County matches just on the back of that link alone.'

'I'll invite him in for coffee and a chat soon. I'll also ask him about those overseas players who couldn't come last year to stay at the Hotel Scarbados. A young Barbadian and a young Aussie if I remember correctly.'

'Yes, that's right, Dad. On paper we have a lot more accommodation to offer now. Jamie, we're going to have to firm-up the plans for your new restaurant. Name? Style? Costs involved. Talk to me!'

'Well, I er, well I want to talk to Samantha Lyon at the TEC first please. I also wanted Pamela's ideas but that's probably out of the question now and …'

'No, it isn't. We are going to use her but it needs some more thought first. We'll chat about that later please, after tea.'

'But I won't be here will I? I'm meeting Chloe down the seafront then I'm going to her folk's place for tea. Sorry.'

'OK we'll leave that until tomorrow then. And don't get lost on your way back, particularly if you've had a drink or two. The Old Town is a myriad of ginnels and narrow streets. And you'd better be on best behaviour. Chloe's Dad was a down to earth sort of chap but her Mum might be quite the opposite. Don't forget – clean shirt, polished shoes and keep your elbows off the table.'

'Your sounding like Mam ten years ago!'

'Well, I'm just saying that's all. Mind your Ps and Qs, you're not in 'Ull now!'

'Yes, Sis. Can I go now please, Miss?'

They both laughed and Jamie disappeared upstairs to polish his best black shoes. Millie ran her finger down the "to do" list and mentally ticked them off. A main PC for the reception and office, TV sets for all the rooms on the first floor. The new sign for the Hotel's exterior. Where were the receipts and invoices from all the work done at the Hotel Scarbados? She went hunting for the storage box she knew she had kept them safe in. The name of the company was *'We are Neon'* from Teesside. They had done a fabulous job of a new sign for the Hotel Scarbados. She soon found what she was looking for. The phone number was on the top of the paid invoice. She remembered the boss's name – Dave Gibson. She dialled the number and waited. It diverted to a mobile.

'We are Neon, Dave Gibson speaking.'

'Oh hello, Mr Gibson. It's Millie Fishburn from the Hotel Scarbados in Scarborough, except that ..'

'Oh hello, how are you all? I'd heard lots of tittle-tattle on the rumour mill about your place. Is it all true?'

'Some of it will be! But listen, we no longer own the Hotel Scarbados. We've bought the Clifftop Hotel up near the Bowling Centre and ..."

'Wow! I'd heard that a new owner had taken over once the Home Office had done all the renovations on it. Lucky you. So what can I do for you? It must be in tip-top fettle now, surely?'

Yes, it sure is but we've decided to change the name so the old outside sign which looks as if has been there for ever will have to come down to be replaced by a high-tech one like you did for the Hotel Scarbados.'

'So what's the new name? Dare I ask?'

'You can. It's new name is the Hotel Koala.'

'Hey, I like that. We can have a field day with the sign. My brain's buzzing already! Is there an Australian connection?'

'There is but we'll tell you about that later. When will you next be down this way?'

'Well, as it happens, I'm coming down to Filey one day next week to quote for a big job on a disused hotel that's being converted to a Nursing Home. Can I give you a call when I've got the day fixed? Folks are only just getting into the swing of working again after the holidays. They just seem to get longer every year. Catch you soon, Millie. My best regards to your Dad please.'

'Will do, Mr Gibson and thank you.'

One more job ticked off the list. Next job was the TV sets. Rather than call them she would pop into that nice electrical shop opposite the Casino on her next walk into town. They had already provided a huge set for their own lounge on approval. It would be only fair to approach them first.

Item by item, step by step, the Hotel Koala as a trading entity was starting to take shape.

She caught sight of Jamie leaving the back door on his way to meet Chloe on the seafront.

'Have a great time Bro. Be good and if you can't be good be careful. You know what I mean.'

She gave him that big-Sis wink and shut the door behind him. She had never seen his shoes shined like that before.

23.

Once he was on the sea-front it didn't take long for Jamie to find the Flamingo Bay Café. It had a huge pink flamingo painted across its facade at least two stories high. He was a few minutes early. Was she here already? He glanced nervously inside and scanned the colourful tables and chairs that were tiny and would look more at home in a doll's house. There was a middle-aged couple occupying the prime window seats gazing out across the beach where an ebbing tide had left a wet expanse of sand all the way down to the water's edge at least thirty metres distant. The only other people in the place were two girls, one behind the serving counter, with auburn hair tied-back, the other on the customer side, wearing a warm-looking parka with a fur hood. They were chatting animatedly. The waitress, whose badge gave her name as Amber, leant across the counter.

'So, Chloe, who's this new fella then? Donna was telling me you've met this new chap from Hull?'

'You mean 'Ull!'

They both laughed and immediately Jamie realised that the hooded girl was non-other than Chloe! He dug her playfully in the small of her back and she twirled round.

'Oi, less of the 'Ull. I'm a Scarbadian now.'

She pecked him swiftly on both cheeks.

'Jamie, this is Amber who's worked here for as long as I can remember. Amber, this is Jamie.'

Amber reached a hand across the counter.

'Ow do! I've heard all about you. But don't worry it's all good. Now, what can I get you both? Has Chloe told you about our famous hot chocolate?'

'Er, no I don't think so. Two of those then please.'

'Flake and marsh mallows on top of the cream?'

'Please. You too, Chloe, I'm guessing?'

'You betcha. We'll grab that table in the window now that couple have gone. Are they visitors or regulars, do you know?'

'Regular customers. We get lots of those in the winter, especially when it's really cold. Why spend money on your own gas and electric when you can use someone else's and sample our famous hot chocolate! Go and sit down and I'll bring them over to you.'

Chloe opened the batting.

'You found this place OK then?'

'Sure, you can't really miss it can you? The whole building looks like an ad for one of those David Attenborough nature programmes.'

'You're right there. Let's take our coats off or we'll not feel the benefit of them outside – like my Grandma used to say!'

'Mine too! Maybe all grandmas are like that?' The chatter was easy.

'Do you come here often?'

'Ha! I was wondering if you were going to say that! Actually I do, when I'm not at Uni of course. Because we live in the Old Town it's not far for me to walk. To be honest I keep my time in the town centre to a minimum – when I'm not at work that is. It's a bit depressing I think.'

'Depressing, why?'

'Well since Covid a lot of shops have closed and are boarded up. Mum and Dad say that the town centre is a shadow of its former self. You know, the usual parental stuff – 'back in the day when we were teenagers, bla bla bla!'

'I know what you mean but there's probably an element of truth in that too. Times have changed, particularly in British seaside towns. Folks don't go into town to just shop any more. They want to be fed, watered and, above all, entertained. They want an experience, not just a carrier bag full of shopping.'

'Gosh, you are in a philosophical frame of mind aren't you? Tell me more about your plans for the Hotel Koala and your own restaurant. Will it be open to non-residents? I sure hope so 'cos Mum and Dad know half the people in town!'

'Oh yes, I just can't stop thinking about it to be honest. I've got too many ideas in my head at the same time. I need to talk to my course tutor, Samantha Lyon, before making any decisions. And Pamela Hesketh too.'

'Who?'

'Pamela Hesketh – you ate her dinner on New Year's Eve! Listen, while we're here alone I think I'd better tell you about Pamela.'

Jamie thought it best to come clean about the Pamela situation – if only to prevent her from inadvertently putting her foot in it on a future occasion. He started at the beginning – how she had done them all a huge favour by using her position as a magazine editor to ingratiate herself into the family's affairs and thence into the clutches of his father, Peter. He rambled on for several minutes before Chloe interrupted him.

'If you don't look out, Jamie, all that extra chocolate and the flake will be forming a mud slide down the side of your glass …'

'What, oh heck. I see what you mean. I'll use the straw. Hang on.'

He slurped and spluttered for ages as the mixture in the glass reduced to a safe level and then he resumed his explanation.

'So you see, Chloe, it's all be a bit tricky to say the least. Pamela is now definitely on the main Board of Best Eastern Hotels plc but she doesn't know we know, if you see what I mean.'

'Goodness me. It's like a TV drama series isn't it? Is your Dad upset, hurt or a mixture of both?'

'You've probably hit the nail on the head there, Chloe. He was probably going to be a bit vulnerable when he and Mam split up. She obviously sensed that and then one thing led to another. You know how it is.'

She was interrupted by Amber.

'Come on you two, it's after four o'clock and I want to shut shop. It's almost dark.'

'Crikey, is that the time Chloe? Drink up. How far away do you live? Quay Street did you say?'

'It's only a few hundred yards although we live right near the end - number forty-three. Let's get our coats on, it looks grim out there and I hate to say it but I think it's trying to snow. I can see a few flakes already fluttering past the street lights - and I don't mean chocolate flakes either. Bye Amber! I'll see you again before I go back to Uni.'

'Bye, hun. And look after him. He's nice!'

'Ignore her jibes, Jamie. Come on, left here then past the Harbour Bar and we'll cut through the car park into this end of Quay Street. It's freezing! Thank goodness we took Grandma's advice.'

They were soon past a car park set back from the sea front and in a winding street boasting a diverse range of properties - new, old and very old. Jamie was impressed.

'Goodness me, one or two of these properties look as if they were around during Shakespeare's days. Look at that one over there – look!'

'That's probably the oldest building in Scarborough still standing – apart from Scarborough Castle that is. Don't ask me when it dates from. Mum's the history buff. She'll talk about it until the cows come home if you let her. Lots of history down this part of town. You know that firm that built the Titanic, Harland and something?'

'Harland and Wolff I think you mean?'

'Yeah, well they started life down here somewhere, outgrew it and so moved to Belfast where they still are today.'

'You're kidding me!'

'Nope. Scarbados has a lot more history than most folks realise. But it's the future now that most business folks are worried about, including my Dad. No doubt he'll tell you more later if I know my Dad. Here we are, nearly there.'

Just ahead, on the left, was a small but double-fronted detached house. To the left and right of the black painted door were two mounted lights in copper housings – one green and one red to denote port and starboard. Jamie smiled. His Dad would approve, to put it mildly. Chloe had barely put her hand on the door handle when her mother pulled it inwards to open it.

'Ah, there you are you two. As soon as it got dark I didn't think you'd be long. Hello Jamie, I'm Sarah, Chloe's mum. Pleased to meet you. Let me take your coat.'

24.

Everyone was on first name terms from the off and Jamie felt very much at home. A gas powered imitation log burner glowed in the old-fashioned tiled hearth. Stretched out in front of it, fast asleep, was a chunky tortoiseshell cat.

'Jamie this Leo. He's getting on a bit now. We've had him for fifteen years now and he was just a kitten when we rescued him. Be warned though, he doesn't normally take kindly to strangers. His tail's twitching so he's probably dreaming about his next dinner. As you can imagine he is spoilt rotten with seafood with Dad being in the trade but surprisingly he doesn't like prawns.'

'Three guesses what's for tea then – prawn cocktails!'

'No! It's roast pheasant with all the trimmings. A little tradition that goes back a while apparently. Dad supplies seafood to a country estate in the East Riding where wealthy city-types pay a fortune to shoot game. They return the favour with a brace of oven-ready pheasants every New Year. Mum's got it weighed off to a fine art now. Ask her later and she'll tell you. Ah, here's Dad.'

'Hey-up Jamie. Good to see you again. Now then, what can I get you to drink? I've a bottle or two of that tasty Wolds Ale in't fridge. Will you join me?'

'Thanks Mr Cammish, er Fred, yes that sounds good. I believe in consuming local produce. It's the way forward, that's for sure.'

'I'll certainly go along with that way of thinking. Your good health. Cheers. Tell you what, let's grab a pew in the living room while the girls finish getting tea ready. We still call it tea in this house. Posh folks call it supper and even posher folks call it dinner!'

'Yes, we still call it tea but with the new hotel opening at Easter we'd better start calling it Dinner and charge accordingly.'

'That's what I like to hear – a young man with a skill and an eye for business. Now, tell me a bit more about your own restaurant and how you intend to operate it. Chloe's told me a bit. Do you mind?'

'No, not at all Fred.'

'I'm not being nosey but you never know I just might be able to give you a few pointers. Since the millennium I've seen quite a few restaurants set up all right but only to see them falter and close within a short period of time – you know, just a couple of summer seasons and that's it. And therein lies the problem – as I see it anyway.'

'You've lost me already …'

'It's the words "summer season" that, I think anyway, is the problem. Not just with restaurateurs but with most of the hospitality sector in general. In this town 'the season,' as they call it, used to start at the Whit Bank Holiday and finished on the last day of the Scarborough Cricket Festival. Five months at the very most – absolutely crazy if you ask me.'

'So most of the year, in fact over half of it, was wasted in terms of income and revenue?'

'Exactly! When I was just a youngster most folks who came here for their annual holiday would stay for a fixed seven or fourteen days and then, on changeover day as they called it, get the train back to Leeds, Bradford or wherever. Those days were manic I can tell you.'

'And today?'

'Short three-day breaks are the order of the day. And the vast majority drive here in their own cars. Scarbados is now the most visited place in England outside of London. Did you know that?'

'Er, no I can't say I did. So are you saying that my new restaurant, when it opens, as a year round trade? Potentially at least?'

'Most definitely. And as we are right next to a stretch of the North Sea, prime quality seafood has to be speciality of the house – your house!'

'All the year round?'

'Almost. Everything has seasons of course, including the shellfish industry and ...'

'Fred, the name we have in mind for my restaurant is the Four Seasons, with the menu changing accordingly four times a year. What do you think?'

'Jamie, that sounds great. Seafood has its seasons too, you know. It's not just adverse weather in the winter. Marine crustaceans lose body weight in the winter and to be honest, many are not worth catching let alone eating.'

'I never realised that. So is a lot of it frozen in the best months and then sold as 'fresh' in the winter when in fact it's anything but?'

'There is a lot of that but I would concentrate on the seasonal aspect of your restaurant and use it as a major selling point.'

'Ah, my sister Millie, who's into all this jargon, would call it a USP – a unique selling point!'

They were interrupted by a call from the kitchen. It was Sarah.

'Tea's ready you chaps! Take your seats in the dining room you two. Let's have the gent's sitting opposite each other shall we. We don't want the banter to be all about football. Now, who's going to pour the wine? Jamie, can you do the honours? I've put a nice bottle of Valpolicella on the table and I did remember to take the cork out an hour ago, like they do on the telly, don't they?'

Sarah grinned towards Jamie

'Perhaps you could give us a little commentary ..' They all laughed. It was so obvious that Chloe had put her mother up to this as a little joke.

'OK, I think I've been set up for this but here goes. This is a classic easy-drinking red wine from Italy's north-eastern Veneto Region.' He took a long sniff followed by a little sip.

'Yes, probably a hundred percent from the Corvina vines with maybe just a hint of Rondinella. Plenty of body and long on the nose. Perfect with red meats – especially game.'

The other three grinned and gave a short round of applause. Sarah was the first to say something.

'Wow! And when is this restaurant opening? Next month? I can't wait.'

'No, Sarah. Not until Easter. Lots of planning and thought has to go into it first. Heck, is this all mine? There's a half a pheasant on my plate. And all these extras too. Bread sauce, fresh cranberries, chipolata sausages and correct me if I'm wrong but are these game chips, shallow fried with a hint of rosemary?'

'They sure are. I do this every New Year's Day, or a day or two later depending how it falls in the calendar.'

Jamie made mental notes. It could be a good idea for the Four Seasons next New Year. Suddenly he felt a nose nudging his lower calf and he glanced down. It was Leo who had just awoken from his feline slumber's. His huge, sleepy lion-like eyes gazed upwards towards him. Fred broke the silence.

'You now have a problem, young Jamie.'

'Really, how?'

'Well, this old cat of ours, despite his years, has got a nose like a blood-hound. He can smell cooked game a mile away. You now have a choice. You either ignore him and he'll go away and never speak to you again, or you give in, offer him a little tasting, and you've got a friend for life. You choose.'

Jamie was genuinely perplexed. Was he being set up again like with the wine? The other three watched him intently. Was this going to be a defining moment in his relationship with the whole family, not just with Chloe? He paused for what seemed like an eternity and then made his move. He sliced off a nice little chunk of breast meat from the generous helping on his plate, picked it up twixt forefinger and thumb and leant down towards Leo who was already starting to purr. He took it into his mouth so gently, swallowed it in one gulp, did a rapid about-turn and headed back to the warmth of the hearth. Had he done the right thing? Only time would tell. The rest of the dinner chatter was smooth and easy. The wine was emptied and plates cleared.

'It's my own special trifle for pudding, Jamie. Chloe always asks for it when she's home. I put lots of cheap Cyprus sherry in it to give it a bit of a kick. Our neighbours brought a litre bottle of it back from a holiday in Paphos a couple of months ago. They have a time-share there and they bring me a bottle back twice a year. Nice folks. We've been neighbours since we moved here over twenty years ago. You'll have to meet them next time you come. Maybe when Chloe's back here at the end of the next term at Easter?'

Chloe smiled inwardly. She was coming back a darned sight sooner than that. She wasn't going to let this one go that's for sure. No way José!

25.

'And what time did you get back last night, Bro? It must have been after midnight because I went to bed just before then and I didn't see or hear you come in.'

They were just clearing away the breakfast pots and Jamie had only just staggered, bleary eyed, into the kitchen. He looked a bit sheepish.

'Well it can't have been long after that because the radio was on in the Nippy Taxi and we listened to the News at the stroke of midnight. So maybe twelve-fifteen at the latest.'

'Well you better look sharp with your brekky 'cos that Inspector Mort from North Yorkshire Police is arriving soon to take statements from us in respect of those two West Indian guys believed to be behind the drugs and money laundering racket at the hotel Scarbados, or the Wendover as it was called then. He said about tenish if the weather was OK – and it is by all accounts.'

'Yeah, that's fine by me. I haven't got a right lot to tell him anyway. I only cooked and served them a nice dinner. It was just small talk – not even banter, but I'll do what I can. He's only ticking boxes anyway. It's their job.'

'You must take it more seriously, Jamie. And when do you go back to college? Do you have any reading or course work to do before it starts again? And your new friend Chloe will be going back to York Uni soon so you won't be distracted in that direction. Will you? You've got to pass that Chef's Diploma, preferably with distinction. The Certificate will have to be framed and prominently displayed ready for the opening night.'

'Sis, you're beginning to sound like Mam on a bad day. Nag nag nag!'

'Sorry, Bro, but it's all hands to the pumps now. We've got ninety days left according to my tear off post it note home-made calendar and, believe me, that time will absolutely fly by. I've made 'to do' lists for all of us. Yours is on the dining room table. I'll leave it with you. I'm into town now and the first port of call is the TV shop opposite the Casino. We need enough tellies for the First Floor only at the moment.'

'Where's Lucy? And how long is her 'to do' list anyway? She seems to get away with doing a lot less than most of us and …'

'Just cut Lucy a bit of slack will you, Bro? Don't forget she's the baby of the family and in a week's time she's starting her work experience at Mr Wilson's veterinary surgery. It's a life changing moment for her and we've got to be encouraging and protective at the same time. Just bear that in mind. Right, where's my coat? I'm off now. And don't forget Mort will be arriving soon. Be nice and co-operate with him. No sneaky jibes like 'ello, 'ello 'ello! And make him some nice coffee. Bye!'

And with that she was gone. Jamie lifted his coffee and what remained of his toast and marmalade into the dining room and grabbed a chair. He slid his 'to do' list towards him and did his best to concentrate. Talk about the twelve tasks of Hercules.

1. Finalise the décor and furnishings for the Four Seasons Restaurant.

2. Carpets and curtains for the same.

3. Check adequate supply of appropriate cutlery

4. The same for glassware and crystal.

5. Place mats – embossed 'Four Seasons Restaurant.'

6. Double check initial supply of beers, wines & spirits. Dad will help with this.

7. Draft a guest list for the opening night.

8. Remake the clock and barometer plaque to effect at least six time zones.

9. Check out the box in which were contained the scroll relating to the old Koala Hotel.

10. Draft the wording for Four Seasons business cards.

Jeez, did big sisters ever give up? Millie was right though, there was a lot to do and with the Christmas and New Year festivities well behind them, time was of the essence. He glanced down the list. Why on Earth did she want no less than six time zones? He made a mental note to ask her after lunch. The Hotel's main doorbell was soon ringing. It was Inspector Mort, on his own. No side-kick this time.

'Come in Inspector and a Happy New Year to you. Coffee?'

'Please, thank you. On your own? Nobody else around?'

'Dad and Lucy have gone out with our dog, Sebbie. I think they've gone to see that Garry Ritson who owns the dog that our Sebbie got in the family way – if you see what I mean?'

'Well, that's nature for you. That Mr Ritson is actually well known to us as a volunteer dog trainer. I'm going to see him soon, later today probably. We're still keeping tabs on your old hotel and it seems that Mr Ritson doesn't miss a trick. Now, let's commence that statement from you please. In your own words ....'

Twenty minutes later and they were done.

'Crikey you haven't told us much have you? I don't think you'd get from Uniform into CID in a hurry. Your descriptions of the two main suspects wouldn't pass muster in a Court of Law. Black, medium-build, six feet two, smart suited with a penchant for Yorkshire puddings ....God help us. Anyway read through it and then sign it please. The chances of them ever being apprehended, let alone charged, are almost nil. Oh well it's a funny old world – and not a very nice one at the moment if you ask me. I'll be off now. Thanks for the coffee and my best regards to your Dad and sister Millie please. It's a pity she didn't have contact with those two suspects. Her statement and description might have been a tad more detailed and thorough. Anyway you've done your best.'

Jamie showed him out and was glad to see the back of him. Cheeky sod. There's one person who won't be on the guest list for the Four Seasons opening night. He glanced back at his 'to do' list and made mental notes. The plaque of wood he had salvaged and on which he had mounted the two clocks and marine barometer would not be big enough to accommodate six clocks. What on Earth was Millie thinking? Then he remembered that there was still some spare rescued Tasmanian oak in the shed at the Hotel Scarbados. He instantly reached for his mobile and speed dialled his father. He soon answered.

'Hi Dad. Are you still at the Ritsons?'

'Yes, why, what's up?'

'Listen, can you check the shed at our old place and see if there's any of those small planks of timber that I removed from the dining room. They were used as shelving above the radiators until we had to have them replaced for Health and Safety reasons. It's not locked.'

'Actually we're just leaving. I'll check now and call you back. Give me five. Bye.'

He hung up but in less than three minutes he was back.

'Hiya. There's about four or five planks each about four foot long and ...'

'For goodness sake Dad, how long is that? Didn't you ever go metric like the rest of the world?'

'Well in your money that's well over a metre and a bit. How much of it do you need?'

'Just pick the plank that you think is in the best condition please and bring it back in the back of the car. I'll explain why later. See you soon. We'll have a chat when you get back.'

Peter just did as he was told. Nothing surprised him about his kids any more. In fact nothing surprised him about anything since they'd left 'Ull. Fifteen minutes later and he was back in the car park of the Clifftop Hotel and opening the tailgate of the family estate.

'Here y'are. Grab it. Is it good enough for what you need?'

'Brill. Now come in and I'll show you these bloomin' lists of jobs that Millie has left us. Your list is a lot longer than mine. They're on the main dining room table. Peter donned his reading glasses.

'Good God. There's over twenty tasks on my list. Task number one is: Contact We Are Neon for the new illuminated sign for the Hotel Koala. How many on yours?'

'Ten. Look at number eight on mine. It's all about clocks. What is she thinking about for goodness sake? Dunno – you'll have to ask her when she gets back. Where the heck is she anyway?'

'She's gone to see about all the new televisions. Then she was going to see about a new computer for the hotel's office and a software package tailor-made for the hotel trade. You know what she's like when she gets the bit between her teeth – there's no stopping her. By the way Dad, man to man, while the girls are out, what's the crack with Pamela? When is she coming back and have you decided how to play it yet?'

Two hundred and fifty miles to the south some not dissimilar soul-searching was in train.

26.

It was a typically miserable January day in central London. The clouds were low and grey and the distant view of the River Thames from Pamela's Juliet balcony, normally pleasant, was anything but. She was not a happy lady, to put it mildly, and yet another bad night's sleep had added to her melancholy. The pangs of guilt were horrific. It had been the cruellest of co-incidences that the first, and thus most important, Board Meeting of Best Eastern Hotels had coincided with the first anniversary of her sister Margaret's death. Exactly a year earlier she had passed away peacefully in a Nursing Home in Isleworth after a series of strokes. First anniversaries were always the worst she thought. Margaret's birthday in the early summer followed closely by her own a week later - both passed without a card received or a card sent. It was tough. The lie she had so recently told Pete about her sister's illness was at least partly true, just a year late. It had made telling the lie slightly easier, in her mind anyway. She knew she would have to come clean, firstly with Pete and then with his lovely family. She hadn't planned it this way. Events had simply overtaken her. Damn that takeover of English Hotels Monthly by an Emerati publishing magnate. And damn that new foreign editor who had squeezed her out. Damn, damn, damn! And what could she possibly know about English hotels for God's sake? The offer to join the Board of Best Eastern Hotels had come totally out of the blue. Talk about the cavalry riding over the hill. There had been no redundancy money – just a P45 and a perfunctory 'thank you for your service' letter with an indecipherable signature from some mogul in the Gulf. She simply had to move on – so she did.

Falling head over heels for Peter during her second visit to Scarborough had not been in the brochure. It was genuine. The redundancy and the new job offer had all happened between then and the invitation to join the Fishburn family for Christmas. It was only then that the deceit crept in. It just happened and was neither planned not malevolent. Human nature and survival simply cut in. After three cups of coffee and umpteen cigarettes she made up her mind. She would return to Scarborough and tell Pete everything – absolutely everything. She went online to the Trainline website and booked a single ticket from Kings Cross to Scarborough, via York, for the following day. Hands trembling, she picked up her iPhone and concocted a short message to Pete.

> *'Pete Dahling – all is well for me to return to "Scarbados" now – in fact tomorrow. My train arrives at around three o'clock. Can you meet me please? Then, first, can we have a quiet hour to ourselves please? Maybe the Watermark Café but I'll leave the choice to you – as long as we're alone. Miss you. Pammie xxx'*

It took Pamela another ten minutes and a final cigarette before her right forefinger finally pressed on the send button. It was like launching a rocket. Once it had gone, it was gone. There was no going back now. She donned a wind-proof fleece, weather-proof shoes and went out for a walk round the nearest park. Of course she didn't know that Peter and his family knew only too well of her duplicity. A few seconds later Pete's phone pinged twice in his shirt pocket. He was sitting at the dining room table pondering over his “to do” list. Ping ping! Ah that was probably Dave Gibson from We are Neon Ltd. returning his call. Wrong! It was, of course, Pamela. He read her message slowly, three times, trying to take it in.

‘All is well for me to return.’ What exactly did she mean by that? And why was she insisting that they met alone? Was she going to whitewash him even further without any possible intervention? And why was there no mention of her sister Margaret’s condition? He was more than a little perplexed. Surely she wanted to keep up the pretence of illness, hospital and Nursing Home? Should he perhaps confide in Millie, the real brains behind the new Hotel Koala project. No, he would wait until he and Pamela had had their tête á tête the next day. He put the kettle on and just before it came to the boil Millie arrived back from town.

‘Hi Dad. Just in time. Put another tea bag in the pot. You know I like it stronger than you. Any news, any developments?’ Pete told his own white lie.

‘No nothing. All quiet on the Eastern front.’

‘Dad, the red light’s flashing on the Hotel’s ansaphone – the land line. We’d all better get used to it being as it’s going to be the main business number. I’ll see who the message is from.’

She pressed the ‘play message’ button and it crackled into life.

‘Hi, Dave Gibson here. I’ll be with you tomorrow tenish. Please check the power supply to the existing exterior hotel sign. See you soon. Cheers.’

‘Oh well, that’s good news, Dad. Only nineteen more items on your list now!’

‘Don’t be cheeky, young lady. What news do you bring, if any? Let’s pour some tea first.’

‘Well the TV issues are sorted. What a fab outfit they are – family owned for over half a century and now part of a huge marketing and supply chain organisation. All the TV sets will be installed and up and running at least a week before Easter. They guarantee it. We'd best tell Garry Ritson too – it was on his recommendation remember?'

'Anything else?'

'Oh, yes, I popped into the Crescent Gardens Hotel for a chat and a coffee with Nadine. I quizzed her about computer systems for hotels and she's put me onto a small company here in town that can help us. It will do everything once it's installed and set up – accounts, bookings, room and table reservations – the lot! We can lease the whole system and if there are any problems they send a member of staff to sort it. The address is Falsgrave Road somewhere. It fact, it's not far from the vet's surgery where Lucy is joining. Nadine rang them while I was there. They'll call soon to make an appointment to come and see us.'

'Well that's marvellous. I don't suppose you mentioned staffing did you? How do they cope on that score anyway?'

'She said that since Brexit and the absence of Eastern European staff it's been tough. Unlike the Care Industry which provides for extra work permits, the hospitality sector has been left to float its own boat, as it were. She advised we start advertising for staff a month before Easter. They maintain permanent staff over the winter months and recruit extras for the summer. So, we'll start from scratch.'

'Well, you've had a terrific morning then I'd say. That's two and half items sorted from your "to do" list I'd say.'

'Oi, watch it you!'

'And I don't suppose you've heard from the Lady Hesketh have you? I wonder what she's up to now. Surely it won't be long before she's worming her way back into your favours, not to mention your bed and …'

'And we'll stop there young lady. You're beginning to sound like your Mam!'

They both laughed. Peter re-donned his reading glasses and considered item number two on his list- Check the stock levels for the Bar and Hotel – liaise with Jamie. And have you checked the Hotel's alcohol licence? No he hadn't. And who was going to be the Registered Licensee anyway? He or Jamie? The Clifftop Hotel hadn't had an alcohol Licence for several years, in fact since it had been used as a reception centre for Afghan refugees. Now that it was back in the commercial sector they would have to start from scratch. Come to think of it the Licence, when issued, would have to be appropriate for Residents, non-Residents and customers of the Four Seasons Restaurant. They didn't want to be outwith the Rules before they'd barely got started. And why on Earth had Millie put this on his "to do" list? Surely she could just as easily have picked up the phone to that nice 'Mel from Licensing' who had been so helpful with the Hotel Scarbados and who was one of the guests at the formal opening night. They mustn't forget to invite her to the similar ceremony for the Hotel Koala. He looked across the table at Jamie's list and Item No. 7 – the Guest List – and wondered why this was on both lists. Perhaps she was doing a belt and braces job in case either of them got it wrong. That's our Millie!

27.

Ever one for punctuality, and just before ten o'clock, Dave Gibson pulled into the car park of the Clifftop Hotel, his sat-nav doing its job accurately. He'd come down the coast road from Yarm and then Whitby. There was still snow to be seen on the moors but the roads had been gritted and he made good progress. He got his bearings as soon as he was within sight of Peasholm Park and the smooth voice of the Tom-Tom was perfunctory. However he still found the 'You have arrived at your destination' comforting. Once outside of his van he took in the sea view and then gazed all round the exterior of the Hotel itself. Wow! It was quite a size compared to the much more modest Hotel Scarbados. This would be a much bigger job altogether and before he even went inside he was doing mental sketches of some initial ideas.

'Morning, Dave. A good drive? What were the roads like?'

'Morning, Pete. Not too bad, actually. Gary Gritter had obviously been out early!' They laughed.

'Come on in. Coffee's on and we'll have a chat first.'

'Great idea. Crikey, this is some place you've got here now. What happened?'

It's a long story, mate. You remember my lad Jamie don't you?'

'Hello, Mr Gibson. I'm here to give you a hand if you need me.'

'Yes, hi, Jamie. I might need a hand with ladders later. Gosh, it's a much taller building isn't it? The main elevation has got to be forty feet at least – plus that turret at the southern end. What was that all about in the grand scheme of things?'

'We have no idea. Let's pour the coffees. Ah here's Millie now, right on cue.'

'Hi Mr Gibson. So what are your first impressions?'

'Well, I've only been here less than five minutes but the first thing that strikes me is that you have three facades to cover – north, east and south. The main length of the hotel faces east and it's visible from the road outside and from the Marine Drive a hundred feet below. Motorists and pedestrians will see it in their thousands. The other two facades face north and south and are much smaller but still offer a visual attraction. What you don't know is that I already have some images that I downloaded from the internet and I have played around with a suggestion or two and I have them on my iPad. Are you ready?'

Pete looked at Millie, Jamie just stared at the iPad and within two seconds an image appeared in colour. The front of the Hotel was impressive with a small 'Hotel' in pale green at a jaunty angle and below it a huge 'KOALA' in dark green hi-viz lettering that extended some forty feel in length between the second and third floors.

'So that's the main neon signage facing east. Good eh? Now, close your eyes and don't open them until I say so.'

He fiddled with a button or two and then gave the OK.

''Right, open eyes.'

They simply couldn't believe what they saw. On both side elevations was a massive grey neon koala shinning up a eucalyptus tree! They would be at least twenty feet tall if they came to fruition. Millie reacted first.

'Oh my God! That's unbelievable! That is simply stunning! Can it be done in practice or are they just electronic doodles? And the cost – what about the cost? It'll break the bank. It's the sort of thing you might see on the side of a hotel in a theme park not a holiday resort. Also, I don't think we'd get away with it, you know, the Council. Think about that.'

Dave Gibson seemed to have an answer for everything.

'The costings might not be as humongous as you might think. I'll work on those and get back to you. And as for planning permission you'll be aware, or maybe not, that Scarborough Borough Council was abolished recently. This area now comes under the jurisdiction of the new North Yorkshire Council in Northallerton. So, we'll do the job, plead ignorance, and then apply for retrospective permission – if indeed we need it all.' Peter was appalled at his nonchalance.

'You must be kidding! We can't do that. The adverse publicity, if it got out, might damage our reputation.' But Millie, not for the first time, didn't agree with her father.

''No, Dad, Mr Gibson is right. The old adage "there's no such thing as bad publicity" is very relevant here. I say let's go ahead, subject to costings, and deliberately take not even the slightest interest in planning, by-laws or whatever. In the unlikely event of any objections from either the Council or anybody else, we'll have a field day. The publicity will be enormous. We'd be in the papers for days, if not weeks.'

Millie kept the rest of her thoughts to herself. She had a little giggle and made a few mental notes.

'Mr Gibson, could you please email me those three images. I'll make good use of them in our pre-launch publicity campaign.'

'Of course, I'll do it now if you like? Now, I need to take

some detailed photos of the exterior and measurements. Jamie, a quick hand with my ladders please, young man. It shouldn't take too long. Half an hour should do it. But come the day of installation, should you decide to accept my quotes, we will definitely require either scaffolding or, more likely, the hire of a suitable cherry-picker. There's a good tool-hire company in town, Andy somebody, I've used them before. The quote will include the cost of the machinery hire.'

'That's fine', chirped Millie. She glanced at her father, who looked as if he was about to give birth to a whole litter of kittens.

'Dad, don't look so worried. Because you spent twenty-plus years working at sea, you were too bound by too many rules and regulations. You're on dry land now and you are the Captain of the MV Hotel Koala. Let's go for it. Mr Gibson, how long will it take for your quotes to arrive?'

'Assuming I get the daily rate for a cherry-picker sorted quickly and then do some of my own internal costings, within a few days. Shall we say by the end of the week? I'll quote you separately for each elevation. With luck we'll only need a cherry-picker for one whole day but if it overruns, say due to bad weather, it might run over into a second day. If we left the installation until after the clocks go forward at the end of March then it gives us a bit more light in the evening and ...'

Millie interrupted him, quite brusquely, which caused her father's eyebrows to rise to hackle-level.

'No, sorry to interrupt, but if we go ahead then we want the lights switched on well before the formal opening. It will be an early message to future customers that within a short period of time the Hotel Koala will be open for business with its new name and under new owners.'

'OK, I'll see what I can do. Come on, Jamie, outside. Let's get the ladders off the roof of my van.'

They disappeared outside, leaving Millie and her Dad alone. Father was not best pleased with his daughter – as they say in Yorkshire.

'Millie love, I know how ambitious you are but don't you think we might just be biting off more than we can chew? How much will it all cost?'

'Who knows, Dad, but without telling Mr Gibson, we could set a limit of ten grand on the project and then just wait for his quote. If we get this right we'll be visible for a very long way and the two koalas will be the biggest illuminated signs in Scarborough – even bigger than the big Theatre in the town centre where you took Lady Pamela to see that production called The Kiss. And speaking of her, don't forget that you're collecting her from the train station at three o'clock. Have you decided how to play her yet? Bitch.'

'Oi, less of that. We agreed to play it by ear didn't we? I'll leave here just after half past two to be on the safe side. I hope the train's on time.'

'You'd better put a clean shirt on and have you shaved this morning? Get upstairs and make yourself look pukka, as if you were still on the Pride of Bruges.'

'Yes, boss.'

What would he do without his elder daughter? She made a short call to Clive White in Beverley and twenty minutes later was outside for the briefest of chats with Dave Gibson just as he was about to jump into the cab of his van.

'Mr Gibson, I need the quote to be well under ten grand. The official invoice must not exceed eight grand and anything over that will be in cash. Are we talking the same language?'

'Right, Miss Fishburn, er Millie. I see where you're coming from, nudge, wink.'

Millie smiled to herself as she went back inside. By 'eck she'd learnt a lot in the last two years.

28.

Filled with trepidation verging on fear, Peter set off for the railway station. Pamela had sent him a message saying 'Just leaving Malton now – train on time.'

He drove the mile and a half to the station in the very centre of town. How many resorts had a train station right in the middle of town? Not many he thought. He was right there. Even wealthy Brighton and Eastbourne didn't come close. He parked his car, without realising it, at the end of a line of taxis, much to the consternation of a white cab whose driver was outside of his car having a quick fag before the York train arrived.

'Look here, mate. You can't park here. You'll have to go round to the proper car park. Don't bother paying – just hover and you'll see the train coming in. I just looked at the 'arrivals board' and it's coming in on Platform One so whoever you're meeting can spot you quite easily.'

'OK, thanks for the tip. Cheers.'

Peter restarted his car engine and pulled out into the main road then took the first left into the car park. It looked almost empty and he was tempted to pull into a vacant berth but suddenly he spotted the silver and blue nose of the train a few hundred yards away. It glided almost noiselessly past the reputed longest platform seat in the country, over one hundred metres, and came to a halt less than fifty metres away from him. The electrically powered doors swished open simultaneously on all five carriages and he glanced from left to right along the platform to see which carriage Pamela was about to alight from. Then he spotted her exiting the last coach. Of course! First Class was at the rear. He should have guessed. She was pulling the same small case with wheels that she had so recently travelled south with. Spotting him, she waved with her free hand, protected from a chill wind by black leather gloves. Her omnipresent Gucci sunglasses were perched atop her head like a fashion accessory, not a protection against the Caribbean sun which was her normal winter penchant. Peter wasn't sure how to play it. A hug? A kiss and a clench or what? Until so recently it would have been at least two smackers on the lips and a bear hug. She solved his dilemma for him.

'Peter, dahling. It's good to see you.'

Two air kisses followed – mwa mwa! He could have sworn she was slightly moist-eyed and not just from the easterly wind.

'Pete, you got my message I'm assuming. Anywhere for a quiet chat, just us, please.'

The damp eyes turned into little rivulets and within seconds had left two visible streaks down her upper cheeks. Not exactly Niles or Amazons but certainly Severns. He turned down the Valley onto the seafront for the fifteen minute drive to the North Bay and their intended destination – the Watermark Café. The tide was almost at its highest, and salt-water spray lashed across the protective wall. Had it not been constructed two decades earlier, then the whole road would almost certainly have been eroded and wiped out for ever by an unforgiving North Sea, or the Oceanus Germanicus as some old maps still called it. They managed to park almost right outside the café and there were very few other cars despite parking fees being waived in the winter months. They stepped inside and Pamela headed to the warmer corner near the wood burning stove. Peter went to the counter to get two hot chocolates. The youngish assistant was friendly but firm.

'We'll serve you, sir, but with the weather looking grim and high tide due in half an hour I would ask you to consume your drinks as soon as you can, if you don't mind. We have some special hoarding to erect just in case and it takes two of us twenty minutes at least.'

'No problem. I quite understand.'

'It's one of the dubious bonuses of working so close to Mother Nature when she gets angry. Hang on a minute – aren't you Lucy's dad? She brings her doggie, Sebbie, in here regularly.'

'Yes, hi. I'm Peter Fishburn and this lady is my er, er, my friend Pamela from London. She's staying a while and helping us to plan the opening and re-naming of the Clifftop Hotel.'

'Re-naming?'

'Yes, its new name will be the Hotel Koala, but keep that under your hat for a while please.'

'Sure, Mr Fishburn. I'll bring the drinks over to you, no worries.'

Why, thought Peter to himself, do youngsters in the hospitality trade always say "no worries" or "no problem?" Why can't they just say "yes certainly thank you?" It was a mystery to him and probably to millions of others. Oh well. The drinks arrived and Pamela took a sip from the hot and welcoming drink with its origins in West Africa. She looked hesitant and without her normal confidence, started to speak.

'Peter, I have several confessions to make. This isn't easy and I want you to bear with me for a few minutes, please.'

She laid her hand on his just as he was about to lift his own mug to his lips. Over the next few minutes the Severns turned into Danubes and several Kleenexes were retrieved from her hand-bag. She told him everything – her dismissal from the English Hotels Monthly magazine following a Middle Eastern takeover, how she was head-hunted onto the Board of Best Eastern Hotels, the white lie about her sister's critical illness – in fact everything. Then she told him how the lie had come easily about her sister Margaret whose death was a year to the day before the crucial Board Meeting. Peter had not expected this. It was a full confession. Only the Priest and the curtain were missing. He found himself gripping her hand, not the other way round.

'I did fall for you, Peter, I promise you. I fell for you head over heels. You were, still are, absolutely charming. A down-to-earth East Yorkshireman and such a refreshing change from the City-types that my parents always hoped I would hitch up with. No chance. And as for your lovely family … what on Earth am I going to say to your kids …'

'Pammie, you don't have to say anything. They already know.'

'What? They can't possibly. How?'

'Our Company Secretary, Clive White, has an enquiring and sceptical mind – not to mention friends in the City. He predicted, almost to the day, that you would concoct a sudden excuse to leave for London and the all-important board meeting. I won't pretend that it didn't hurt, Pammie, because it did. To be honest I still haven't recovered from it. Maybe I was vulnerable following my own redundancy, the huge move from Hull and the change of direction, not just for me but for the whole family. Looking back it was just crazy. The effect it had on my ex-wife, Mandy, must have been unbearable in the long run. I still feel a tad guilty and …'

'Peter, guilt is the one emotion you should not feel. Didn't young Lucy say she was disappointed in her Mam and all she seems interested in now is "Bingo and Cruises?" Well, didn't she?'

'You're right, she did. Unlike the kids she couldn't cope with leaving Hull. My kids are just wonderful, all three of them, all different but all wonderful in their own way.'

'So what's happened while I've been away? Can you tell me or am I now persona non grata?'

'Pammie, lots has happened, all good, but it's one step at a time. We now have less than ninety days before the Clifftop is opened and re-named the Hotel Koala. It's all go. Millie seems to have everything in hand and has even given me and Jamie long "to do" lists. It's like she's already done this in a previous life. If Hotel Koala was a plc I reckon she'd be on the Board before she's twenty-five.'

That last sentence was not lost on Pamela.

'So, Pete, what are we going to say to your family in half an hour's time?'

'Pammie, just leave it to me OK? I will be as candid with them as you have just been with me.'

'But what about the future, Pete? What about us? We can't just pretend nothing has happened. Do you think it's best if I check into another hotel? You can take me to the Crescent Gardens if you like.'

'No, let's have a chat with the kids during and after supper. Then we'll decide as adults what to do. Your old room's already made up for you when we get back. Give me a short time alone with them first. I think Jamie's knocking up a tasty supper for us all.'

'How is he coming along with the planning for the Four Seasons Restaurant, by the way? And when will he finish his Chef's Diploma? Has he finalised the décor and ..'

'So many questions! You can ask him yourself.'

'I can't wait to see them all again. And Sebbie? How's Sebbie?'

'He's just fine. I hope you've got some of his favourite treats in your bag?'

'Did you think I would dare come back without any?'

Two hours later and it was almost as if nothing bad had happened between them. Pete asked the kids to try and understand Pamela's predicament and to understand her duplicity. They did their best, albeit with reservations. Sebbie was overjoyed to see that an additional source of treats had returned to the fold.

'So, Lucy, tell me, when is Sebbie's son going to join him here at the Clifftop – er I mean the Koala?

''Thanks for asking. Well, next week I'm starting my work experience at Mr Wilson's veterinary surgery so I'm going to ask him for his advice. Young AlfieBoy is growing nicely but still dependent on his mother Candy for milk of course. And what do you call a cross between a Yorkshire Terrier and a Labradoodle anyway? Anyone got any ideas?'

Nobody did. After Jamie's excellent Beef Stroganoff washed down with a glass of Argentine Malbec, the conversation got around to the future and how Pamela could help. She explained to them that Best Eastern Hotels was in an acquisitive corporate mood and was looking, in the not too distant future, to invest heavily in the East Coast hospitality industry. Millie cottoned on immediately and looked straight into Pamela's eyes like a cobra about to spit.

'Do you mean to say that their interest might include the future Koala Hotel? Us?'

'Millie, I can't rule anything out with these people. Their coffers seem to be stuffed with Hong Kong dollars, Singapore dollars and Thai baht. I can tell you, in confidence, that Kenneth Chan, whom you met at the Lucky Dragon, is also a fellow director of Best Eastern Hotels. They're taking the corporate point of view that following Covid and the reluctance of thousands to travel abroad for vacations, then the east coast of England is the next Costa del Sol. Add to that the now undeniable affects of climate change, global warming or whatever you want to call it and it's the opposite of a perfect storm for this area. The Mediterranean is now almost unbearably hot in the summer for most people, especially those with kids. So where are they going to go? I'll tell you where. They're going to head for Whitby, Bridlington, Cleethorpes and all the way down to Ingoldmells, Skegness and of course .... Scarbados! Good, profitable businesses will be snapped up left, right and centre over the course of the next few years. Trust me on that score.'

There was almost total silence until Jamie announced:

'Who's for coffee. We've got Java from Indonesia, Kilimanjaro from the upper reaches of Tanzania, Columbian from the mountains of north-west South America or ...'

'Shut up Jamie! Your restaurant's not open yet. Instant will be fine.'

Everybody laughed and Millie had hit the nail right on the head. 'Project Koala' was back on stream and now, with Pamela's help, they would make it the success it surely deserved to be. Millie took the initiative once again. Didn't she always?

'Pamela, welcome back. Things might not be quite the same as before but let's all work together shall we, please?'

She held out a clenched fist towards Pamela.

'Pax!'

'What does that mean?'

'Literally, it means peace. Just do it. It's a Yorkshire thing – Grandad once told me.'

They bumped fists. Normality of some sorts had returned. The future was going to be very, very exciting.

In bed that night, alone, Pamela pondered about the envelope that she had retrieved from her London flat – the one with Belgian stamps on and postmarked Brugge. When should she give it to Peter? After all, he was the addressee. The time had to be just right – and that time was not now.

29.

The next few weeks, in fact the rest of January, was a frenzy of activity. The "to do" lists had mostly ticks alongside the tasks outlined.

All the public, and first floor guest rooms, were now equipped with high quality "smart" TVs and Peter had tested each one individually himself. The installers had also supplied, as part of the deal, two spare sets in case any developed a fault. They would wait until they had completed at least a full three months trading before ordering for the second, let alone the third, floors. The local computer supplier had installed the specialist desktop PC complete with the required software. All they needed to do now was test it. They had acquired a new website domain – hotelkoala.com – and Millie's friend Katya, back in Hull, was commissioned to design the new website. It would be very different to the one she had built for the former Hotel Scarbados. Exit palm trees, enter eucalyptus trees – not to mention a couple of the actual marsupials themselves, virtual of course. Dave Gibson's quotes for the neon lighting had come in at £6,700 plus VAT which they had accepted, knowing there was a two thousand pound "wiggle room" if required. That latter factor was just as well as when Pamela had asked Jamie why there was no external advertising or lighting for the Four Seasons Restaurant his reply of 'Oh my gosh' had not gone down well. Dave Gibson came back to take some more measurements and had come up with just a simple Four Seasons Restaurant in gold neon this time. They would be affixed on the Hotel's frontage spread across the two adjacent dining rooms. It would only be illuminated when the restaurant was actually open and serving, unlike the remainder of the hotel's lighting. This oversight had swallowed up a thousand of the two grand "wiggle room" and it had earned Jamie a severe ear bashing from his big sister.

'You'll have to buck up, Bro. It's all very well bashing on with your Diploma but you need to concentrate on the long-term. And can I suggest that until you've finished that course and got the Certificate on display, that you only travel to York to see Chloe every other weekend?'

'Yeah, yeah, yeah. Stop nagging. You're beginning to sound more like Mam as you get older.'

Their mother, Mandy, was away on a relatively short winter cruise with her sister Gwen, This time 'only to the Canaries' she had said in a brief phone call before a private taxi had taken them to Southampton to join the liner Aurora. Her parting words had been:

'And don't forget to make arrangements to sell my shares in the company. Two hundred thousand wasn't it?! I'll sign all the paperwork when we get back. And who did you say the buyer is? Not that I'm bothered any more.'

She hadn't bothered to ask after Lucy in her new job or Sebbie. In fact she hadn't enquired about anybody. Would she have objected if the transferee was one Pamela Hesketh? Probably not but at this stage of the game no-one cared. Before very long Pamela would replace Mandy Fishburn as a twenty-five percent shareholder in Hotel Koala Ltd. Clive White would have all the paperwork ready for when Mandy returned to Blighty and he had already reminded her, in writing, that without the financial transfer for the agreed consideration then Pamela's shareholding would be invalid.

Pamela herself had absented herself on several occasions in the past few weeks, at least once to London for another Board Meeting of Best Eastern Hotels, and twice down to Lincolnshire to look at Hotels in Skegness and Cleethorpes. She seemed to have a reconnaissance role for the company akin to a Scout for a Premier League Football Club, awash with money, looking for new talent in which to invest. She had discovered lots of little gems, mostly family owned, and had often stayed in them posing as a genuine customer. None of them however, in her opinion, could match the potential of the soon to be reopened Hotel Koala. She simply couldn't wait to get hold of that share certificate in her name. Only then would she feel empowered to light the blue touch paper to guarantee its future prosperity – not to mention that of its owners. She had made the necessary arrangements with her own Bank in London who were on standby to effect the two hundred thousand pound transfer at twenty-four hour's notice. When the time came she would offer a little prayer of thanks to her sister Margaret whose legacy a year ago would make her acquisition of the shares possible.

On returning from her last mission, a visit to look at a motel near Humberside Airport, she sat down after supper and relaxed with the whole family, including Sebbie, who had missed his extra treats during her temporary absence. Lucy seemed a bit quieter than usual and sensing this. Pamela decided to try and cheer her up. Assuming the role of her absent mother, who was somewhere between Madeira and Lisbon and awash with gin and salt water, Pamela took the plunge.

'Lucy, how's the work experience going at the Vets? And has Mr Wilson advised when AlfieBoy might be allowed to come here with Sebbie?' She sensed that something was wrong.

'It was a bad day today, very upsetting. We had to put two little doggies to sleep. There had been too many in the litter Mr Wilson said, and the weakest two weren't going to make it and it was kinder to put them to sleep.'

Tears rolled down her little cheeks and she reached out to Sebbie who looked as if he was going to cry too.

'Mr Wilson got me to hold them while he injected them. It was awful, just awful. Before I came home he had a little chat with me and told me that it was the hardest part of his job. Afterwards one of the qualified Veterinary Nurses told me that Mr Wilson had deliberately picked me to assist him and that he had regarded it as a sort of test. In fact, he did whisper in my ear 'Well done Lucy' just before I came home.'

'Oh Lucy, that is so sad' said Pamela. 'But think of it this way – you helped the two little puppies on their way to Rainbow Bridge and possibly right now they're hopping around chasing butterflies.'

'Do you believe in Rainbow Bridge, Pamela?'

'Of course I do, Lucy. I was brought up on the edge of the South Downs and we always had two golden labradors in the family, sometimes three. Whenever one passed away we always had a little ceremony for them. Anyway, Lucy love, on the brighter side, when did Mr Wilson say that AlfieBoy can come home?' Immediately her face lit up like a thousand candles.

'I've saved that bit until last. This Saturday. He's coming home – AlfieBoy is coming home!'

This time the tears were for joyous reasons and not sadness. Jamie seized the initiative.

'Prosecco time folks! I'll get a bottle and five glasses out. That reminds me, Dad, you and I need to finalise those stock lists very soon. Agreed?'

'Yes son, we do.'

All was going roughly according to plan but there were now less than eighty days left before the Grand Opening – even fewer in terms of working days if there were any weather-related delays. Surely not. The days were already starting to lengthen and as one of the Grandma's had always told them: 'By the second Sunday in February, you can have your tea without putting a light on.'

They all retired early that night and none of them noticed the little red light light flashing on the answer-phone on the Reception desk.

30.

The next morning and hardly before the breakfast pots had been cleared away, there was a noisy commotion in the hotel's car park at the rear. It sounded as if a farmer was driving a combine and had lost it's way. Peter opened the back door from the kitchens to find a small low-loader being towed by a Land Rover. On it was mounted a bright yellow cherry-picker. The driver got out and shouted towards Peter.

'Morning – it's a good day for it. It's dry and hardly any wind – unusual and lucky for this time of the year. Isn't Mr Gibson from Teesside here yet? We promised we'd be here by eight-thirty and we are. Well, just about anyway. Where is he? Which side does he want to do first?'

'What? Today? I didn't even know he was ...' A cry out from Millie at the kitchen door interrupted him.

'Dad, there's a message on the hotel's answer-phone. I just spotted the flashing red light. It's from Dave Gibson at *We are Neon* and ...'

'Don't tell me, he's coming today?'

'How did you guess?'

'Because the hired cherry-picker has already arrived. Look!'

'The message says he'll be here around nine o'clock.'

'In fact here he is. He must have left Teesside at first light.'

He waived to the large white Transit van pulling into the car park. Dave Gibson waived at Peter and then at the driver of the Land Rover. It looks as if they had worked together before. Dave took charge.

'You look surprised – as if you weren't expecting us. Do you remember my apprentice? This is John. He's no longer an apprentice. He's full-time staff – couldn't do without him now. Since Covid finished, business is booming from Redcar right down over the Humber Bridge. We're booked up with business to Easter and beyond. Business is amazing, never known 'owt like it – hotels, guest houses, you name it.'

'I'm pleased to hear it. Yes, hello John, of course I remember you from when you fixed the new signs at the Hotel Scarbados. As you can see, things have moved on a bit since then. Coffee everyone, before you make a start?'

'That'll be great. We'll be doing the north facing side first because although its quite calm now winds forecast for later, if the MET Office is correct, will be northerly so just in case they're right …'

'Now that's what I call planning, Dave! Coffee's coming up. Let's all go into the warmer kitchen.'

Fifteen minutes later and the cherry-picker was in position and its platform carried a three metre high koala shinning up a similar length of highly realistic green eucalyptus branch. It's true realism would only become apparent at dusk when the natural daylight dimmed. In all it took two hours to affix it's one hundred kilogram weight and everyone breathed a huge sigh of relief when the supporting frame did its job and it all held fast. The electrical wiring, mostly on the inside of the main wall, would be done later, whatever the weather.

Two hours later and the exact same exercise was completed on the south facing wall. It was cleverly done with both Koalas facing out towards the sea so they faced and climbed in opposite directions. They all took a short break for a packed lunch which they had brought in their vans. Millie was upset as, had she had notice, she would have insisted they had a cooked lunch inside. Jamie would have rustled up something nice for them – and then she realised that he was at College today. Boy, would he get a surprise when he got back around fiveish!

The lighting at the front of the hotel was rather more straightforward. The main lettering for Hotel and then Koala was erected without any hitches but there was more than a bit of a palaver when it came to the gold lettering for the Four Seasons Restaurant. If only all three words had the same number of letters it would have been straightforward. They had to fix the 'Four' first and then a reasonable gap before 'Seasons' and then because of a narrow downpipe coming down from the roof there was a slightly bigger gap before the ten letter word 'Restaurant.' It would only really be noticeable in daylight and only a pedant with a measuring tape would be critical enough to make any remarks. Surely!'

The milky winter sunshine earlier had completely disappeared. The predicted northerly breeze had duly arrived and a slow, persistent drizzle had set in. No matter. All the hard external work had been done. All that remained was the internal wiring and connections. The cherry-picker and its operator departed back to their depot on the other side of town. The job being completed in one day had kept the hiring costs to a minimum. The decision to choose that route, rather than scaffolding, had been a sound one.

It was almost dark at 5pm and it was time for the test – the big switch-on. It immediately brought back memories of watching the town Christmas Lights being switched on almost two months earlier. Dave Gibson barked his orders.

'Right, everyone, coats on. It's not nice out there now. I want you to gather outside the north side and in precisely one minute I'm going to switch on the first koala using the master switch that I have installed in the Reception area behind the main desk. Can one of you dial my number on your mobile please and keep the line open. This is why we often use Walkie-Talkies on site.' Lucy volunteered. She had only just returned from the Vet's after a happier day than yesterday. 'Off you go.'

Dave Gibson waited a full minute then threw the switch. He didn't need the use of a phone. The collective screams of delight could probably have been heard as far away as Flamborough Head.

'Now go round to the south side please.'

The relevant switch was thrown and the second koala burst into life like the opening scenes of a David Attenborough documentary from Down Under. More screams and more absolute delight.

'Right, Lucy, now ask everyone to go to the front please. I'll do the main sign first, wait thirty seconds, then I'll illuminate the Restaurant sign. OK are you ready?'

The main Hotel Koala sign burst into life followed shortly thereafter by the gold signs of the Four Seasons Restaurant. A mile out to sea the Scarborough Lifeboat was heading south from an exercise at Scalby Mills towatds its base in the South Bay. The Skipper turned to the Coxswain and said:

'Did you just see what I saw?'

'What's that, Skipper?'

'I could swear I just saw a huge grey koala bear illuminated on that old hotel up on the cliff. You know, that one that was closed for a couple of years. I heard on the radio that it had recently been bought. Did you?'

'I can't say I did Skipper, no. And as for a koala bear, it's not a bear by the way, it's just a koala. It's a marsupial. Are you sure you've not had a nip too many of that Pusser's Rum left over from Christmas?'

'No, absolutely not you cheeky beggar. Oh my God look! There's another one!'

'By God, you're right. I can see it too. It's gone out now. Well, it's two months too early for an April Fool. Maybe we'll read summat in't paper about it. I reckon it's just someone having a laugh. With the right kit you can project anything you like onto the side of a building. Anyway, look sharp, we're almost home now.'

Back at the hotel Dave Gibson was just tidying up his tools and explaining to Peter the switch controls for the four separate signs. The end one, switch number four, is for the Four Seasons only. That's why I did it like that – easy to remember eh? What time is young Jamie back from college?'

'I can hear his motorbike outside now.'

'Right, without telling him why, take him right round to the front of the hotel. I'll do what I did before – Hotel sign first then the Restaurant sign. Three minutes later and Jamie was in the kitchen and almost in tears. He shook Dave Gibson's hand until it almost fell off. There were still many days to go before the formal opening but to Jamie it was an indication that the end result was in sight.

'Prosecco time everyone!' he cried, for the second time in twenty-four hours.

For the first time since moving in, the whole family, including Pamela, felt they were making good progress. Now, where were those "to do" lists? There were still a few more tasks to be ticked.

31.

An incoming call from Clive White in Beverley advised them that the documentation for the transfer of Mandy Fishburn's shares in Hotel Koala Ltd. to Pamela, had been partially completed. The partially completed Stock Transfer pro-forma had arrived at his address, duly signed and dated by Mandy. A week earlier he had posted it to Mandy's address in Nosely Way, Hull, enclosed in a stamped addressed envelope to return it to himself. It had come back sooner than he had expected. Perhaps her latest cruise had been curtailed early. No matter.

'Hi Millie. Yes, all is well here thank you. Your mother has completed her formalities so now, if I may, can I have a short chat with Pamela please? Is she in, or on one of her scouting trips?'

'No, she's here. Right now she's chatting away nineteen to the dozen with Jamie on their plans for the Four Seasons Restaurant. Hold on, I'll get her for you, Clive. By the way, when will we see you again?'

'Possibly tomorrow actually, if Pamela is around. Your mother is desperately keen for this transaction to be processed quickly, I can tell you.'

'How do you know that?'

'Because on the Stock Transfer Form she's stuck a yellow post-it note with "as soon as possible please" written on it!'

'Mmm, that sounds like Mam. She's morphed into a

different animal from the Mam we knew as younger kids. Anyway, here's Pam. See you tomorrow then, Clive. Bye.'

She handed the telephone handset that normally resided on the Reception desk to Pamela.'

'I'll leave you to it, Pam. I'll go and keep Jamie company.'

'Thanks, Millie. Hello, Clive. This is an unexpected call.'

'Hello, Pamela. Yes, well it's taken me by surprise as well.'

'What's up?'

'It's good news. Mandy, Peter's ex-wife, has signed the Transfer Form for the twenty-five shares in her name. She wants it done as quickly as possible.'

'Great stuff. Was there any argy-bargy about me being the transferee? After all, she doesn't like me one single little bit."

'Well, to be honest, I left that bit blank and she didn't query it. In any event the other three shareholders would have had first dibs at buying her shares and they have relinquished their option to do that. By lunchtime tomorrow, you will be a one quarter shareholder in Hotel Koala Ltd. with the proviso that the money transfer goes through. Can you make the necessary arrangements by say, twelve noon tomorrow?'

'Sure, I can transfer funds online into my current account as soon as we finish this conversation. I take it you have Mrs Fishburn's bank account details to receive these funds?'

'Gosh, you've got me there. How could I possibly have forgotten? I'll call her now and tell her what the arrangements are going to be. So, if you like, tell the rest of the family that I'll be coming mid-morning tomorrow to complete the formalities. If that's OK by you and everyone else?'

'Thanks, Clive. I'm sure it will be. See you tomorrow then. Bye.'

Pamela breathed a huge sigh of relief and made her way into the lounge only to be met by Sebbie on the lookout for another treat from the nice lady from London.

'Great news everyone. By this time tomorrow I will have replaced your Mam as a shareholder in the Hotel Koala. Clive's arriving mid-morning to complete the formalities. He says if the weather's bad he'll come on the train from Beverley. What is the forecast anyway?'

Peter was on the ball as always, having listened to a thousand forecasts on board the Pride of Bruges. Old habits died hard and he did his best to imitate the voice of the Shipping Forecast:

'Tyne, Dogger, German Bight, one thousand and ten, rising. Visibility ten miles. Wind northerly, backing easterly …'

'Put a sock in it, Dad. Is it gonna snow or not?"

'I'm not sure. Put the telly on and well see!'

In fact the forecast was not at all good. Rather than take a chance driving on dodgy roads, he might be well advised to plan the short train journey from the outset. In fact, Clive was watching the forecast on TV at the same time and immediately decided to leave the car at home and take the train. He looked online at the Hull to Scarborough timetable. There were several stops en-route of which Beverley was the second. The ETA for Scarborough was given as ten minutes past twelve so he immediately texted Millie with the time together with a request that one of them collect him at the station. Millie immediately had an idea.

'Listen, Dad. How about me, you and Pamela all go to the station to meet Clive? We can find somewhere for a bit of lunch within walking distance and then surely the minimal formalities can be completed over a bite of something nice and a glass of something to complement it? Just the four of us.'

'What about Jamie and Lucy?'

'Well for a start, Lucy will be at the Vet's and Jamie will be at College. He's only got about ten weeks left hasn't he? He doesn't need "time out" at this stage of the game. Well does he?'

'Has he any idea how he's doing with his grades? He never talks about it much – at least not to me anyway. You?'

'No, never. But I am in touch from time to time with Samantha Lyon, his course tutor. She would tell me if he was slacking. We know each other quite well now. And that reminds me, she and some of her students will be very much a part of our opening night – just as they were when we launched the Hotel Scarbados all those months ago. It will be great publicity for her Department too. In a few months they'll be starting to recruit new students for the next academic year. I'll call her tomorrow. Would you like to meet her sometime, Pam?'

'Thank you, yes I certainly would.'

Pamela hadn't played all her cards yet but after tomorrow, when she was a bona-fide Director and shareholder, some of her ideas and intentions would be made more apparent. They all had a fairly early night. Lucy had already retired and was in bed reading some notes that Mr Wilson had given her on basic animal care. She was taking to it like a duck to water.

Before drifting off to sleep herself, Pamela had yet another read of the letter in the envelope that had arrived at the office of English Hotels Monthly. Deep down she knew that one day, in the not too distant future, she would have to hand it over to Peter, the addressee. It was only right that she did so. But should she go even further than that? Should she contact the writer to advise of Peter's new address? She had mulled over this dilemma a thousand times. Yes, she would, but not just yet.

Next morning brought forth quite an angry vista out to sea with "white horses" right across the Bay. At least Force Four thought Pete and he was glad he wasn't on duty on the Pride of Bruges approaching the River Humber. Many a time over the years he had been delayed docking at King George Dock by adverse weather conditions – usually easterly gales making entrance to the narrow lock difficult to say the least.

Lucy had gone off to the Vet's and Jamie was long since gone on his motorbike to college. Peter, Pamela and Millie had a minimal breakfast of coffee and a single slice of toast and marmalade. Millie had yet another idea – didn't she always?

'Listen, after we meet Clive at the station, let's walk round to the Crescent Gardens Hotel for a spot of lunch. Yes? We can complete the formalities in that nice little side lounge and then go downstairs to the Public Bar. They do a nice selection of lunch dishes. I also need another little chat with Nadine about staff. After all we're at opposite ends of the town and hardly in competition are we?'

Both heads nodded in mute acquiescence.

'Good, that's that then. I'll order a cab for eleven forty-five. No point in going on the bus when there are three of us. Millie couldn't help but smile at the bemused look on Pamela's face at the mere mention of a bus. A bus? A bus? She hadn't been on one since she and her late mother had gone shopping in the West End Sales a quarter of a century earlier.

They arrived at the train station just a few minutes before Clive's Northern Rail train arrived exactly on time. A short ten minute walk to the Crescent Gardens and they were in the welcoming warmth of the lounge, with coffee and shortbreads courtesy of Nadine and her staff. Clive opened the batting.

'Right, Pamela. This is your new certificate for twenty-five percent of the shares. All I have to do now is sign it as Company Secretary. Now, here are the banking details for Mrs Mandy Fishburn's bank account in Hull. How are you going to make the transfer of two hundred thousand pounds exactly?'

'I've brought my own laptop and Nadine has already given me the in-house WiFi password – 'Atrioofyorkshirepuddings' indeed! You wait while I tell Jamie!'

Less than a minute later and Pamela B. Hesketh was a one quarter shareholder in the company and Mandy Fishburn was history, as far as the Hotel Koala was concerned anyway. A short but delightful lunch followed downstairs but Clive made his apologies earlier than expected. He said that a member of Northern Rail staff had hinted that if the gales worsened and snow arrived then the last two trains of the day might be cancelled.

Nadine joined Peter and Millie for a chat after lunch on the thorny topic of staffing – something that affected the whole of the hospitality industry. She had some welcome and surprising news.

'I saw a report on the lunchtime News that the Government is considering relaxing the rules for young people in Europe to come and work in the UK, for a period of up to three years. Apparently there have been strong representations from the Hospitality and Care industries who fear that unless a sort of "reverse Brexit" was put into place, then too many people would suffer real hardship.'

'So how do we as hoteliers make sure it works for us?"

'Just do what we did – put a notice on your website. You'll be inundated, trust me. Just be careful though. Interview them online first via Zoom. Some will claim to be good English speakers when in fact they are barely adequate. When are you formally opening anyway?"

'It was going to be a week or so before Easter but we might bring that forward a tad ..' Peter looked surprised.

'You never mentioned that to me, young lady and ..'

'Dad, you don't listen to half of what I say to you.'

She exchanged a wink with Pam. Had they secretly discussed some plans between themselves? Peter would never know but there again he didn't need to know either. One thing was certain. With two very ambitious women effectively running the show, there would be no let-up in the project to turn the Hotel Koala into one of the best known and envied hotels on the East Coast of England. If Pamela had her way, then within twelve months of trading it would be a jewel fit to mount into the crown of Best Eastern Hotels.

The weather was definitely worsening and Clive had wisely decided to get an early train back to Beverley. Nadine ordered a taxi for them and twenty minutes later they were back at the Hotel Koala. The brisk easterly had increased to at least Force Five if not more. Even Sebbie didn't want to venture far and after a call of nature he was soon keen to get back into the warmth of the kitchen. Re-donning his warm fleece, Peter decided to do a quick inspection of the newly fixed neon signs around the exterior. He switched all four switches to "on" and stepped outside. A couple of minutes later and he was back.

'All's well. Those signs look absolutely fantastic and haven't budged an inch. A top man is Dave Gibson. We mustn't forget to invite him and his wife to the opening – whenever it is. Now, what's for tea? When's Jamie back? Or shall we rustle something up as a surprise for him? After all, he did miss out on the Trio of Yorkshire Puddings today.'

32.

Between them they rustled up a "Spag Bol" for tea without Jamie's help and they remembered to do a smaller Quorn version for Lucy at the last minute. This was very much to Sebbie's advantage who ate the portion originally intended for Lucy. He turned his cold nose up at the 'spag' bit but the 'bol' bit, being mostly butchers-grade ground beef, always went down well. If only he could tell them to go a bit easier on the oregano next time. Since Jamie's enrolment on the Chef's Diploma course he was becoming a tad too discerning. Would his offspring, AlfieBoy, take after him? They would soon find out. Lucy had a little announcement to make.

'Great news everyone. Alfie Boy is arriving on Saturday! Mr Wilson has cleared him and he's had his first injections. Mr Ritson has kindly offered to bring him late morning. Can we have some sort of a little party for him please, Dad?'

'I er, well I don't see why not, Lucy. Are we prepared for him yet? He'll need his own bowls, not to mention his own basket and blanket. And as for house-training …'

'Dad, Mr Ritson has been training dogs for even longer than you were at sea on the Pride of Bruges. AlfieBoy is already house-trained. I was hoping that he could sleep with me in my room and …'

'No, Lucy! It's going to be the same rule for AlfieBoy as Sebbie: dogs are not allowed upstairs. We don't want any smart-arsed comments on Trip Advisor reporting that their room smelt like a kennel.'

Lucy looked devastated and glanced pleadingly at Pamela hoping for some support. It didn't come.

'To be fair I think your Dad's got it right on this one, Lucy. There's a big difference between a hotel noted for being dog-friendly and one that resembles a kennels. Looking ahead, one of those outbuildings at the rear might be suitable to convert to overnight doggie accommodation but no doubt there will be rules and regulations to look into first – you know, Environmental Health and the rest.' Lucy soon got over her initial disappointment.

'Right, I'll look into it but I'll ask Mr Wilson for his advice too.'

This time it was Jamie's turn to look a little crestfallen. He'd earmarked one of the outbuildings as a workshop. He was going to make some raised planters from some of the Tasmanian oak planks salvaged from the Hotel Scarbados. Spring was just around the corner and he wanted to build his own herb garden. Home-grown mint, rosemary, basil, chives, garlic and other less-know herbs would look very good on his seasonal dishes and provide extra verbiage for the menus themselves. Of course, he would consult with both Pamela and Samantha Lyon nearer the time. How many restaurants could boast their own herb garden within fifty feet of the kitchen door? Not many he warranted. Pamela changed the subject from dogs and herbs to the website.

'Millie, did you say that your college friend, Katya is she called, is going to construct the website for the Hotel Koala? What a great job she did on the Hotel Scarbados didn't she?'

'Yes, she is, Pam. Actually I took some shots on my iPhone a couple of days ago and emailed them to her. I tried to get the koala's in full glow just after dusk but she told me they were inadequate and blurred. So, she's coming up from Hull on the train tomorrow with her tripods, cameras, lenses and God knows what. She'll be staying overnight to get the best evening shots. I thought maybe we could go to the Lucky Dragon for a change – you know a sort of thank-you to her. What does everybody think?'

There were smiles and nods all round, particularly from a very relieved Pam.

'I hope Mr Kenneth Chan is there. I won't have to pretend I don't know him this time.'

The smiles and grins were slightly luke-warm. This was all taking a little getting used to.

The next day was a Friday and Lucy went on the bus to the vets as usual and Jamie drove his motorbike to College. With Lucy out for the best part of the day the remaining girls set about erecting some bunting that they had bought online to welcome AlfieBoy to his new home. They had a surprise for Lucy in that Garry Ritson had brought the 'delivery date' forward twenty-four hours as he and Shirley had decided to attend a matinee performance of "Brassed Off" at the Stephen Joseph Theatre on the Saturday. They would be bringing AlfieBoy just after lunch so that he would already be settled in and feeling 'at home' before Lucy got back around four o'clock. A specially decorated cake had been bought with AlfieBoy's name iced onto it, with a removal doggie bone containing treats on it. It was placed on the dining room table with side plates and knives and small cake forks. Six champagne flutes were polished and two bottles of "champers" taken from the hotel's stock were placed in the main fridge. First though, they had to collect Katya from the station.

'Good God, Kat, what have you got here? No wonder you were the last person to get off the train. You look like you've got enough kit for Attenborough to go on tour with!

Come here and give me a hug. Lovely to see you again. It's been a while hasn't it?'

'Yeah, it sure has. As you can see I've brought everything except the kitchen sink. What's the forecast for this evening? Any idea? If I can I want a shot of the sun going down behind the hotel with one of the koalas illuminated and silhouetted in the foreground and ....'

'Kat, we'll bow to your better judgement on that. Right now we have to get back and arrange the decs for AlfieBoy's homecoming. It's a surprise for Lucy. Hey, come to think of it, you can do a thirty second video of his arrival and maybe put a link to it on the website? Yes? It would enhance the dog-friendly message that Lucy wants to portray.'

'Sure, why not? Here, grab these tripods will you?'

Katya was very impressed with the new hotel and did a sweeping survey of the whole of the ground floor before she had even opened any of her numerous cases, mostly containing her equipment.

'Wow, Millie, you didn't tell me this place was so big! The reception area is simply magnificent.'

'Thanks, well we have a lot more space here of course and we learnt a lot of lessons from our time at the Hotel Scarbados. It seems like ancient history now, to be honest.'

'What's in that wall-mounted glass frame over there?'

'That's the document that was dug up from under the eucalyptus tree in the old garden. It tells the story of the old hotel and why it was called the Hotel Koala by the original owners, the Jewitt family, who came here from Victoria, Australia before the Second World War. We also have the original hand-made box that it was buried in. We're still thinking of the best way to display it to be honest. It's too chunky to put into a fancy display cabinet and ...'

'Millie, can I make a suggestion? I won't be offended if you poo-poo it.'

'Sure, Kat, go for it. I'm all ears.'

'Well, admittedly I have have never seen the box but from the description of it you gave me months ago, I think it might be about the right size for a suggestion box. You could leave it on show on top of the Reception desk. It's big enough for the role if you cut a wide enough slot in it, you know, a bit like a letter box. Does Jamie have the necessary woodwork skills to do the job do you think?'

'You bet he does. Look up there. That's the new clock plaque he made which houses six clocks now, not just the two we had before for Barbados and Scarbados times.'

'How come?'

'Well, we're really going to aim for the cricketing fraternity now that we're a whole lot nearer to the Cricket Club itself. We've developed even closer links. Dad had lunch with the Treasurer, Miles Carter, last week. We've got two overseas players staying with us as soon as the new season starts – one each from Barbados and Australia. Events just worked against them last year.'

'So why six clocks?'

'They'll be set at Barbados, Scarbados, Capetown, Karachi, New Delhi and Melbourne time zones, representing the major cricket playing centres. Any overseas players will always feel at home that way. It's just a bit of PR really but the clocks do look smart don't you think, Kat?'

'They look amazing. I'll draw particular attention to them in the short 'round robin' video of the hotel. It'll look brill when it's finished and online. Trust me! Tell you what, I'll dump my bag in my room and then I'll make a start while the daylight is still good. It always looks better that way – brighter and with no shadows.'

'Right, I'll show you upstairs and then I'll pop the kettle on. Pamela is very keen to meet you, by the way. Did I tell you that she's bought out Mam's shares in the Hotel? She and Dad are no longer an item, if you know what I mean. Just good friends now.'

'With or without benefits?' They both laughed.

'The latter I think. She's also on the board of Best Eastern Hotels now and is away a lot eyeing up new prospects for the company to either buy outright or substantially invest in. They have stakes in over fifty businesses in the hospitality trade all down the east coast from Alnwick in the north to Cromer in the south. It's all foreign money of course.'

'Yeah, but why does it take the business acumen and wonga of foreigners to see opportunities in our own country?'

'I know what you mean, but sometimes it takes new eyes to see new opportunities. Scarborough is now only just rebuilding itself after the Covid disaster. In just a couple of years time Scarborough will be marking four hundred years as a seaside resort. Can you Adam and Eve it?'

'Gosh, well I hope the Tourist Board, or whatever it's called these days, are planning a major celebration when the time comes?'

'You never know these days. One thing's for certain though, the Hotel Koala will be be marking it. Just think, it's a golden opportunity that can last a whole year. Anyway, we've got a year to get our heads around it. That sounds like Dad's car coming back. He's been out for a little ride with Pamela and Sebbie – up to the edge of the Moors I think now that all the roads are relatively clear. Let's have a cuppa first, you can meet Pamela and then you can start filming. We've got two hours before Lucy comes back from the vet's surgery and Mr Ritson will have brought AlfieBoy by then. I thought we could put both doggies in the dining room just before she arrived. Then as soon as she's taken her coat off

I'll tell her that there's a surprise for her in there. It is such a huge moment for her.'

Sure enough, Lucy arrived on the bus which stopped just around the corner and entered through the rear door into the kitchens.

'Hi Sis, where's Sebbie? He's always waiting for me at the door. And where's everyone else?'

'Sebbie's waiting for you in the dining room. He wants to introduce you to somebody.'

'What on earth are you talking about? Pour me a cuppa first will you? I'm dying for a drink.'

'Lucy, please just do as you're told for once. You won't be wanting tea. Go!

Walking through the main hall, then Reception and towards the dining room door, she thought she heard a bark followed by a little squeal. The lights suddenly came on to reveal a banner in red and gold letters strung across the hall. It read:

"Welcome to AlfieBoy – home at last."

Gingerly pushing the door open, another light came on to reveal two doggies, one big one and one tiny one. Sebbie rushed towards Lucy with his tail wagging, followed closely by his son, AlfieBoy.

Lucy cried like Niagara Falls. It was the best day of her life. She hadn't even noticed Katya in the background recording the event for posterity.

33.

The dinner at the Lucky Dragon that evening went down well with everybody. Lucy had been a little concerned that AlfieBoy was left behind for an hour or two but she had taken both him and his father outside for a piddle just before setting off on the ten minute walk. It was Sebbie's first test at being a "dad." How would he cope?

Just after sundown Katya had taken all the outside shots she needed of the Hotel. They looked good in her camera's viewfinder but how would they look on the website when it was put together? She fended off questions from nearly all of them over the aromatic crispy duck starter.

'You'll all just have to be patient. When I get home tomorrow afternoon I'll start to built the website proper OK?'

Pamela could not spot Kenneth Chan, her colleague on the board of Best Eastern Hotels. She made enquiries at the desk near the main entrance. The smartly uniformed head waiter, a Hong Kong Chinese, was firm but polite.

'Mr Chan is absent on business duties. Can I help you?'

Pamela craned forward to read his shiny brass name badge which bore the Best Eastern logo, BE in a circle. She wondered if Peter had noticed it as it reminded her of the Belgium Railways logo, one which Peter would have been familiar with from his many visits to Bruges and Ostend in his previous life. She thought better of mentioning it to him but it was a sharp, if silent, reminder to her that it was only a matter of time before she had to give him that letter. Apart from the writer, she was the only person in the whole world who knew the contents. She would have to choose her moment carefully but would there ever be a truly opportune and sensitive moment? She had agonised over it but she knew that in the not too distant future she would have to come clean. She was snapped out of her daydream by another waiter who asked them if they were all ready to receive the next course – sweet and sour pork or chicken with egg-fried rice. Lucy pulled a face but her disappointment was short lived.

'And it's sweet and sour tofu for you, young lady, with deep-fried artichoke hearts with the manager's compliments. He remembered you are a vegetarian from your first visit before Christmas.'

Lucy beamed like the searchlight on Flamborough Head twenty miles to the south. She loved it here. In fact they all did. Pamela started to engage Katya in conversation who was sitting on her immediate left.

'Katya, I just can't wait to see the completed Hotel Koala website. Is this sort of thing a full time job or what?'

'If only it was. No, it's a sideline really while I work towards the end of my Accounting and Business qualification at Hull. I'm on the same course as Millie. Didn't she tell you?'

'Er no, but I'm a bit of a "Johnny come lately" as regards the Fishburn family enterprises. Their rise in business fortunes has been meteoric. I have recently bought out Millie's mother as a one quarter shareholder in the whole business.'

'Oh wow, well lucky you, is all I can say. Strikes me that the business has massive potential – if it's done properly. I like to think I'm switched on with all aspects of online marketing. If you ask me any business that isn't these days is doomed. Do you agree?'

'Totally, Katya, totally. Listen, give me your mobile number and we'll have a chat over a spot of lunch one day soon. I've got a meeting in Hull to attend one day next month. Do you know somewhere where we could meet and have a quiet chat?'

'Sure, I'll write it down for you. Got a pen?'

By ten o'clock they had all eaten more than their fill. Peter paid the bill and they set off back to the Koala. Lucy strode out about fifty yards ahead of the pack, so keen was she to find out how Sebbie had managed on his first babysitting shift. She need not have worried one jot. Both pooches were fast asleep in their adjacent baskets and there wasn't a piddle or a puddle in sight. Lucy slept like a log that night and dreamt of one hundred and one Dalmatians – all in residence at the Hotel Koala. No such luxury for Pamela whose disturbed sleep was dominated by images of a map of eastern England with enamelled BE pins stuck into it at regular intervals. Thus far there was only one pin in the Scarborough area representing the Lucky Dragon restaurant. One day soon there would be one more, preferably inserted into that part of a koala where the sun doesn't shine. Then she would be quids in, big time. And so would the other shareholders.

It was starting to get lighter in the mornings but mercifully the flocks of herring gulls didn't awake everyone too early. They did however awake AlfieBoy who was unused to these squawking aliens who were never a real problem at his former residence at the Ritson's. It was something that, like his Dad, he would just have to get used to. Sebbie was still hard asleep and dreaming about BBQs and nice sausage handouts – let alone some nice canine female company. Candy had been his first female conquest. It was just as well he didn't understand more than a handful of English words or the word "snip" would have terrified him.

After breakfast Katya took a few more photographs of the seascape immediately in front of the hotel and a few more of the castle in the distance. This girl was a perfectionist, no doubt about that. Almost as an afterthought she remembered to photograph a few of the guest rooms on the first floor.

'Right, I'm done! Can anyone give me a lift to the train station please?'

There were fond hugs at the door as luggage and equipment were put in the back of the family estate car. Twenty minutes later and the Northern Rail train pulled out of Platform number Four. Katya wasn't going to waste any time on the sixty-five minute journey and she pulled out a small notepad and pen from the outside pocket of her case. She jotted down a few ideas while they were still fresh in her mind. Despite being very "tech savvy" she had little or no time for so-called electronic Notebooks. What's wrong with a good old-fashioned pen and paper? Sometimes the old ways were the best. She wrote down bullet points:

- *Website completion date*
- *Link to Cricket Club*
- *Interior photographs*
- *Exterior photographs*
- *Sebbie and AlfieBoy video*
- *Sea views*
- *Link to booking calendar*
- *Four Seasons Restaurant feature*
- *Advertise for staff*
- *Meet the family*

It was that last point 'Meet the family' that caused her a touch of consternation. Peter, Millie, Lucy and the two doggies were fine but what about Pamela? And why did

Pamela seem so keen to meet her outside of the Hotel and even in another town? She would have to wait for the answers to that but not for very long as it transpired.

Meanwhile, back at the ranch as they say, Millie and Pamela were sat at one of the smaller tables in what would soon become the Four Seasons Restaurant. Without the two men knowing it they had acquired both of their "to do" lists and were both shaking their heads at the number of items still to be ticked off. Pamela raised the first issue.

'Dear me, Millie, there are how many days to the launch party or opening ceremony or whatever you want to call it, and neither of them have seemingly made a start on the all-important guest list. Did you keep the old one from the Hotel Scarbados by any chance?'

'I certainly did. I'll go and get it from the file in the Reception desk. Hang on a mo. Here it is look. Forty odd folks but we know a lot more people now, that's for sure. Any suggestions?'

'Well yes, but I think you're going to have to be a bit more calculating this time round. Only invite people who you think might be useful business contacts – you know, folks who'll bring in business, not just friends like the Ritsons. In the trade they're known as KBIs – key business influencers.'

'Such as?'

'Well I've done a bit of research and following the most recent North Yorkshire Council Elections there are seventeen new Councillors. You must invite all of them except one.'

'What? Why? We don't want to make any enemies at this stage of the game for goodness sake. Do we?'

'No, but Councillor Kelly has already made you the enemy. He's been pressing hard for dogs to be banned from the beaches all year round, not just in the summer. He has already made himself deeply unpopular and is looking to garner support for changes to By Laws. It will do us a lot of good as we seek to promote the Hotel as "dog friendly" to put it mildly.'

'Well one thing's for sure, Lucy will be over the moon if we kept him off the guest list.'

'That's settled then. Now, about the rest of the list. I think we could easily entertain getting on for a hundred people on the night. Don't you?'

'Wow, that's an awful lot of folks to feed.'

'Not really. Jamie can do a running buffet. They won't all want to eat at the same time. And what's this seafood connection he's made? His girlfriend's father or something?'

'Oh Mr Cammish? Yes, he's Chloe's dad. I wouldn't say they were an item just yet to be honest. Chloe's gone back to Uni in York but no doubt she'll want to be here for the party.'

'Well I got the impression he was totally smitten. Is she nice?'

'She seems a really nice girl to be fair. But we've told him, in a nice way of course, that both of them have to concentrate on their qualifications before anything else. Actually, Pamela, she ate your supper on New Year's Eve when you were visiting your very ill sister in London.'

They both laughed like hyenas then carried on making the guest list. Friends again for sure.

34.

Millie and Pamela had, they thought, just about finished the guest list when Peter returned from a doggie-walk, for the first time with both Sebbie and AlfieBoy.

'Hi Dad. What's it like taking two dogs for a walk?'

'Twice as hard to be honest with you. One wants to go this way, one wants to go the other way! I can trust Sebbie to go off the lead for a short time but do you know what, he didn't seem to want to leave AlfieBoy for very long. He's very protective of his offspring I'll vouch for that.'

''As soon as the Hotel is fully open you know that Lucy is going to start asking questions about how many guests can bring their dogs along and ..'

'Lucy can ask all she likes but we all know that we can't accept any responsibilities along those lines for a long time. And, to be fair, when you think about it, the Hotel Scarbados was much more dog friendly than where we are now! It was closer to the Park and the beach – and of course a large lawn at the rear which was a very effective canine loo. Here is not so easy is it? And once Jamie has constructed and planted his herb garden he won't want any dogs, whether they're ours or not, sniffing round his mint and bay leaves, now will he? We must try and discourage this 'dog development' for the foreseeable future. Let's face it, we've enough on our plates already, well haven't we? What's that large piece of paper on the table top anyway? Not another invoice I hope?'

'No Dad, it's the suggested guest list for the opening night party. Here, run your eyes down it while I put the kettle on.'

'Good God. Every man and his dog's on this list …'

'Dad, you just said no more dogs!'

'OK but you know what I mean. And who the heck are all these people? I've never heard of any of them.'

'They're new councillors and their wives or partners – thirty two in total as we've already deleted Councillor Kelly from the list. He doesn't seem to be influential in any way so it's no loss. The rest are what Pam calls KBIs – key business influencers. We need to make friends. Something's puzzling you, Pamela. What is it?'

'I've just had a thought. Are any of the names on this list on the Planning Committee?'

'No idea. Why?'

'Let's take a look on the North Yorkshire Council Website. Hang on, where's my iPad? Give me a couple of minutes.'

This time it was Peter and Millie's turn to look a tad puzzled.

'Bingo! Councillor Elsie Thompson is actually the Chair of the Planning Committee! End of problem – potentially anyway.'

'What problem? You've left me in the starting blocks. Has she you too, Dad?'

'Right, we've got to get the invitations out fast. And I mean fast in her case. Send her an email today in fact with a 'Save this date' message.'

'But have we even got a date yet? Come on, we're slipping. Jamie's crucial to this bit as he's in charge of catering. What time is he due back from College? Soon?'

Yes, within half an hour at the outside. You're right we need to tie him down. In fact is that his motorbike I can hear outside right now? Maybe he's early today? Yes it's him. Right, grab the calendar.'

Jamie had barely got his protective clothing off before the two women regaled him and dragged him into the dining room. A mug of tea, the all-important calendar and a pen were thrust under his nose in less than a minute.

'Calm down you two. You can relax. I had a long chat with Samantha Lyon this afternoon. The Saturday evening before the Easter weekend is all clear in her diary. She also asked for four student volunteers to come and help on the night. Guess how many came forward? Sis?'

'Er, two or three maybe.'

'Pamela?'

'All of them. Say twenty plus?'

'Wow, well you're right Pamela. The only one's who declined are those on genuine Easter holidays with their parents. The rest are just itching to come along. I was gobsmacked, to be honest.'

'Well you could have predicted that, Jamie. You can't see the wood for the trees. You're too close to it. You are are in an enviable situation. You will effectively be owning and managing your own restaurant before you have even gained your Diploma. Your fellow students aren't just green with envy – they are looking at you and this hotel as a potential future employer. Had that even occurred to you by any chance?'

'No, to be honest, it hadn't at all.'

'Look Jamie, if this whole project takes off there is no way you can do all the chefing on your own. You're going to need sous-chefs, perhaps two or three. But it's definitely one step at a time. Let's get the launch party sorted first. Now we've got the firm date we can start planning properly. All the Councillors' email addresses are given on the website. We'll get the "Save this date" message out by the close of play today. Are you all happy to leave the wording to me?'

There were nods all round.

'And excuse the metaphor when I said 'by close of play' but where are the Cricket Club contacts on this list? Isn't our proximity to the second biggest ground in Yorkshire one of our USPs?'

'Huh? USPs?'

'Unique selling points! You guys are all going to have to buck up. Where are Malcolm and Marlene Morgan's names on this list? They're not are they? Just because he's no longer the High Commissioner for Barbados doesn't mean he can't influence people. He was just in the wrong place at the wrong time with all that criminality regarding the old Wendover Hotel. I had read somewhere that he might have been in line for a Knighthood a couple of years ago. Again it was just bad luck that Barbados became a Republic and then when our beloved late Queen Elizabeth died that was probably the end of it. So, we must make an extra special effort in his direction. All Barbadians are mad keen on cricket. Is his nephew, Courtney was his name, still scheduled to come and play a season for Scarborough in the Yorkshire League?'

'Well as far as we know, yes. Let's check with Miles Carter, the Club Treasurer. Oh God, we haven't put him on the list either. That's two more, folks.'

'Two?' Why two?'

'He'll be bringing his long suffering wife to make sure he gets home. Remember how much Prosecco he drank last year at the Hotel Scarbados? He's a bit of a lad! Good chap to know though, Pam. And what's the significance of Councillor Elsie Thompson's position as Chair of the Planning Committee?'

'It's quite simple really. On the assumption that she accepts our invitation, and I'm sure she will, then we ask her to officially switch on the hotel's illuminations – the koalas especially.'

'I still don't see …'

'Don't you get it? Dave Gibson from We are Neon said there was a possibility of needing to get special planning permission for the new signs which could cause problems later. If we asked the Head of Planning to ceremoniously switch them on just after dusk then if there were any complaints from that direction she would look very silly. Well wouldn't she? You can just see the headlines in the Scarborough News now – 'The Councillor in charge of planning is complicit in etc.' No, it just wouldn't happen. Any objection would be swept straight under the County Hall carpet. End of problem. Now, where were we? Any more tea in the pot?

35.

Two days later, just before breakfast, Katya texted Millie to advise that she had largely completed the construction of the Hotel Koala website and had sent her a link via email for them all to look at. There was still lots of time to make any amendments if necessary. It was just a "first peek" so to speak. Millie lifted her laptop onto the dining table and switched on. They all gaped at the screen – mid tea, toast and cornflakes. Millie clicked on the link and within a couple of seconds, the hotel as they had never seen it before unfolded before them. The back-drop, or wall paper as it's called these days, was a seascape of cliffs and waves with Scarborough Castle in the distance. She had even caught a herring gull mid-flight as it screeched overhead, atop the hotel's turret. Then slowly, as they watched, the main view of the hotel changed and, as if by magic, dusk appeared and the neon koalas glowed like a zillion fireflies. It was awesome, simply awesome. They all smiled, particularly Pamela. She had plans for Katya but would keep them to herself for the time being.

There were various "links" all over the website.

'Click here for a virtual tour' it said, so Millie did just that. The camera took the viewer through the main entrance of the hotel and into the Reception area, zooming in to the highly polished mahogany main desk upon which the newly made Suggestion Box proudly stood. It had taken Jamie several hours with a keyhole saw to fashion the slot like a miniature letterbox. The brass corners gleamed like cats' eyes in the dark – testimony to Brasso and a not inconsiderable amount of elbow grease on Jamie's part. The camera continued on its tour. Next in view were the six brass clocks from the six nominated time zones of the chosen cricketing venues from Barbados in the west to Melbourne in the east. On the wall opposite was the brass ship's barometer with the tag SVG beneath it. The needle was pointing well to the right indicating fair and very dry weather. They all hoped it was an omen for future success. Peter gulped when he saw it in full view. Only he knew its true significance or did someone else too? If she did then she certainly kept it to herself.

The camera continued its journey through the main lobby and into the two separate dining rooms and the lounges. Moving upstairs to the First Floor, several guest rooms were entered to maximum effect with the sea views and en-suite facilities shown in their best light. The whole tour lasted sixty seconds and was very, very impressive. Despite Katya being fifty miles to the south and out of audio-range they all give her a round of applause.

'Oh wow, wow, wow!' exclaimed Millie. 'Katya deserves a free weekend with us after that, don't you all think? Amazing!'

Pamela brought the gathering to some sort of order and assumed a directorial role within seconds.

'Now, is the Guest List fully complete now? By the way I sent off that email to Cllr. Elsie Thompson asking her to keep that date free. That reminds me I haven't checked my emails yet this morning. Where's my iPad, I'll do it now. Give me a couple of minutes please.'

More tea was poured, more toast made and even more marmalade and butter consumed.

'Yes! She's coming and also bringing her husband Derek. Looks like we're in business but we must keep this lark about switching on the lights a secret until the very last minute. Mum's the word,'

They all nodded.

'Now, we've still got around ten vacant slots on the Guest List, if indeed we are going to invite a hundred people. Let's go through it again shall we? Woe betide us if we've accidentally forgotten anybody important. Any ideas?'

'Oh yes, the Coates's from Skipton! Lovely folks and cricket mad. They so enjoyed it when they came to stay at the Hotel Scarbados. They're friends of Miles Carter at the Cricket Club too and very influential in cricketing circles. They've been coming to watch cricket at Scarborough since the year dot. We've got their phone number so I'll give them a ring. I hope Babs picks up the phone and not Fred. Do you remember how deaf he was until he put his hearing aids in? He drove her bonkers a few times I recall.'

Pamela kept quiet. She hadn't recommended lengthening the Guest List for nothing but she kept a few cards up her sleeve. This wasn't the time. It certainly was the time to perform another task though and the sight of the barometer in such detail on the video had reminded her. She would do it tonight, in her own time and the privacy of her own room.

The rest of the day was full of activity across all fronts. Katya called late morning to ask for some feedback to the proposed website. Pamela actually took the call which was to the Hotel's landline number – the one advertised on the website.

'Katya, we are all over the Moon here. It is just wonderful. Now, when did you say it could 'go live' as it were?'

'Tomorrow, if you like. You did say that you were concerned about the availability of staff didn't you? Between you and me, I don't think that Peter and Millie have really grasped the seriousness of the situation. It can't all be last-minute, unlike the famous website. If the first floor rooms are all going to be open on the date we set, and if the necessary staff aren't in post, it will be a disaster. And there's another point. Nobody gave me the date. It needs to go on the website as a big banner.'

'Katya, I'll let you know within the hour. Now, is there any chance that we can meet for a lunch tomorrow? I'll jump on the train to Hull to save you travelling. What's the name of the main Hotel at the train station?'

'It's the Mercure. What time?'

'Say twelve-thirty?'

'That's fine and the new website will go live while you're on the train.'

'Great. See you tomorrow, Katya.'

Pamela looked up to the "countdown calendar" that Millie had put in the kitchen. She peeled ten days off with one fell swoop and immediately thirty-one days became twenty-one. She hoped that nobody else would notice – not yet anyway. This lot just weren't "on the ball" enough for her liking and they needed a little jolt. Her mind soon wandered onto other matters and she decided to take a solo walk down the slope to the Watermark Café. The queue for a cuppa was quite long so she decided to keep walking until she came to the two blocks of newish apartments known as "Sandpiper Heights" which she thought was rather an odd name to give to up-market properties. Mind you, the two blocks were of substantial height compared to the Forties-style Council owned entertainment complex it had so recently replaced. Spotting a Sales Office she popped her head in. The office girl behind the desk was doing her nails, drinking tea and listening to Smooth Radio all at the same time. She looked surprised that somebody had actually had the brass neck to disturb her. She reacted immediately.'

'Alexa, switch off please!'

The music, a full length version of Prince's Purple Rain, stopped as if a transmitting mast had just collapsed in a gale.

'Hi, sorry about that. Can I help you? Are you looking to buy or rent? There are three apartments currently on offer for sale – all on ninety-nine year leases. They're currently for sale with vacant possession. Or, if you're prepared to wait, the new Penthouse Suites will be available within six months. The plans are over there on the wall and …'

'Thank you er, Jo is it? I can't quite see your name badge from here.'

'Yeah, Joanne, but everyone calls me Jo. And your name is?'

'Pamela, Pamela Hesketh, but plain Pam's fine. I know this is very cheeky but I don't suppose you've got a spare cuppa have you? I did look into the Watermark but there was one helluva queue.'

'Yeah, there often is, Pam, at this time of the day. Lots of dog walkers too. Look, I'll make us a fresh pot so why don't you take a look at those plans while I make a brew?'

Jo wasn't long and Pam was still studying the plans on the wall. She was beaming.

'So when did you say the Penthouse Suites will be available to buy?'

'I'm told by the bosses to say that by the end of June the first two will be open as Show Houses, if you know what I mean.'

'Have the prices been fixed yet?'

'Not officially, no. But the whispers from above are talking about a half a million pounds. Each that is. There hasn't been any interest at all yet, between you and me. Milk and sugar, Pam?'

'Just a drop of milk please.'

Pamela tried to look expressionless. She succeeded.

'And you mentioned letting apartments. What's the situation with those, if I may ask?'

'Well, we're always letting those to visitors, whether it's by the week, weekend or a calendar month. We won't reach maximum turnover until the summer season really and truly gets underway. Are you interested?'

Pamela certainly was interested and in more ways than one.

'So, as regards the letting apartments, what is availability like right now? And do they all have sea views?'

Joanne was eager to please and if possible make a sale. After all she was on a commission based salary.

'Tell you what, let's finish our cuppas and then I'll take you on a little tour shall we? There are currently two very similar apartments on the third floor right above us – a two bedder and a three bedder with just slightly different views. Come on, drink up. I'll get the keys.'

Ten minutes later and Pamela had made up her mind. She would rent the smaller apartment for a minimum of three months and await the completion of the penthouses. Views to the southeast of the Castle and North Bay were stupendous – not to mention the Hotel Koala just four hundred metres away as the herring gulls fly anyway. After all she might as well keep an eye on her investment.

'Jo, I'll have my London solicitor contact you as soon as details are clearer for the penthouses.'

It was a white lie. It would be the Finance Director of Best Eastern Hotels but Jo didn't need to know that just yet.

'I'll pop back in to see you in a few days about taking a minimum three month let on the apartment – from the first of next month if possible please. I'm currently staying in a hotel and it will be good to have some space of my own again. Thank you again and see you soon.'

Jo was on the phone to her bosses within seconds of Pamela leaving.

'I think we've got a bite on one of the penthouses – when they're finished. And the lady in question is going to rent one of the apartments for at least three months before buying.'

Jo was at least partly right. Pamela climbed the steepish slope back to the Hotel Koala. Already she was plotting the next chapter in her life. But first she had to deal with 'that letter.' She had made up her mind exactly what to do. After supper she soon retired to her room, pleading that too much sea air had made her sleepy.

36.

Lying prostrate on her bed, Pamela unfolded the letter from Belgium that had been in her possession for many months. She knew that what she had done, or not done, had been morally indefensible. She read it again for the umpteenth time.

Dear Peter

This is the hardest letter I have ever had to write in my life. In fact, my first three attempts have already ended up in the litter bin – or the "gash-bin" as you would call it. You taught me so much colloquial and slang English in our long relationship. As we all know that relationship was brought to a cruel end by the Covid epidemic. It devastated so many lives and not just from a medical point of view but emotionally too.

I knew from Ena at the Railway Station Brasserie that you had come looking for me on your ship's final visit to Zeebrugge and Bruges. I also learned that you had tried to find me at my brother's restaurant in Ostend when I was running it for him during his illness. Sorry to say he passed away and the restaurant was closed and eventually sold. The reason you couldn't find me was that I was in Liege seeing my mother who had been looking after my daughter, Natalie.

I know this will come as huge shock to you, Peter, but there is no other way to tell you. Natalie is YOUR daughter. She is now almost ten years old. I deliberately didn't tell you because you were married and already had a family of your own in Hull. I see Natalie almost every weekend and my mother absolutely adored her as her only grandchild. Sadly she too fell ill and passed away a month ago and Natalie lives with me in our small apartment in St. Kruis in Bruges.

Some time ago an English tourist accidentally left a recent copy of English Hotels Monthly magazine in the Brasserie. The centre-feature was about the Hotel Scarbados in Scarborough. Is that near to Hull, I don't know? Anyway the photographs were beautiful and within seconds I spotted the brass ship's barometer engraved with my initials – SVG. I knew then it was your hotel. I wrote this letter to you via the Editor of the magazine, Pamela Hesketh, and I asked her to forward this letter to you. If I don't hear from you then I will quite understand.

Perhaps though you would like to learn a little more about Natalie? She is growing up fast and is doing very well at school. She has just started elementary English lessons and her teacher tells me that she is the brightest child in the class in the subject. She can count from one to one hundred already, can you believe that? I'm sure that if her English father was around she would be bilingual by now but that was not to be.

I hope, dear Peter, that this letter finds you happy and healthy in your new life.

Yours forever,

Stephanie.xx

P.S. Natalie has your eyes and the reddish tint in her hair that you teased me was inherited from the Vikings that invaded the Humber centuries ago. My email address is above if you want to get in touch. SVG x

Pamela carefully refolded the letter for the last time and gingerly slipped it back into the envelope. It was now time for her to write the hardest letter of her life. She reached for her laptop and started typing. She decided to keep it short and as truthful as possible.

Dear Stephanie

Until a few months ago I was the Editor in Chief of English Hotels Monthly magazine. You wrote a letter to a Mr Peter Fishburn care of myself. To my shame and embarrassment I did not forward that letter to Peter. The truth is that I was in a relationship with him and I didn't want any complications. Peter was legally separated from his wife Mandy when we started seeing each other. He is now divorced with no complications. Our liaison is now over, I want to assure you of that. We remain friends and business partners but that's all. I am hoping that by the time you open and read this email tomorrow, Peter will have read the letter from you.

I simply cannot tell you what his reaction will be but being the warm-hearted man he is I think I know what he will do. I had to smile when you mentioned that Natalie has a reddish streak in her hair. Both his daughters here in England do too but I think he should tell you about them, not me. I assure you they are both fine young ladies.

Sincerely

Pamela Hesketh

Pamela paused for what seemed an eternity, her right index finger hovering over the "send" button. Should see wait until the morning and think twice before sending it? No! Go for it. Less than a second later and the letter was in Stephanie's inbox in Bruges. An hour ahead of Greenwich Mean Time, Stephanie and Natalie were already fast asleep. By the time they had finished their croissants and coffee the following morning their world would change forever. They just didn't know it yet.

Pamela realised that in order to complete her mission she now had to pass Stephanie's letter to Peter. Should she do it now or wait until the morning? She decided to do it now. Trembling with trepidation she almost tip-toed down the corridor to Peter's bedroom. She knocked gently twice. Thankfully he was still up and he came to the door.

'Pamela, are you OK? What's up?'

'Peter, this letter came to you at my London office many months ago.' She passed it to him.

'Please don't say anything tonight. Just take it and read it. I am so, so sorry. Please forgive me. Night night, Peter.'

She scurried back to her room. Peter could have sworn she was crying. What the heck was this? He closed the door, lay down on his bed and opened the envelope. He immediately knew who it was from by the handwriting and the Belgian postage stamps.

He read and reread the letter so many times that he lost count. His brain was a maelstrom of memories of his passion for Stephanie and times past. How on Earth was he going to tell his two daughters and a son that they had a half-sister on the other side of the North Sea? Should he tell them now, later or never? He lay awake half the night. By the time he had showered, shaved and got dressed he had made up his mind what to do.

Pamela had made it easier for him. She had risen early and taken both doggies out for a long walk before any of the family came downstairs for breakfast.

It was the hardest talk he had ever had to give to his children. It was even harder than telling them that he was being made redundant all that time ago. To make it slightly easier for himself he decided to read out Stephanie's letter word for word. When he came to the bit about Natalie he simply lost control and tears rolled down his cheeks and onto his cornflakes. It broke the ice, not to mention the silence. Lucy reacted first.

'Oh God, Dad, you mean I've got a little sister? With hair like mine? In Belgium? Oh wow. Now I'm no longer the baby of the family! That's brill, Dad.'

She launched herself at his neck and clung to him.

'Two new members of the family in such a short time – AlfieBoy and now Natalie.'

Millie and Jamie's reaction was slightly more muted. It would take both of them time to adjust to the news. How would it affect them in the longer term?

37.

The great day of the launch party had arrived – and so had lots of guests. Those that were travelling from afar had been offered overnight accommodation and breakfast the next morning – a Sunday. They included Fred and Babs Coates, Mr & Mrs Clive White, Katya and Inspector Mort and his wife from North Yorkshire Police who resided in Northallerton. It had been a borderline decision whether to invite them or not but "Morse" had hinted heavily at their last meeting that he would like to be there. After all, police officers were quite well paid and North Yorkshire was the biggest county in England. They all had to take weekend breaks somewhere and word of mouth advertising was free and effective. He had also hinted on the telephone that he might have some news for them about the old Hotel Scarbados which he would divulge privately later.

Dave Gibson and his wife made the journey from Teesside and he had been tipped-off that a Councillor would, at the last minute, be asked to turn on the exterior lights. He thought that, purely as a precaution, it was a great idea. Also travelling from afar were Malcolm and Marlene Morgan, the former High Commissioner from Barbados. They were now permanently resident in London and retired. It was a long way for them to travel but they had accepted the invitation with alacrity. Malcolm was hoping to receive news, not give it. He was not going to be disappointed. All in all there were nineteen overnight guests spread across ten rooms, Katya being the only single occupant. Those arriving early were shown to their respective rooms and then offered tea and biscuits in the lounges. No appetites were going to be spoiled before the sumptuous buffet later that Jamie was laying on. Malcolm Morgan couldn't wait to repeat his walk with Sebbie to the Cricket Club that he had done last year with Jamie. Peter had told him that the Club Treasurer had already offered to give him a personal tour of the ground on the Sunday morning.

'You never know, Malcolm, Miles Carter is the Treasurer and you can chat personally to him tonight That is if he doesn't go overboard with the Prosecco like he did last time.' He deliberately kept schtum about the bit of news to which he was already privy. He would leave that pleasure to Miles.

Also invited locally were Kenneth Chan, the de facto Chairman of Best Eastern Hotels and his wife. From the hotel trade, Nadine Murray from the Crescent Gardens Hotel was amongst the first guests to arrive. Unexpectedly she didn't bring her husband.

'I hope you don't think its impertinent but my hubby isn't really into "dos" like this so I've brought Marina along. You remember each other, I hope, when you spent those few days with us before you settled in?'

'Of course, hello Marina and welcome to the Clifftop Hotel which will be renamed the Hotel Koala within the hour. Let me get you both a drink would a …'

But Nadine, who was dressed in the most revealing dark green cocktail dress that she had ever worn, had already made a beeline for the free Bar. Marina whispered discreetly in Peter's ear.

'I don't think she even told her hubby about tonight's function. In fact I know she didn't. She told him a white lie about a birthday party that was being held at the Crescent that she felt obliged to attend. She's a right one when she gets going, I'm telling you. You'd better look out, Mr Fishburn. Any male with a pulse is fair game and ..... look out she's coming back.' Her Midlothian lilt gave her away at ten paces, twenty if she'd had a few.

'Cheers, everybody. Marina, ask him now. Go on, now!'

Peter was puzzled. What was this? Nadine disappeared to go and chat with Inspector Mort, well until his wife appeared from the lift in the lobby and glared at him gazing into Nadine's ample cleavage.

'Mr Fishburn, Nadine said it was OK for me to ask you so, er here goes. Confidentially, my husband and I have recently parted company and ...'

'Oh I'm so sorry but sometimes these things are for the best. Speaking from experience I can ...'

'Yes, that's true but the consequences can be cruel and unexpected. I have recently had to seek accommodation away from the original family home and I'm renting a nice flat overlooking the entrance to Peasholm Park, just a few hundred yards down the road. My future ex is a chef at the Crescent Gardens and it would be better for both of us if I got a job elsewhere. I'll quite understand if you have already recruited a Head Housekeeper but if you haven't then I would be very appreciative if you would consider me.'

'Wow, Marina. Talk about being in the right place at the right time. As you can see we are all really busy tonight. How about I speak with Millie in the morning and we'll take it from there?'

'Oh that would be great, thank you so much. Now where on Earth has Nadine gone? Gosh, she's ditched the Inspector and now she's chatting up a bloke over there in the pin-stripe suit. Who is he do you know?'

'Er, I think he's one of Pamela's colleagues from Best

Eastern Hotels but I'm not sure. Oh yes I can see now. He might be their Finance Director, Toby somebody. A Londoner. I've not met him before. Pamela has invited several of their "bigwigs" – goodness knows why.'

In fact it wouldn't be too long before he found out why – just a few days in fact. Folks were filing in and out of the dining room clutching plateful's of delicious food. Samantha Lyon, as promised, had supplied much of the fair and several of her prize students to assist in carving from the sides of ham and ribs of beef that would not have looked out of place at a Texas BAR-B-Q. Jamie's preferred choice of Spring Lamb would have to wait a few months before it came into season. Lucy was having a field day, or even a field evening, introducing AlfieBoy to everybody. He was just lapping up the attention, not to mention little slivers of beef that were accidentally dropped under his nose. No wonder he didn't want much breakfast the following morning. The whole evening was going swimmingly but then, just as daylight was fading fast, Millie tapped her father on the shoulder and gently reminded him of the main reason for the occasion – the official opening of the hotel under its new name and new management. He brought the gathering to attention by sharply clanging a knife from the buffet table against the side of a sturdy looking wine goblet. Ding, ding, ding! Had Peter had a musical education he might have known it was a 'D flat' – very flat in his case as twice he banged his thumb instead of the glass. The animated conversation, accentuated by generous quantities of social lubrication of the liquid kind, slowly but surely died down to zero. Well almost to zero as a well-oiled Nadine was already deep into the charms of 'Toby from London.'

'Ladies and Gentlemen, your attention please. Thank you. I hope it's not too late to welcome you all this evening to the newly-named Koala Hotel. Some of you have travelled a long way to be here and my family is truly appreciative.'

He nodded towards Malcolm Morgan who was already engaged in conversation with Miles Carter and easily identifiable by his green cricketing blazer displaying the SCC logo on the breast pocket.

'For those of you who aren't aware of the reasons that we changed the name of the Hotel to "Koala" can I suggest that you spend a few minutes of your time this evening reading the document enclosed in the glass frame in the Reception lobby. A Mr & Mrs Walter Jewitt, originally from the State of Victoria, Australia, were the original proprietors of the Koala Hotel near Peasholm Park. It is a fascinating story, if a little sad. Like many other family owned hotels in Scarborough, it was requisitioned by the Air Ministry following the outbreak of War in 1939. So, in their memory, we named this hotel the Hotel Koala. So now you know. And now we have a surprise for you all. Would you all please put down your glasses for just a few minutes and gather outside on the other side of the road. Councillor Elsie Thompson, may I please ask you to do the honours and formally switch on the new exterior lighting?'

The Councillor positively beamed.

'Mr Fishburn, I would be absolutely delighted.'

'Thank you. In a couple of minutes time my two daughters will start the countdown which I hope will be loud enough for the Councillor and I to hear it from the inside. Thank you.'

People started shuffling towards the main exit door with one or two pausing for a quick look on the way at the framed document that Peter had urged them all to read.

'Councillor Thompson, if you would like to come with me please. The master switches are just behind reception.

We'll wait until the countdown starts and then I'll ask you to throw those switches in order from one to four with about a five second gap between each one. OK?'

'Oh how exciting! But I won't actually see very much from in here will I?'

'Don't worry, it's all being filmed by a young lady called Katya and she'll replay it later on a big screen in the dining room. She's making a condensed ten minute video of the whole evening to put on the hotel's website at a later date. Right, get ready it won't be long now.

'Ten – nine – eight – seven – six – five – four – three – two – one – zero!'

Outside the hotel, first the main Hotel Koala sign came on followed five seconds later by the green letters of The Four Seasons Restaurant. There was much cheering and polite clapping outside. But when the first and then the second koalas exploded into life there were sharp intakes of breath followed immediately by raucous cheering of the sort that you would normally hear only at football matches. It was unprecedented in the history of the Scarbados hospitality industry. What would Mr and Mrs Jewitt have thought of it all if they were hear to see it?

Two miles out to sea the same crew of the same lifeboat were once again returning to base but this time almost an hour later than previously to compensate for the clocks having moved forward to British Summer Time. The Captain and Coxswain turned to each other and smiled.

'Now we know those koalas were for real. It must have been a dummy run for some opening ceremony tonight. Pass me those Zeiss bins will you?

He trained the best binoculars that money could buy towards the Hotel's lights that shone like beacons.

'Wow. Looks like they've opened a restaurant too. I might even take "her indoors" there for a bite on her birthday.'

With everyone back inside the Hotel the atmosphere seemed to change. Everyone was in high spirits. Small talk, so prevalent at many similar functions, had evaporated. Miles Carter seemed to be telling the Morgans a non-stop string of jokes and Peter offered up a silent prayer in the hope that they were "suitable" and not of the type for which he apparently had a reputation. He need not have worried. Miles had just told him that the Club's Finance Committee had given the green light to cover the costs of his nephew Courtney's contract with the Club for the new season. They had also passed a similar motion for the young Australian player to join them too. Unfortunately, so full of Prosecco, beef and Malbec was the Treasurer that he clean forgot to inform either Peter or Millie of the good news.

Pamela had meanwhile managed to prise the more than tipsy Nadine away from the pin-striped Toby. She had had already obtained the green lights she wanted from him about the future of the Hotel Koala but nobody else needed to know just yet. He would get his reward from her in Room 118 later on that evening. Nobody needed to know about that either.

Towards midnight the guests started to drift off, either by taxis to local destinations or upstairs to their rooms. Marina had walked the few hundred yards home to her flat at the bottom of Victoria Park having first made sure that Nadine had got into the right taxi for the right destination.

Peter was the last person to retire. It was gone one o'clock in the morning in Bruges and he wondered if Stephanie had received his email and, if she had, how would she react. He was too tired to lay awake thinking about it. He dreamt about the fun times they had shared for years. But overriding all of them were images of a young girl he had never met – his third daughter, Natalie.

38.

By mid-morning the following day all the overnight guests, bar none, had left. Peter had given the Morgans a lift to the railway station. Thank goodness they hadn't brought the same amount of luggage as their stay at the Hotel Scarbados last year. They had decided to have a two night stopover in York on the way back to London to see the Minster and other attractions. Inspector Mort and his wife had actually been the last two guests to physically leave and he had taken the opportunity to have a quick word in Peter's ear just before his car pulled out of the car park.

'Thanks for a great evening, Peter, really enjoyed it. But listen, a quick word between you and me.'

Peter craned forward to his car's window as it lowered.

'The word coming down from the Home Office is that now that all criminal investigations are complete at the former Hotel Scarbados, it will now be sold at public auction. The only CCTV evidence we gathered was of you going into the shed to come out with a plank of wood. Why on Earth did you want that anyway?'

'Jamie needed it to mount those clocks on. Didn't you see them in the hall near Reception? They're for the cricketing fraternity's benefit once the season gets under way.'

'Yes I did notice them – very eye-catching. Just think on about that news re the Hotel Scarbados. If you still owned it you could maybe utilise it as a sort of annexe, or spillover when the Hotel Koala is full. Anyway cheers and thanks again. See you soon I hope. I'll spread the word at County Hall for you. Cheers!'

And with that they were off. They turned down towards the seafront for a last look at the ocean before setting back inland to the land-locked County Town of Northallerton. Peter was so pleased that he and his family were living in the fresh air of the North Sea. If the "climate doomsters" were correct then zillions would be flocking to live by the coast, let alone just go there for a cooling break. Peter went into the kitchen to find everyone round the table with a fresh pouring of coffee. Everyone that is except Lucy who was already half a mile away with the two loves of her life.

'Dad, we're just having a sort of "round robin" meeting about last night – you know, how it went. What did we do right? What did we do wrong? Could we have done better? Lessons to be learnt, that sort of thing. I'll get you some coffee, Dad.'

'Thanks, Millie. Shall I open the batting?'

''Go for it but just give me a few ticks to get your Nescafé instant as we …'

'What? Since when have we ever used instant coffee?'

'Since now. By eleven last night we had run out of Java, Kenyan, Columbian and whatever else will be on Jamie's menu. So that's lesson number one! Stock control.'

She gave a sly wink to her brother who smiled back.

'We also ran out of clean wine glasses and champagne flutes by ten o'clock and the dish-washer was working overtime. If Marina hadn't been kind enough to give us a hand we would have been reduced to plastic cups and drinking straws. She's going to be a wonderful asset when she formally joins our staff. I'll talk to Nadine about it when it's convenient for the Crescent Gardens too. After all, we still have fourteen days to our formal opening when we take guests permanently. By the way, Pam, I spotted your little trick when you peeled off ten days from the countdown calendar. It did do us good though! Now, ideas and comments from others please. Pamela?'

'Well, I might as well tell you now, while all the stakeholders are gathered together.'

She swallowed hard on the last mouth-full of Nescafé left in her mug.

'Tobias Fairweather, the Finance Director of Best Eastern Hotels, was mega impressed with what he saw last night. Very impressed indeed. He reckoned that if this was Brighton or in Devon the hotel would be worth between two and three million pounds, and possibly more.'

She didn't tell them what he had seen "after hours" in Room 118. They didn't ever need to know.

'He's going to recommend to the Board next month that the company makes an offer for a fifty percent stake in Hotel Koala Ltd.'

Millie and Jamie were simply stunned. Their father was reduced to stone like a wizard's spell. He simply couldn't get the news from Inspector Mort out of his head. What if …

'Dad, wake up. You look as if you're miles away.'

In truth he was. Two hundred nautical miles away to be precise.

'So what's going to happen now, Pam, if anything?'

'Well look, we hold all the cards if you think about it, don't we?'

'We do?'

'Sure we do. Between us we own all the shares. Do we want to sell part of the company or not? We come at this from different angles don't we? Millie, you and Jamie are youngsters with your whole lives ahead of you. Your immediate futures are here at the Hotel Koala. Of that I have absolutely no doubt. Mine is different. I'm a "Johnny come lately" who by immense good fortune has fallen on her feet. Peter, your situation is a whole lot different, isn't it?'

She didn't mention the newly discovered family ties across the North Sea. She didn't have to. The ensuing silence was proof that everyone knew what she was inferring. She decided to change the subject.

'Anyway, look Jamie, you have done far too much cooking over the last couple of days so let's go to the Scalby Manor for the carvery lunch shall we? Hands up!'

Jamie's reaction was instant.

'Great but can I ask Chloe to join us please? She missed out on the launch party last night as she had a family function to attend and she goes back to York tomorrow. We can't get any more people in our car but I'm sure her Mum or her Dad will give her a lift.'

'Of course she can join us. I'll call the Manor now and book a table for six people for, shall we say, one o'clock? Everyone happy?'

Two hours later and they all rendezvoused in the substantial car park of a hostelry that decades earlier had been one of the town's premier locations. Today, it was owned by a national pizza chain but at least it ensured it's commercial survival and was well kept and properly staffed. An oval shaped table for six had been reserved for them by the duty manager and it wasn't long before their table number, No. 17, was called out. Lucy took one look at the joints of beef, pork and turkey and immediately complained.

'I'm a vegetarian! Don't you have a veggie option.'

'I'm sorry Miss, but had you called earlier we could have prepared something special for you. However the choice of vegetables on offer is excellent – even if I say so myself. Look!'

Lucy's eyes panned from left to right across a range of tasty looking veg and then she smiled at the chef clad in his whites with carving knife and steel in his practised hands.

'Tell you what, Miss, do you have a dog by any chance?'

'Yes I do – two actually. Am I thinking what you're thinking?'

'Choose your selection of veg to eat now and I'll make up two separate doggie bags for you to take home. What do you think they'd prefer, Miss?'

'Well Sebbie, the eldest, is a beef or pork boy. Not sure yet about little Alfie Boy as he's only a nipper at ten weeks old.'

'Right, Miss, I'll bear that in mind and give him a little bit of everything. I'll cut it up small for him. I'll stick to pork for Sebbie as it's really luscious today and ...'

'Heavy on the crackling please, he loves it.'

'Certainly, Miss, always happy to please a dog lover. I've got two of my own and ...'

'Move along please! The rest of us in the queue are famished!'

The voice belonged to a burly gentleman at the back who looked as if he'd already consumed several lunches. Five minutes later when he took his own plate to Table No.16 his plate was piled to the gunwales so high it was a wonder that half of his roast potatoes didn't fall off. Jamie was tempted to ask him if he had planning permission for it but thought better of it. He didn't want to create a scene did he, particularly in front of Chloe? He was always on best behaviour in her company. It did however give him a few ideas. Maybe the Four Seasons Restaurant could establish a "Sunday Carvery" of its own. Why not, after all they were very popular these days? He kept the idea to himself for the time being.

39.

By late afternoon they were back at the Hotel Koala, well most of them anyway. Jamie and Chloe walked hand in hand all the way round the Marine Drive and ended up at the Flamingo Bay Café for another special hot chocolate. Amber, the waitress, recognised them from last time and smiled and winked at Chloe.

'Got yourself a nice one there love. You cling onto him. I would if I were you. Let me guess, two special hot chocolates? Coming up! I think I'd better give you one of our loyalty cards.'

Back at the Koala, Millie and Pamela were almost falling asleep watching an old black and white Humphrey Bogard film.

'I'm glad we're on our own Millie. We can have a little chat. I know that you probably have mixed feelings about me, that I can quite understand. The events of the last twelve months have been astonishing, haven't they? It must be so hard for your Dad, mentally I mean.'

'You can say that again, Pam. The latest turn of events with Stephanie and the revelation that he had a third daughter would have caused emotional meltdown to most men his age. I think he's secretly delighted, to be honest. Do you agree?'

'I just know he is, Millie. He told me himself. I can now tell you something else. He has written a heartfelt letter to Stephanie within the last twenty-four hours. I don't know whether he's received a reply yet but the gist of his letter was to explain his situation today. Ok I might as well tell you the rest – he's invited Stephanie and Natalie to come over for a week's visit before the Hotel is open to the public.'

'Wow! Oh my God! But why didn't he tell me? After all, I'm his eldest child and …'

''Because he wanted to tell his youngest child first, that's why. This will affect Lucy more than anyone else in the family. Look at the way she cried when he told us about Natalie. She cried all over him did she not? You and Jamie were somewhat impassive. Remember?'

'So when will he tell Lucy about the invitation to visit?'

'Probably about now. That's why they have taken Sebbie and AlfieBoy out for a walk – up towards the Castle I think. Now let me tell you a bit more about what I think, indeed hope, will happen.'

Over the next ten minutes Pamela told Lucy more about Best Eastern's plans and how, if it all came about, it would affect all of them. The company would purchase the shareholdings in Hotel Koala belonging to herself and Peter. "BE" was cash rich and eager to snap up Hotels like the Koala.

'What it will mean Millie, is that your Dad will have oodles of wonga in the bank and be free to do as he pleases. Did he tell you that the old Hotel Scarbados is going to be sold at public auction by order of the Home Office?'

'No, did he "eckerslike." What's he thinking of. You've floored me.'

'Well, Millie, I might be wrong but I'm pretty sure that he's made up his mind to bid for it. If he's successful then I think he's minded to take Lucy with him and hope that his new family, currently in Belgium, join them. Think about it – it makes sense. You and Jamie stay here and you would have all the resources of "BE" behind you – money, people and expertise. And your Dad and little sister, no two sisters now, will not be far away will they? The problem of finding the money to fund the other two floors in the hotel would be over. Think about it in your own time.'

Pamela knew she had sown some major seeds in Millie's mind. Half a mile away, in the shadow of Scarborough Castle, a middle-aged man, his daughter and two dogs paused for a rest at a bench overlooking acres of green shrubbery and a concrete skateboard park.

'Are you tired, Dad? Too much lunch? I've saved those doggie-bags for the boys later. Dad, say something. What's up?'

For the next few minutes Peter told Lucy of his plans.

'So, if it comes off, me you, Stephanie and Natalie will live at the Hotel Scarbados and we'll turn it back into a lovely boutique Guest House. What do you think, Lucy? If you're not in favour then I'll scrap the whole notion. What do you think?'

'Can Sebbie and AlfieBoy come with us?'

'Oh Lucy, of course they can! In a way they'll be going home won't they? AlfieBoy was born next door! Also the big back lawn was always Sebbie's playground wasn't it? And if he hadn't dug that hole underneath the eucalyptus tree then we wouldn't be where we are now, would we?'

For the second time in a few days Lucy threw her arms around Peter's neck.

'It's a deal, Dad, but there's one condition.'

'What's that?'

'We build proper kennels at the back. There's lots of space. So can we?'

'Of course we can, and come to think of it when you've passed your Veterinary Nurse qualifications in in couple of year's time it will look really good to potential customers who are dog owners.'

'Of course it would! And we'll be back living next door to the Ritsons. Oh how exciting! Just cast your mind back to that awful freezing day we arrived. Remember how kind they were?'

'Of course I do, we couldn't have had nicer neighbours.'

'Can we tell them yet, Dad?'

'No, Lucy, sorry. First of all I have to sell my stake in the Hotel Koala and then there's the little matter of being the successful bidder at the auction.'

'When is it?'

It's next Saturday at the Crown Hotel on the Esplanade. I'll speak to the auctioneer tomorrow to try and get some sort of estimate from him as to the likely figure it will realise.'

'You're the best Dad in the world. Come on, let's walk back to the Koala. Tell you what, I'll text Millie right now and get her to illuminate the neon koalas even if it isn't dark yet.'

The next few days were just a blur to them all. Not all the paperwork for the sale of the shares to BE Hotels had been completed but the consideration of £1.2 million had not even been queried. Six hundred thousand might not be enough to buy the Hotel Scarbados. Peter didn't even wonder why BE Hotels hadn't struck a harder bargain. He would never ever find out that Miss Hesketh's extra-curricular hospitality in Room 118 was responsible. Pamela was on schedule to buy her penthouse suite at Sandpiper Heights and announce to them that she was meanwhile going to move into one of the apartments until it was completed. Toby Fairweather had negotiated to buy both penthouses at a considerable discount and was in turn selling one of them to Pamela at a slight loss to BE Hotels. Room 118 had been responsible for quite a lot of shenanigans. Everyone was happy so what harm did it do?

40.

It was the day of the auction for the property formerly known as the "Hotel Scarbados." Peter had obtained a copy of the Prospectus from the Auctioneer's office in York. It was a four-page colour document supposedly to show the former hotel in its best light. It didn't really succeed in that objective. Quite the opposite. The main photograph of the hotel looked a bit depressing set against a dark grey sky. Clearly it wasn't being sold as a going concern, just as a 'property suitable for a variety of uses – a guest house, a residential summer retreat or even a private dwelling. Needs considerable upgrade to bring it up to modern standards.' Peter was not impressed. After all the hard work and sheer love that the family had put into it too.

Still, they wanted it back in the Fishburn fold. Clive White had offered to come up to Scarborough to attend the auction with Peter who was now cash rich following the sale and transfer of his shareholding in Hotel Koala Ltd. which went through two days earlier.

The "Hull Train" from Beverley pulled into Scarborough station on time, just after ten-thirty. With the auction scheduled for eleven o'clock there was heaps of time to drive across Valley Bridge and up to the South Cliff area of the town. They soon found a parking space not far from the Crown Hotel. It was one of the few venues in town that still maintained a modicum of Georgian splendour with six Corinthian pillars proudly protecting the main entrance like giant white soldiers. Inside the lobby a temporary notice read "Auction – Consort Suite" with a temporary gold arrow pointing the visitor in the right direction.

Fifty chairs had been arranged in five rows of ten, theatre-style, on the main floor. A wooden lectern and a microphone had been erected on a raised dias about twenty feet behind the front row. Peter was anxious to sit down and made to grab a seat in the front row or the "three and sixes", as he called it.

'No, Peter, back row. We're going in the "one and nines." Just trust me. In any case, we can see exactly who's doing the bidding from back here. Have you registered and got a bidder's number?'

'A what?'

'Oh never mind, I'll do it.'

Clive went over to the desk where a member of staff, a thirty-something strawberry blonde, was officiating.

Her name was Emma by the name on her badge, her title was "Events Manager" and she took the personal details of everyone registering.

'Your name please, Sir?'

'White. Clive White.'

'Contact telephone number?'

He gave it. After all he was acting as Peter's agent wasn't he?

'Thank you, Sir, and do you have a copy of the order of today's sale?'

'Sorry?'

'Aren't you aware there are over thirty lots for sale today? Is there a particular property you're interested in, Sir?'

'Er, well yes – the former Hotel Scarbados. Isn't everybody?'

'The first couple of dozen lots are repossessions and from the looks of many of the bidders here I suspect that they're builders looking to make a quick killing. Between you, me and the garden gate I think there will only be a handful of serious bidders for the former "Hotel Scarbados."

'Really, do you think so?'

'Oh yes, definitely. We have these auctions nearly every month, except in December when we're too busy with Christmas functions. Looking around, I'd say that the only other serious bidders are those two Oriental gentlemen in the front row. They're here on a frequent basis. I think they buy up cheap accommodation for, you know, irregular immigrants. Anyway, you'd better sit down as here comes the Auctioneer himself – Mr Arthur Price from Arthur Price & Co. of York.'

In a broad pin-striped suit he looked like a cross between David Dickinson and Arthur Negus – an image he always tried to cultivate.

'Good morning everyone. It's just after eleven so let's get the proceedings under way as quickly as possible shall we?

Lot Number One. A two bedroomed terrace house in the Old Town badly in need of modernisation. Can I start the bidding at one hundred thousand ....

Lot Number Two. A three bedroomed semi-detached house in the popular district of Osgodby on the south side of town ....'

Peter rapidly started to lose interest and almost dozed off. Slowly but surely the place started to empty as bidders secured the properties they wanted. He day-dreamed about Belgium, Stephanie and the little girl he hadn't even seen yet. Suddenly, he was brought back to the real world by a sharp dig in the ribs from Clive.

'Wake up! We're almost there.'

The ambience changed as the Auctioneer reached for the colour prospectus of the what was expected to be the most expensive lot of the auction.

'The final lot today, Number Thirty-three, the former Hotel Scarbados.'

There were only four bidders left in the room – Clive, Peter and the two Orientals.

'Can I start the bidding at three hundred thousand?'

One of the Chinese stuck up his placard – No. 8.

'Ah, that's a give away. He's definitely Hong Kong Chinese. I'll bet you he slipped somebody a tenner tip to make sure he got No. 8 – a lucky number in Chinese folklore.'

'Clive, you are such a cynic.'

'Maybe, but I'll bet you lunch I'm right.'

'"Thank you, gentlemen. Am I bid three hundred and fifty?"'

'Go for it, Pete. Stick your placard up – now.'

'Thank you, Sir. Am I bid four hundred thousand?'

'Once again the No. 8 was raised towards the ceiling.'

'Thank you gentlemen. Do I have four hundred and fifty?'

'No? I'll take four two five. Any more for any more? Do I have four two five?'

'Wait till I tell you, Peter. Just wait …'

Mr Price reached for his little brass gavel and commenced his final ritual. The Chinese chaps looked ecstatic. It was like Lunar New Year all over again.

Going once, going twice …

'Now, Peter, now!'

The No. 16 shot skywards as if propelled by a rocket as the gavel came crashing down.

'Sold to the gentleman on the back row. Thank you all for coming. That concludes our business today.'

The Chinese chaps almost started a fight between themselves.

'Dew lay lo mo! You idiot! I told you we could go up to half a million didn't I?!'

'Yes but I thought it was in the bag at four hundred. Then, suddenly, that fat Gweilo at the back stepped in. I didn't even see him. Did you? Oh well, we'll come back next month.'

'Right, Peter. It's time for some lunch. I've booked a table for three in the Taste Restaurant right here in the Hotel.'

'Three, why three?'

'They walked through the main lobby of the Hotel and into the small but smart little Bar. It was time for a little pre-lunch aperitif. The third member of their lunch party was already seated with a glass of Harvey's Bristol Cream sherry.

'Ah, Peter, may I introduce an old school chum of mine – Arthur Price?'

'Delighted, delighted.'

Peter reached into his jacket pocket for his mobile phone. He had promised her a message.

'Hi Lucy – start designing those kennels. We're going back to the Hotel Scarbados. Dad xxx'

EPILOGUE

It was a lovely late Spring day in the gorgeous City of Bruges. A friend had kindly given them a lift from St. Kruis to the railway station. They had a small suitcase each, both with wheels, and made their way through the arcade of shops to the escalator which would take them upstairs to Vertrep No. 6 – the platform for the next train to Brussels where they would change trains for the Eurostar to London. Stephanie had done the trip once before with girlfriends on a Christmas shopping trip to London. Who didn't want to shop at Harrods and come back sporting the famous dark green carrier bags with the gold lettering?

For little Natalie, it would be her first trip away from Continental Europe. She had journeyed with her mother and grandmother by coach to the south of France the previous summer. A school trip to the Alps where they had made the film *The Sound of Music* had been her only other foreign venture. This was different. She was really going across the ocean, even if she was going under it and not over it.

'Mama, how long will it take us to get to London? All day?"

'No, darling, only a few hours. Then we get off the Eurostar at a place called St. Pancras.'

'That's a funny name. My teacher says it's almost as beautiful as Antwerp Station. Is she right?'

'I've no idea, Natalie. We'll take some photos with my iPhone when we get there OK? Then you can show them to your father.'

'Why, hasn't he been there himself?'

'I don't think so. He always sailed to Belgium on a big ship. He never went by train. But you'll be able to ask him yourself.'

'Mama, when we get to London, what shall I say to Papa?'

Stephanie's eyes moistened up. She hadn't been expecting this. She paused and thought for a few seconds that seemed like an eternity.

'I don't think you'll have to say anything honey. The smile on his face will tell you everything you need to know.'

BY THE SAME AUTHOR

Novels

Your Country Needs You
A Very Special Relationship
Her Place in the Sun

The Takeaway
The Maltese Mandarin
Hocus-Pocus AUKUS

Hotel Scarbados

Non-fiction

MALTA My Island
One Thousand Days in Hong Kong
From UK to Belgium and Back
Sunburnt Pom's Tales of Oz

www.mvhbooks.com